HER PRIVATE WAR

DAVID LAWS

www.bloodhoundbooks.com

Print ISBN 978-1-5040-7654-8

To Eleanor, Richard and all the grandchildren

CHAPTER ONE

MONDAY 6TH JULY 1914

W hy is it that only men and boys are welcome at the dare?

I grind my teeth at being confined to female spectator status as my young brother is done up like some diminutive alien from outer space in tight leather helmet, goggles and a huge leather jacket several sizes too big for him while being strapped into this fragile machine.

Not so long ago I'd bested him in bike races, climbing trees, hurling sticks over the river, any ball game you can name. As kids, this was allowed; now, as adults, it's forbidden. Natural ability is being overridden in favour of the male and he's the one in the flying seat. I'm looking at the Farman biplane. It sits on a muddy little patch of countryside. It may seem unimpressive, a strange contrivance of wire and cotton, but I know – I'm certain beyond any possibility of doubt – that the Farman III represents the future. And it's been decided. It's my brother's future.

As usual Mother is fussing. 'Sure you've got those straps tight? Don't let them work loose, don't want you falling out.'

The instructor looks to the sky and it isn't to check the weather.

'I'm okay, really I'm okay,' Marcus insists.

I can't hold back. I lean forward. 'For goodness' sake, this is his tenth flight, he should know all that by now.'

I wonder that Marcus can stand all the cloying attention – but then, he is the beneficiary of all Mother's enormous ambitions for her children. He loves his; I hate mine.

'Ready?' Aleksander Nowak, a monosyllabic instructor at the best of times, is getting impatient.

There's a jerky thumbs up from the co-pilot position, we move back and the Gnome motor bursts into noisy life. Every time the revs increase in pitch the tiny craft shudders as if it feels uncomfortable sitting on this muddy patch of the countryside surrounded by a car racing circuit. Then the howl of the Bugattis and Leylands across the turf at Broadlands is blotted out as Nowak opens the throttle wide and his ungainly machine begins to move – hesitantly at first, as if unsure it can really win its battle with gravity.

At this point I retreat to my favourite observation point – the stump of an old tree by a grassy knoll, the same spot from which I've watched so many take-offs, right back to my early teens, back when Marcus and I were first bitten by the flying bug. I clench a fist, look away and try to ignore my mother. She's exultant, almost clapping with joy, putting her hands together as if in prayer.

'He's really got a talent for this, hasn't he?' she gushes, a smile lifted to the sky.

I say nothing.

We continue to stare up at the little craft, all doped-up fabric, finger-thick mahogany struts and thrashing propeller. It flies a circuit of the field, dog-legs above the motor racing circuit, turning this way and that in a series of quirky turns, and then disappears from view.

Watching this somewhat shambolic performance, I

momentarily forget the official script of unalloyed admiration and rashly remark: 'Oh dear, not a graceful soar into the sky today.'

At this Mother rounds on me and snaps: 'You just stop carping. We all know you're jealous. Not a nice thing to be. Resentful of your own brother.'

I turn away, repressing the urge to reply, eyes no longer seeking out the buzzing dot in the sky, striding back towards the flying school – in reality, a rickety hut without facilities. No sanitation, no electricity, no washbasin, not even a can of water to rinse dirty hands. Aviation Village it's called, an absurdly bombastic name for a muddy little track between a line of sheds the flyers rent out at £10 a month. It's probably because I'm holding my temper in check that I don't notice until the last moment a Blériot XI being manoeuvred out of a neighbouring shed. One wheel is already stuck in a rut. I try not to make my interest too obvious. The aircraft is one of the most prized in the village, the original having made the first Channel crossing and this machine a veteran of countless races around Britain. Its owner, Dan Jackson Forbes, is a jeering thorn in the side of Mother's flying operations and her pride and joy, the Dovedale School of Flying. He scoffs loudly at our rather basic Farman, calling Nowak the instructor 'a damned amateur' or 'Huh! Some teacher!' or 'Don't know how you've got the brass neck to charge 'em five shillings to go up in that old thing.'

'Ignore him!' she says, but the braggart Jackson never passes up a chance to taunt. He can certainly read the Dovedale family runes, calling loudly to me as he pushes his machine: 'Not taken you up yet then, Charlotte? Tut tut!'

I ignore him, keep a neutral expression in place and enter Shed No.6 with its flamboyant copperplate sign over the door. Perhaps that's what really irritates Forbes. Then I begin to think of the many women who already fly – brilliant aviators who'd give Forbes a run for his money. The papers are full of them: Ruth Law, Harriet Quimby, Hilda Hewlett and a host of others. Most have money and you need plenty of that to become what the newspapers are apt to describe as an *aviatrix*. This is an old dream of mine and a persistent one. How I would love to add my name to that list of aviation greats. Forbes's taunt just now in the avenue is, to me, like a row of bee stings. This is the simmering dispute between us that has soured mother-and-daughter relations since the day Marcus took his first lesson. And now I'm in the mood for confrontation.

She starts it. Says: 'Don't let Forbes upset you.'

'But he's right, isn't he?' I say. 'Definitely right. So – let me ask you this... when do I get my chance to fly?'

She stops what she's doing and looks up abruptly. 'You? Don't be daft!'

'And why not?'

'Told you before. This is for Marcus. He wants in at the very beginning of military flying.' We both know the government has finally bowed to pressure from the aviation lobby and the Army's Royal Flying Corps is just getting started. Marcus has set his heart on this pioneering venture. 'It's his big ambition,' she says. 'What he wants more than anything.'

'Me too.' I almost shout the words.

'No way! The military won't have you. A girl? Don't be ridiculous. Besides, I've different plans for you.'

I explode and stalk to the back of the shed. The place reeks of aviation fuel. There's a table with a metal chair in one corner and in the other a bench littered with tools.

She tries to be placating. 'My hopes and ambition for you are to become what I was not,' she says, her tone all reasonable and concerned. 'A lady with servants, a good husband and a lovely house. Dinner parties, high society...'

'Then wish it on someone else.'

4

'I want you to marry well. What about that lovely boy you knew at college? Lionel... wasn't it?'

'Marry well? What me, a shopkeeper's daughter?'

She turns back to her business. She's sitting at the table with a single ledger on which she checks off her flight pupils. 'And another thing.' She's waving a pencil in my direction. 'You need to pay Marcus more respect. He's not your little playmate anymore. Soon he'll be an officer, the holder of the King's Commission no less.'

'He's still my brother. The King's Commission won't make him someone else.'

'Of course it will, he'll be a man of substance and that demands respect.'

'You don't demand respect, you earn it.'

'I don't like your attitude.'

What do you say to that? But I won't leave it. We square up, stony-faced, eye to eye. It isn't the first time. Then I say, perhaps a shade more belligerently than intended: 'You have two children, Mother, and I intend to prove that I'm every bit as capable and every bit as deserving as my brother.'

CHAPTER TWO

The lines appear in a great rush. Quick broad strokes flash across the sketchpad and the scene takes shape on paper just as I remember it. The old Boxkite, all struts and canvas, skims across the grass field at the altitude of a mere three feet, sometimes just inches above the blades, before hitting the bank a few hundred yards across the meadow. A real grasscutter indeed, fashioned by my favourite 2B. Shade and shadow, form and faithful outline. I've never been short of a decent set of pencils and this is graphic recall of those days when Marcus and I were first gripped by the craze for flying. The thrill of watching a heavier-than-air machine defying gravity, the magic moment of the first lift, the initial loosening of the earth's grip, then up and away like a bird. An indelible memory and how we cheered! The two of us had been regulars at the aerodrome back then – me thirteen, he two years younger.

A short swish of movement overhead disturbs this recall and reminds me of Marcus's lesson. I look up to see the Farman coming in to land, a mere wispy purr with the revs cut right back. No need to worry, he's not going solo. There's a short burst of the trademark bark of the Gnome motor, then the Farman puts down well past the chosen spot, close to the far edge of the racetrack right next to the raised banking. Instinctively, even though I've never been up, I reckon I could have managed a better landing. We two, my brother and I, we've always been competitive; running, climbing, biking, puzzles, riddles; through childhood to adulthood. How I wish fervently I could be competitive with Marcus now.

I put down my pencil and look critically at the sketch. Art has always been my release from tension and I simply had to get out of that shed, away from my mother, to calm an acute sense of frustration. Collecting my pad from the dickey seat at the rear of her Fiat Tipo Zero, I'd walked clear of the avenue, well away from the rutted tracks churned up by the wheels of other aircraft to find a convenient spot and consider the taunts of the irritating Dan Jackson Forbes. He, of course, is a crude braggart and an affront to decent conversation but occasionally he speaks the truth and, I have to admit, is especially enviable for his achievements in the air. 'One day...' I say out loud, screwing up my eyes and clenching a fist, 'one day!'

'Well, hello there,' says a strange voice over my shoulder.

It's a shock and I spin round. A tall man, must be nearly six foot, is smiling quizzically in my direction. I can tell from his clothes and the way he holds himself he's no penurious flyer from our line of sheds.

'May I inquire,' he says, 'what will happen one day?'

The voice is deep and mellifluous and the well-modulated tone speaks of Eton or some similar institution. I give him a long stare. 'The sky,' I say, 'one day I'll be up there.'

He turns his gaze to a spot beyond the rickety rooftops to where Marcus has been dog-legging back and forth above the aviators' circle of grass and asks: 'Someone you know?'

'My brother.'

'Ah yes, I spotted the Farman taking off. Of course, it's from the flying school.'

Silence. I resist the temptation to enlarge on the subject, to say anything about the Dovedale Flying School. Why should I reveal to any stranger the shabby truth of our family background? That Mother has shares in Nowak's ramshackle outfit; that she's probably propped him up when he should have gone bust; that they're almost certainly having an affair. I can feel my eyes going to slits. I seethe with unspoken disapproval at this last thought.

'If you'll forgive me for saying so,' the man beside me says, 'you have that far, far away look, as if you really want to be somewhere else, but there can't be many people at Broadlands who want to be somewhere else. Most simply can't wait to get here. It should be a place of enjoyment, excitement and fun.'

'It is for some.'

'May I ask why it isn't for you?'

I shrug.

'Forgive me,' he says suddenly, extending a hand. 'I should have introduced myself. Scott Fanshawe.'

I take it, looking at him more closely, noting the amused openness of him, the fine cut of his waistcoat, the leathery tang of his shoes. 'Charlotte Dovedale.'

'Been up in the Farman yourself?'

There it is again. Another bee sting. 'They let me sit in it and look at the controls, but precious little else. No instructions, more on sufferance...' My words trail off. Again, I don't want to expand on my second-class status when it comes to aviation, so I bounce the ball back to him: 'So, what do you think of the Farman? As a learner aircraft, I mean?'

He draws in a breath and considers. I can sense him trying to find something positive to say.

'I reckon it's a very good starter aircraft,' he replies at length, 'but once the novice pilot has a feel for flying he would be well advised to move on to something more adventurous, more challenging, more up to date and suited for longer flight.'

'Figures,' I say. 'Nowak refuses to answer any of my questions. Mind you, he's hardly the most loquacious of instructors.'

'You don't like him?'

A so-so gesture, a weave of the head. I don't want to be too revealing about our situation. Nowak, a monosyllabic refugee Pole who's fled a pogrom, a dodgy teacher, a failing flying school, a shambolic chaos rescued by Mother's much vaunted business acumen...

'Well,' Fanshawe says, 'I'm more than happy to talk about flying, in fact, if you would like, I'd be glad to show you over my own aircraft.'

I can't repress a smile. A definite improvement of mood. I've already clocked the gleaming Avro 504 at the far end of the row but didn't realise it was his. To see over such an advanced and superior machine would be a privilege. Certainly one up on another young man who's just been lumbering around the sky in the Farman.

I must have made my pleasure a shade too obvious because he smiles, turns and indicates back along the avenue.

We're walking eastwards towards the end of the line of flight huts and for once I silently give thanks that I'm not in riding breeches or any of the ridiculous flying pantaloons favoured by other women. Today it's a pale-blue-and-white batiste dress with horizontal and vertical stripes. He indicates right and as we approach the end of the line I realise that there's a pecking order even for sheds. At our end, battered and ill-fitting bare wood doors; further along, painted fronts and nameplates and now, at the far corner, what appears to be more in the way of a sprawling, expansive bungalow.

That's when it becomes obvious he has a slight limp, carrying his right leg somewhat awkwardly. I pretend not to notice and look up at a veranda of blue-painted slats. I can make out a table and several easy chairs with cushions and somewhere behind is the sound of metal on metal.

'Tea suit you?' he asks, then calling to the unseen hand, 'Put the kettle on, Tom.'

Tom? Is this a mechanic, perhaps even a chauffeur? Just visible parked at the rear of the property is a blue bull-nosed Bentley.

'Better than that fly-blown café, eh?' he says with a grin when we're seated. The Aero Café of Broadlands has a certain grubby cachet for racing mechanics and flying enthusiasts who see themselves as the engine house of the future. Laid out on Fanshawe's table, however, is a well-thumbed newspaper and I glimpse an article about Mrs Pankhurst and the suffrage movement. Down the page several squares of the crossword grid have been filled in.

'So you have time for this too?' I say, pointing.

'Keeps the grey cells working. Helped by a mind filled with the clutter of infinite nonsense, so I'm told.'

By now the dark mood caused by my mother's rejection has receded, to be replaced by light-hearted banter over china teacups and clotted cream scones. The conversation turns to cars (none of Mr Ford's Model Ts in this family!), cinema (Charlie Chaplin, Mary Pickford and D.W. Griffith's *The Birth of a Nation*), the state of the nation (strikes, votes for women and the many pronouncements of Prime Minister Asquith) and, of course, aircraft. How is it that this man is so urbane and altogether and has the leisure to fly his own plane at such a young age? Perhaps he's just read my thoughts. Perhaps the question is written too plainly on my features, because he says with a grin: 'Old money.'

Then he eyes the sketchpad clutched under an arm. 'I take it that's not just for show.'

'Just a hobby.'

'Not only a flying enthusiast, but an artist as well! Do I get to see?'

Soon he's flicking through the pages of my most recent work: predictably, Marcus looking small and uncomfortable perched at the controls of the Farman; a close-up of him in his helmet, the strap hanging loose; then other subjects, mostly faces. Some, serious studies in shading and shadow; others, comical, funny, cartoonesque.

'I shall have to look out,' he says, 'if I see you with a pencil in your hand.' Then, quite suddenly, he's serious again. 'But I'm holding you up. You want to see the 504.'

I smile, itching to get down those steps to the apron, making up my mind as I go. I will not allow this moment to become a casual stroll around the machine making anodyne, polite or complimentary remarks. I want to demonstrate my practical knowledge, my grasp of all things aviation, that I'm quite capable of getting my hands dirty. And I want to know all about the Avro. Absolutely everything.

He's walking me part by part around the machine, explaining each item. The Avro is one of a type that's already received the blessing of the War Office, meeting the demands of the Military Aeroplane Competition, reaching a height of 2,000 feet in five minutes and covering seventeen miles in twenty minutes.

An odd thought strikes me, although perhaps this is not the

right moment to mention it. Nevertheless, I'd still like to know how Fanshawe just happens to be flying around in the 504 when the Flying Corps and the Admiralty have made this plane their own. I determine to find out later. Perhaps my brother Marcus will get to fly one – if he makes it into the military. I chew hard on this thought.

Fanshawe is pointing out the single long skid, the steel-framed tailplane, the observer sitting in front of the pilot, the dual controls. 'Shut me up if you already know all this,' he says, but I just smile.

'Want to sit in the cockpit?'

Do I?

It's how I expected. Hard, unforgiving and wonderful. When I get settled I feel excitement, exhilaration and at home. I touch the fabric, fingers rove over the controls, I stroke the tautness of the wires, try out the warping lever. I sniff the fuel, imagine myself done up in a big padded flying suit as protection from the cold. This is where I should be. This is meant for me.

Then it's time to concentrate on what he's saying. There's an easy conversation between us. He's talking about his plans for longer flights. He wants to take off to some distant point and meet a friend who is parked up ready and waiting with the necessary fuel to make the return flight. Good idea, I tell him, I'd like to do that.

But the hint falls flat. He's into stargazing mode. Talking about the future of aviation. Aircraft will soon develop even more, he says; longer flights and bigger loads. 'Newer machines are coming along, it's only a matter of time before things advance way beyond what we're familiar with today. Aviation will change everything, it's definitely the future, whatever the old brass hats say.'

Odd! I look at him questioningly.

'The French chief of staff,' he says, 'thinks aircraft are just toys, of no use on the battlefield. How could he be so dumb? To fly over the enemy's front and see what he's doing – that's going to be a huge advantage for any army.'

I make a face, a discordant note interrupting this moment of sublime exuberance. 'Let's not talk of war,' I tell him.

'It may come. Sooner than you think.' Then, seeing my dubious expression, he adds: 'It's what I'm hearing from my father. He has his finger on the pulse. An old hand from the Foreign Office.'

Fanshawe, I decide, is a breath of fresh air. He treats me as an equal, doesn't talk down to a mere girl, doesn't patronise. I like his shape, how he moves, his voice, his smell – a hint of soap that distinguishes him from the sweaty multitude who do not have access to the luxury of a bathroom. There's a natural sociability, a quiet chortle, a gentle humour. He responds agreeably to all questions about speeds, take-off, stalling and landing. 'I love your machine,' I say. 'Wonderful, so modern, exhilarating, marvellous. Not enough words to describe it.'

He looks thoughtful, pensive even. 'I register all this great enthusiasm of yours,' he says. 'And a strong determination. Shame to waste it! Sometimes, I know only too well, families can be difficult. Sometimes friends can be more accommodating.' Then he smiles. 'So, there's only one thing for it.'

I do my best to look earnest and guileless, holding my breath.

'I'll just have to teach you to fly,' he says.

CHAPTER THREE

I declare this now: you won't get softly-softly from me. I'm a suffragette, a break-free personality, and I've no intention of adopting the quiet, polite, reserved tone of a young lady who knows her place. There's going to be no holding back. It's no surprise to me, therefore, that there's trouble the minute I step inside my mother's shop next day.

'Don't think I don't know what you've been up to!' She's in full voice. 'I saw you with that man.'

We're back in Bury St Edmunds and I always make it my business to call in at the Artists' Emporium on Kings Road every day after lessons.

'No use getting upset,' I snap back, 'it's quite simple. If you and Nowak won't teach me to fly, then Scott will.'

'Scott!' she scoffs. 'You be very careful there. He's not the right one for you.'

'I thought you wanted me to find a man.'

'He's a playboy. Not serious. I know his sort. Only after one thing, then he'll dump you.'

'Difficult when flying at several hundred feet.'

She turns from counting sets of brushes and gives me the

full-on glare. 'Why can't you leave it alone? Flying's not for you. And haven't I been good to you? Good school, nice clothes, bicycles. Isn't that good enough? Not many young ladies look like this...'

She's pointing at my blue rayon jersey day dress with the silk lining. I'm also quite keen on the rounded pompadour hairstyle and flower-decorated hat. Actually, hats are my thing.

I look at the ceiling, examine the light fittings and peer out of the window, then decide to be a shade reasonable. I have, after all, benefited quite considerably from my mother's business acumen. 'I'm grateful,' I say, shrugging a conciliatory shoulder. 'I know you mean well, but really, your idea of heaven isn't mine. Servants, big house, boring husband...' I affect an admittedly over-the-top stage shudder.

'And then there's Marcus,' she says.

At this I draw in a deep breath. Now we're getting to the core of it. Mother hates any hint of sibling competition in the matter of aviation. She has this massive sense of ambition for dear Marcus. In her eyes, my brother is going to be the star in a great flying firmament, but I can't help it, I resent all the maternal bragging, not least because I know my brother. He's a gawky member of the awkward squad.

'Don't you go making him nervous,' she says, wagging a finger.

'I won't. I won't go anywhere near him.'

Not actually entirely truthful, I admit. We'll soon be flying from the same aerodrome, I'll be in a far superior plane and with a much better instructor. However, Marcus has a ten-lesson start on me and we'll just have to see who wins out. Like always. It's a competition, natural rivalry. Nothing nasty about it, just how it is. I think about the nature of our relationship, my brother and I, right from childhood. I was the older sister showing him how – how to climb trees, how to ride a bike, how to shin up a drainpipe. There were races and I nearly always won – until adolescence, that is, when suddenly Marcus no longer wanted his Big Sis around. But our naturally competitive natures don't fade with adulthood. It endures. It isn't jealousy, as our mother claims, simply a natural thirst for being first. After all, if you're not first, you might as well be last.

By this time the shop is getting crowded and Mother is busy serving, so I wander over to the shaggy sofa situated in one corner where I find old Goff staring into space. He's a dreamy sort of fellow who fits the furniture and this is his normal perch. I'm amazed she doesn't turn him out, knowing her strictly business pound-shillings-and-pence attitude, but he does buy the occasional brush and paint pot. And the shop is a kind of home from home for the artists round here. There are several colonies of them in this town. They live in cramped and overcrowded rooms in houses given over to them by moneyed people happy to patronise the arts. Big old draughty places in Victoria Street and Cemetery Road. Years ago Mother was her clever self, spotting a business opportunity, supplying art materials to the growing numbers. It's what you'd expect. Trade is in the family bloodstream. Grandfather was a butcher, and Uncle a draper.

But here's a strange thing. Despite all that business acumen, I know that at heart she despises her customers. She hates me talking to any artist. 'Don't want you mixing with them, nor God forbid, becoming one. It's not a good life. Dissolute, immoral, free love. Not having you anywhere near any of that.'

Goff's not very conversational, as per usual, so I walk out of the shop and into the big square at the centre of the town. Some of his friends are seated on tiny wooden stools, painting the Moyse's Museum and the Victorian Post Office, always with the statue of the fallen soldier as the centrepiece of their townscapes.

'Why don't you try your hand?' It's Big George, a craggy fellow who's taken a shine to me. 'I know you've got talent,' he says.

So for a while I do, pencilling in details of the roofs and chimneys and the people in the street below. But soon patience runs thin and I switch to a quick sketch of George's head and shoulders, much to his amusement. 'What a subject!' he exclaims. 'I'm an ugly brute for sure, but you've caught the face wonderfully and the expression with amazing exactitude.'

We laugh. He's encouraging, a bit of a flatterer, but he's interested in people as well as painting. His wan smile tells me he knows my situation, has worked out why I'm in the square and not in the shop. Oh for a perceptive parent! Just the sort of encouraging person I might have liked for a father.

I give him the sketch as a souvenir and look up to see my friend Katie crossing the square toward me. She's the one I lodge with and a fellow warrior, like me, ready to fight the good fight. 'Fantastic news,' she shouts as she gets within earshot. 'Just heard. Mrs Pankhurst is coming to Bury.'

'To speak?'

'Of course. Big rally in the square outside the Abbey Hotel on Friday evening.'

I make a snap decision. Despite my job – teaching at the commercial college in Friars Lane – I'll take the afternoon off and to hell with the consequences. Every red-blooded woman in town will be there. No way I'd miss it. Climb a mountain, wrestle a bear, even plump Mother's cushions. Do anything to get there.

'Is it love and hate, cat and dog?'

Old Morty, the tenement tramp, is grinning at us from

across the doorstep. Fancies himself. A bit of a wiseacre. 'I mean,' he persists, 'how do two such different people get along, you know, living bunched up together in this same household?'

He's not the first person to query our friendship and I suppose he has a point. Katie's from the poorest quarter of the town while I hail from Guildhall Street – 'the nobby end' as she insists on calling it. My mother's place has an arched front doorway, geranium flower pots, white canopy, bright-blue door, six-pane fanlight and the brass knocker that goes with all her middle-class pretentions. Social circles that normally don't mix in this town.

So it's our personal histories that are intriguing the old rogue. He's peering in at us through the open front door while we sit on hard wooden chairs around the kitchen table, hemmed in by Katie's cramped surroundings – a grim old stove and a tiny scullery.

'You're a bit of a mystery,' Morty insists, pointing at me – but the answer to how Katie and I met is really no puzzle. It is, of course, our shared interest in the cause of women. We hit it off back in May at a meeting in the Athenaeum, Bury's huge yellow hulk of classical architecture situated at one end of the Abbey square, at a meeting of the WSPU. A transformative moment for both of us.

A woman in a flowery white dress overlaid by the suffragist colours of purple, white and green was on her feet. She suggests, in a whiny sort of upper-crust tone, that the campaign for the female vote should be confined to women of property over the age of thirty. This select group, she says, will be the spearhead for female emancipation.

What rot! But before I can interrupt a tiny figure in a tangerine shawl sitting in the next row of seats leaps to her feet. 'That's a wrong 'un!' she calls and two-dozen frozen expressions turn in her direction. 'Got to say no to that! It's just not right!'

Pause, a shocked silence, then: 'Everyone, just everyone should be treated proper. We're entitled. I say the vote is for everyone. For all classes, all society, no matter who they are.'

White dress is justifying. A select female suffrage will be the answer to the government's fears of 'being swamped by the uneducated masses', she says.

'But you can't shut us out!' The little one is on her feet again. 'There's millions of us. Ordinary folk... and we won't be quiet. We won't stay silent,' she shouts in another intervention.

'Bravo!' I cry, clapping furiously to encourage others, and later make the acquaintance of the tiny figure from six seats away – who, of course, is Katie.

After the meeting we have a long conversation out in the square and decide that white dress is a government toady. We have a laugh and a giggle and in the course of our chat I discover that Katie is looking for a lodger. I draw in a deep breath at this news and consider. Guildhall Street has become unbearable to me. I'm fed up with its stultifying atmosphere, the simmering hostility and wounded relationships. Everything about my life seems transitory. I don't see a long-term future in teaching, I shy away from the traditional route of matrimony, and all I want to do is to fly.

I make a decision. 'I'm your new lodger,' I tell Katie.

She looks askance, then shamefaced. 'Gawd! It's nothing like you've been used to,' she says.

My reward is an easy, lively friendship, an empathy based on mutual goals; her reward is the rent to help her make ends meet. Since then we've been getting along fine, though she can be a trifle preachy at times and is quick to take offence. She and Rufus haven't got much in the way of crockery so one day I liberate a big serving dish from one of Mother's cupboards. She hasn't used it in years, and I try to make things right with Katie by saying I bought it cheap in the market.

'I ain't a perishing charity,' she snaps. One of her little flare-ups accompanied by a reddened face.

'Can't a person give a friend a gift?'

In the ensuing fraught silence broken only by the clink of cutlery as we devour our beef hash, I consider the morality of my actions. Can deceit ever be acceptable for the greater good, a kindly sort of white lie? It's a subject I'll return to in later days.

Over time Katie relents on her ferocious sense of personal pride and allows me without protest to bring in the occasional goodies from the market: meat, fish and vegetables for the stew, items to improve their meagre diet, recipe suggestions and cooking tips. We grow closer. I bring newspapers – well, copies of *The Planet* – into the house and we exchange details about our different worlds. She's a nurse at the local infirmary. Lots of young girls. Some are staff from the kitchens used on an occasional basis without formal training. It wouldn't happen at more prestigious hospitals and there's talk of registration for nurses at some time in the future.

My friend screws up her pretty face in a moment of angry recall. 'You know what that old dragon of a matron said to me the other day? "Keep quiet, know your place". Why should I? I only wanted to speak to the doctor, but apparently he's on a higher plane. They treat us like skivvies. Like dirt.'

'You're a victim of the system,' I say, 'a system that doesn't recognise half of the population as people. That makes us powerless like some subspecies.' Now we're getting into our stride on our joint enthusiasm for the cause. 'You and I have as much right to be on this earth as any man,' I say, 'so why should we be treated as lesser beings?'

'Power to us!' she says banging a fist on the table, then goes quiet. We can hear her husband moving about upstairs. She points to the front page of *The Planet* and says more quietly:

'They're at it again, arresting her, putting her in jail, doing terrible things to her.'

The *her*, of course, is once again Mrs Pankhurst, lifted like a small toy into the arms of a huge brawny policeman at the latest protest rally. Reports appear daily of arrests, convictions, imprisonment, force-feeding, illness; a brick wall of resistance to the cause. 'It's not right,' she says, 'that horrid great brute mauling her about.'

I bring out my old photos. No one at Guildhall Street had the slightest interest in my childhood holidays spent with a school friend in Belgium, but Katie enjoys looking at them: lots of outdoor fun, trekking, walking, running, climbing, swimming, picking wild flowers, scrumping apples, visiting art galleries.

'You're lucky to have such a friend,' she says – until I tell her we met at boarding school. 'A bunch of posh girls!' she accuses, then can't resist another dig: 'And I bet you have servants back in Guildhall Street.'

'Of course we do.'

'And cars!'

I shrug. 'Naturally. One of Mother's obsessions. Actually, mine too... as well as bicycles.'

'I know, I've seen you whizzing about on that bike, it's a wonder that big hat of yours don't blow off in the wind.'

'Artful hatpins,' I explain, and show her my favourite, the Charles Horner amethyst with its long stem and a sharp point.

The occasional spat doesn't stop her being intrigued by my ability with plain paper and pencil. Great hilarity greets caricatures of her husband – but then Mooseface, as I call him because he's so morose and moody, is easy to cartoon. These sketches are liberally spread around the kitchen table in his absence but hurriedly tidied away when footsteps are heard outside, lest he be offended at my sense of humour. I tell her: faces are my thing. I love the quirks nature throws at us: beetle-brows, ski-jump chins, glaucous eyes, all the facial tics that can be exaggerated to individualise a person and make them memorable. Study faces, I tell Katie, everyone's character is written there.

She's giggling. 'And another thing,' I say, 'we're not put on this earth to be miserable. I can't stand weary willies. Enjoy!'

One day I even try to inveigle her into a gallery – 'Well, you like art, don't you, you endlessly encourage mine,' I tell her – but she complains I'm patronising her, so instead I buy a picture of a Norfolk cottage and hang it on a nail, my attempt to brighten the place up and am upbraided once again for being posh. We both love animals and yearn for a dog or even a tiny kitten, but there's no room to swing the proverbial pet at No.4 Tenement Row. It has a tiny backyard curtained off by high brick walls and half of that space is taken up with Mooseface's pigeon coop. 'I'm not having any damned cat near my birds,' he insists, and that's that.

However, lively company is just the tonic I need, plus removal from too much interaction with my mother, and I have a very bright light beckoning me at the weekend: a flying lesson at the Broadlands aerodrome with my new friend Scottie Fanshawe.

Wonderful. I simply can't wait.

CHAPTER FOUR

A huge blanket of mist rolls in from the direction of the river and blots out everything. What a huge disappointment! I've been waiting for this day with so much pent-up excitement but now my very first flying lesson is not to be. No one can take off in such a murk. Disappointing for all the aviators – but for me, Charlotte Dovedale, anxious novice pilot, it's a huge downer.

Scott and I arrived at Broadlands by late morning but have been stuck here ever since. How do I cope? How I always cope! I get out my pencils and sketchpad and begin to draw. I have him don his helmet and goggles, adopt an urgent pose and sit completely still on a chair while I get to work. Never pass up the chance of capturing a fascinating face, that's my motto, and just now the aerodrome apron is looking more like a portrait gallery than a showcase for aviation. Like me, Scott has an eye for form and shape, which is just as well, because he's a good sitter and we begin to talk. I decide that what I like about him most of all is his complete lack of snobbery. He doesn't reflect the superior attitudes of his family. As I scale up the picture I become fascinated by the details of what I'm hearing; a picture, it seems to me, of the most absurd formalities of home life. The gong, dressing for dinner, prayers and addressing his father as 'pater'.

Families! But who am I to criticise with my disjointed background? He tells me about his unforgiving brothers and their scorn for anything other than the military art. Brothers? You don't choose them, I say, you choose your friends. It seems to me that Scott is the odd one out in his household. The others at home have little regard for what interests him: photography, music and the arts. He's also keen on architecture; tells me about all the wonderful buildings he's seen and the latest trends. However, before we can go any further down this road my thoughts are interrupted by a loud voice from behind and I turn to see a big woman with crooked teeth bearing down on me.

I stare at her. She's wearing a green jumper but that's not all. She also has on a startling pair of mannish brown riding breeches and high lace-up black boots.

'That's good,' she says, pointing at my pad. 'Very good. You've got a gift.'

We've never met but I recognise her instantly. My friend Katie has told me all about her. This is the newspaper correspondent Maggie Melrose, a staunch supporter of us suffragettes. Melrose, Katie says, represents the controversial – and some would say sensationalist – daily picture paper, *The Planet*. They've met at WSPU rallies.

I put down my pencil and turn full circle on the stool to give Melrose an inviting smile. 'Keeps us occupied while we wait,' I say.

She leans closer to examine the sketch in detail, nodding as she does so. 'Did you know the paper I work for runs a special daily feature for sketches of relevant current events? Called Sketch of the Day. Why don't you submit?'

'Relevant?'

'Flying. Isn't that relevant?'

I nod enthusiastically. Don't let the chance slip. 'Certainly! Aviation, perhaps the most relevant development of the age. Great new things are on the way...'

'Can you write?'

'Of course. I'm a constant diarist.' Not quite true – but half true, given my propensity to letter writing.

'Then submit the sketch and a short commentary. A sketch like that... might be worth, perhaps, maybe if you're lucky, half a guinea.' She thrusts out a card containing numbers and an address. 'Only, get the aeroplane fully in the background.'

With that, she turns and begins to stride away. I'm enthralled by this development, not least by Melrose's attire. Those riding breeches will be a constant shock to the traditionalists, and what nerve! Not for her the absurd get-ups – vast baggy pantaloons – I've seen worn by some women flyers I admire. So, if she can do it...

After four steps Melrose – 'call me Mel' – stops and turns back. 'Nearly forgot!' she says. 'Pankhurst is here on Friday. Are you going? Could be a good subject.'

I grin and turn to Scottie. 'We're both going,' I say and stare at him, daring him to disagree.

He coughs and says: 'Absolutely!'

'See you there,' Mel says, resuming her walk. I watch her go. Large confident steps. A woman without fear. Down by the track she approaches a parked motorcycle. I recognise it – a Douglas 350. She's donning helmet, goggles and gloves as she goes, then flicks the bike off its stand with an almost aggressive arrogance, kick-starts the engine and roars away in a cloud of dust and fumes.

This is a person of supreme purpose, I decide. Katie has filled me in on the background. Mel is a former car racer with a history of prangs and wears her scars like badges. A veteran of the circuits at both Broadlands and the Isle of Man. Completely unselfconscious. A gait that says everyone should take her for what she is: an emblem of the modern woman who's thrown off the antediluvian Edwardian baggage of thick skirts down to the ankle. Then I think of that other dominant woman we've been discussing, Emmeline Pankhurst. Now there's a brave one. I'm in awe of her. All that defiance and reckless disregard of her own safety. She even trumpets that she's ready to lay down her life for the cause. You have to admire her, even if I sometimes puzzle at her excesses, but then I ask myself if there isn't a common thread running through all these obsessions. I compare her do-or-die spirit to the urgent compulsion I feel to fly. Is the same sort of restlessness propelling me into the air?

I go back to my pad but my heart isn't in it. I simply cannot be excluded from the world of aviation. The flying bug is an intoxication. It's also a belief in the future with a touch of danger and recklessness thrown in. So what does that say about the spirit of the age?

Perhaps we'll find out at next Friday's rally in Bury's big square.

CHAPTER FIVE

I bang the door shut behind me and set off along Tenement Row with a sense of eager and excited anticipation, wearing something deliberately dull and conventional: an ankle-length tweed suit, silk velvet hat and high lace-up brown boots.

Tempting, of course, in the spirit of this day of challenge and change, to make the statement of a fashion rebel. If only I had jodhpurs to flout convention, or perhaps some item borrowed from my brother's wardrobe. However, I know the suffragette marchers always appear in immaculate long dresses sporting the colour code of purple, white and green, signals of feminine rectitude even in the face of threatening confrontation.

A crooked smile. Rectitude is not normally me, of course, but Mother's malign influence still persists. She's forbidden me to attend the rally but cannot enforce such an absurd stricture. I'm coming up to my twentieth birthday and no longer live at the family home. I'm not going to be dictated to and I'm not waiting for my twenty-first to be a truly independent woman. What person of spirit could survive the restrictive regime of 29 Guildhall Street into adulthood? Typically, Marcus can.

The light is beginning to dim toward evening and there's a chill in the air. I'm not alone. Lines of women are heading towards the big square and I note how the roofs, walls and pavements of Cemetery Road – never a beautiful place – have acquired a grey grittiness that is tribute to the industrial endeavour of maltings, factories and workshops in our town. Crossing into Woodhall Street, I'm encouraged to see three of the new motorised charabancs, all done out in dazzling bright orange, parked haphazardly among the hansoms, growlers and broughams that have brought supporters in from the country.

I'm making for our rendezvous and Scott, like the reliable fellow he is, waits for me on the steps up to the Corn Exchange. Today, however, he is not wearing his habitual smile and I know why. Like me, he's the outsider. One brother is at Dartmouth, the other at Sandhurst and the family has a big place out on the Risby road. Such an uptight military cast would be aghast at the notion of his attendance at a Votes for Women rally.

We enter Abbeygate Street, passing the carcase-festooned Barwell butchery and Ridley's grocery store. The boss is standing outside, wearing his top hat, joined by several white-aproned staff, arms crossed, staring poker-faced at the female procession. There's more mute hostility from other spectators and I can feel an atmosphere of menace building as we descend the steep incline past familiar names – Groom's bookshop, the Music Warehouse and Jarman's photography. I spot a familiar pallid face behind a first-floor window at Cowper and Jelling's shuttered department store and give my friend Rose a wave. At the bottom of the slope I can already hear the hubbub that is Angel Hill, people spilling on to the street like water gushing from a burst pipe. If Scott had not been present, despite all my resolve, I might have faltered. Crowds are not my natural territory. A single-handed battler against the forces of gravity – hopefully, that'll soon be me, excitement aplenty in a flimsy cockpit – but this intense, raucous, clamouring mass of bodies is a new and frightening experience. However, I won't turn away.

We push, shove and ease our way into the big square, to be greeted by a sea of bobbing hats – extravagant 'bird nests' full of bows and lace, silk velvet turbans in blue and yellow, ostrich feathers, panamas, straw boaters, top hats, bowlers, flat caps and police helmets, all moving but stationary, it seems, as if the owners are dancing on the spot. I've stripped mine of its usual wild flower decoration. Nothing so frivolous for this occasion.

To my right I can just see the top half of the portentous Doric columns and bright cream paintwork of the Athenaeum subscription rooms and the huge brewery chimney far beyond; closer still, the flower-bedecked grey-faced Angel Hotel. The police are everywhere, beefy, strapping fellows stationed around the hotel entrance, positioned, I suspect, to carry away those they will arrest, and above the continuous racket of a thousand voices is the clatter of hooves on cobbles and the snorting of police horses.

What will happen next? We've all seen the reports of arrests and violence at suffrage marches in London. Will the authorities in Bury allow this to pass without hindrance?

I turn to see, on the far side of the square, by the huge Norman tower gateway which is the entrance to the Abbey Gardens, a cluster of people, mostly in flat caps, whose banners do not fit the expected theme of the occasion. *A Woman's Place Is In Her Home*, says one; *Women's Suffrage Means Higher Taxes*, says another. Perhaps most galling of all is a female figure holding a notice proclaiming: *No Votes Thank You*.

'They're the antis,' Scott whispers, as a tall woman in a plain crown hat puts some amplifying gadget to her lips and above the resulting shrieks of dissent I make out the words 'this wicked foolishness...'

Scott is still close by my left ear. 'That was Queen Victoria's opinion on the votes campaign. Now being put out by Gertrude Bell.'

A name I know: noted archaeologist, explorer, imperial emissary to the Arab lands. Not a woman, surely, to be dismissed as an unintelligent loon.

Perhaps I've moved too close to this counterdemonstration by the Anti-Suffrage League, because a bucolic middle-aged man addresses me directly. 'You don't really believe in all this, do you?' he shouts, pointing at the ranks of purple, green and white. Before I can reply he ticks off a list of objections to the militant tactics of the campaigners, using the splayed fingers of his hand: 'Bombing the homes of prominent people, setting fire to churches, incinerating post boxes, slashing old masters, smashing department store windows...'

His voice is lost as a louder chant is heard. The suffragettes have spotted the tiny figure of Emmeline Pankhurst. This is the person I and the vast crowd have come to hear, now mounting the steps to a small canopy outside the entrance to the Angel Hotel, gripping metal railings to keep her from falling. Cheers are contrasted to a low grumbling from others in the crowd. I can smell gin on the breath of a stout man; another looks beady-eyed; fists are shaken, insults shouted. Excitement is all. I move further into the throng to see and hear this tiny heroic figure of a woman.

The clamour dies, reduced almost to a hush. Behind Pankhurst hangs a banner urging attendance at a House of Commons demonstration. In the pause before the speech begins, I try to bring to mind some useful phrases to be used in a report, and my artistic eye photographs the essence of the scene for a later sketch. I'm also aware of a possible personal conflict. I'm meant to be an observer as well as a supporter. My friend *The Planet* correspondent has warned me against putting belief before objectivity.

Then the voice we've been waiting to hear is high and sharp and heard despite repeated catcalls from the antis. 'We are called militant,' Pankhurst proclaims, 'and we are willing to accept the name.' I'm surprised by this directness. 'Be militant each in your own way,' she says. 'Those who can express your militancy by going to the Commons – do so. Those of you who can break windows – break them. Those who can still further attack the secret idol of property – do so.' A pause before the final declaration: 'And my last word is to the government. I incite this meeting to rebellion.'

An answering roar. And threatening activity below the hotel steps among the constabulary. The antis begin to push into the crowd, lashing out with fists. There's a clash of banners, missiles begin to fly and arrests look certain. I can visualise another sketch of Pankhurst being carried away by some seven-foot uniformed giant. I'm conscious of the pungent odour of fresh horse dung, the dull smell of well-worn heavy serge, steam rising from a thousand agitated bodes. It's a toxic mix of fear, wonder and anticipation.

At this moment I feel a tug on my sleeve and turn in surprise to see my friend the correspondent beckoning me to move away. Maggie Melrose is a tough one, that's for certain, with scars visible on hands and arms, but this time she's shouting words of warning. 'It's getting dangerous,' she says, 'those horses are going to charge the crowd. Hell to pay, broken bones, heads smashed... don't get yourself under those hooves.'

'I won't,' I assure her.

But she's not finished. 'And don't get yourself arrested, or the paper won't look at you. Keep well clear, the police aren't too particular about who they arrest and what for.'

But suddenly fear and caution flee my mind. I'm no longer tentative or frightened. Instead, I'm outraged at the actions of a mounted officer in a flat cap on a huge white horse. He's leaning right over to one side and using a baton to thrash someone with unremitting ferocity.

'Why?' I ask out loud and a voice answers from the crowd. 'She's got a pair of secateurs, trying to snip his traces, trying to drag him down.'

I can't stand back and play the impartial observer. I'm enraged at the spite and aggression of this officer. I've lost my fear of the crowd. Now I'm part of it. I shove people aside, the antithesis of caution, and move closer. There's something familiar about this scene and I soon understand why. The woman with the snips is my landlady. Katie Snow is cowering on the ground, groaning, holding her side, a bloodied hand shielding her head.

It's a shock to find her so. I thought she was on duty at the hospital, but it looks as if she'll soon be back there as a casualty.

Heedless of Melrose's warning words, I grab Katie's other hand and begin dragging her away, backing into a hard thicket of bodies. Others in the crowd are remonstrating with the beater but he looks set to win his war. I can smell his horse, its hot breath, leather and the brasses. I'm not afraid of horses but know the damage they can cause. Despite this, the horse skitters, moves nearer, treads on my foot. Amid the shock and pain I let go of Katie's hand and the next thing I'm conscious of is a wedge of constables grabbing Katie and pulling her away. Beyond my reach, beyond my rescue.

Now someone is dragging me too. I go limp, feel the brutal roughness of cobbles on unprotected skin. The sting and pain from my foot is more than anything I've known. Limp and helpless, I'm pulled roughly through a forest of legs and bodies away from the thrashing baton. A disembodied part of my brain registers another collision – my knee with a hard object – and a rip and tear to my clothing. I assume the firm grip and big hands belong to my saviour, most likely the supportive and trusty

Scott, taking me away from all this, but when I turn I find they're all wearing blue. They dump me in a heap, minus my hat, at some temporary cubicle being used by the police.

'Another damned troublemaker,' a voice says. 'Another arrest.'

Arrest! I'm aghast. This means the end. No more *Planet*. No more sketches or commentary. What a blow. And my foot feels like a piece of squashed meat that belongs to someone else.

There are many of us, victims of the police charge, the fallen detritus of a day of protest, crowded together in a meagre carriage, pressed against the sides as a labouring horse drags us clattering and jolting over the cobbles to the courthouse. I do my best to control my fear, to accept the crush of bodies. 'That darned horse!' I complain to my neighbour, a sour woman with a torn dress. 'My foot is on fire. I need an arnica compress on it.'

She snorts. 'Some hope in here!'

I look at the others; blanched features, scrawny limbs and hunched shoulders. How will I cope with the humiliation – inside and later, when I am out? This has to be the nadir of my fortunes. Arrested, perhaps jailed, and the life I had planned – flying, writing or teaching – now wrenched away from me. A dead end, a non-future in a cul-de-sac of life.

I can see the others eyeing me, assessing me, judging me. So now, among my new companions on society's bottom rung, I need to hold my head high.

'They'll have those nice clothes off you, soon enough,' scoffs an old crone with absurdly bad teeth. 'Wait till you have to fight to get into prison garb.' She looks away, chuckling at this prospect.

When we arrive in the courthouse cell block I search

everywhere for Katie, pushing my way through the crowd, but there's no sign. They must have her in another building.

Then I begin to plan; how will I plead when I get to court? How shall I make my protest at the injustice of the situation?

There's no ceremony to this. The court system has obviously been geared up and waiting in anticipation. Driven up a steep set of stone steps and into a crowded dock, I realise there's scant prospect of a fair hearing. Naively, I await my turn to speak among many voices and much shouting.

'Forty shillings,' barks the beak and we're herded back down again like a flock of condemned sheep.

The cells are rank. No light, agricultural smells and a space surely meant for one which now holds twenty. 'I need to go somewhere,' a voice wails, unavailing.

'Dovedale!' Someone is shouting my name above the hubbub. It is repeated several times as we await another conveyance, presumably to the jail.

'Dovedale.'

I push to the front of the crush and wave a hand.

'Get her outta there,' intones a rough voice belonging to a figure in blue serge. 'Lucky bitch, someone's paid her fine.'

CHAPTER SIX

I'm in pain. My foot still throbs but I have much to be grateful for. Maggie Melrose promises I've not blown my chances at *The Planet* – forgiven as 'a victim of police action' – and I owe my freedom to Scott who paid the fine. Now I'm wondering how I can repay him. He's proving to be Mr Dependable, my steadfast supporter. Perhaps he's becoming more than that. I see him as a sitter for a serious future portrait. I picture his shape, the nose, the chin, those perfect teeth and the ready smile. And the voice, eloquent and articulate, that contributes to the easy manner and complete absence of class consciousness. In short, a modern man, though I insist to myself that this is a purely artistic appraisal.

My immediate worry is Katie. She's not been so lucky, ending up in Bury's bleak jailhouse for assaulting a police officer. I assure her husband that somehow – I don't yet know how – I'm going to bust her out. Never a happy soul, Mooseface is moping about, wandering from room to room, mumbling and asking how on earth he's going to manage without her wage.

Look, I feel like telling him, I've done my bit. Got up at six this morning, despite the aching foot. Did the dishes, emptied the ashes, laid the fire. All the normal routine in this household where I lodge. Now it's your turn, chum! But no, I don't say this. Katie's my friend as well as my landlord and I'm playing the discreet supporting role. I'll be round the town jail on Wednesday morning to see what I can do. That's the first chance I'll get, as they only allow visitors once a week.

Besides, I've got my own worries – principally, that this foot injury may put a damper on my big day at the aerodrome – the day I've been longing for over all these years, but damn it, I'm determined; pain or no, nothing is going to stop me now Scott has agreed to take me up.

I look around Katie's dingy kitchen and scullery. Of course, some of my friends think I'm mad to have moved out of the comfort of Guildhall Street to live in this tiny place in the poorest street in town. Mother asks me why I've spurned her home comforts; demands 'what's the attraction of slumming it?' Does she really need an answer?

Besides, I want to connect with people, not isolate myself as she does, creating a barrier by staying in class. I've made a vow to socialise everywhere and I make a conscious effort to share all the chores and show Katie and Mooseface I'm not above getting my hands dirty and I don't care about crossing boundaries.

Right now I'm sitting at the kitchen table with my pad and pencils. On the back wall are a couple of my previous efforts; people I've had fun with; beetle-brows, double chins, bulging eyes. I look down, fingers exploring a crack in the table and the rough underside, and consider my new subject. This is going to be serious, a very special sketch. No fun today: the horse, the battering cop and the falling woman. Then there are the words to accompany the work. I craft these with equal care, especially proud of my description of the opponents of Votes for Women; merely fringe malcontents, I say, the left-behinds of history. I have a vague worry about my correspondent friend wagging her finger on the subject of objectivity. *You're supposed to be an observer,* she insists, *not a believer, keep some balance, even if you do think the other side are a bunch of rascals.* I shake my head. No, this has to be about feeling, the I-was-there theme. What it felt like entering the huge press of bodies, the anticipation, the dreadful insults, the pain and the drama of it all.

I've promised Maggie Melrose I'll have it done by lunchtime and on the dot of twelve she's at the door. 'Coming along nicely,' she says, leaning over my shoulder. 'Love the way you've got the startled crowd. Yes, we should get this down to London as soon as you're done.'

She's going to put it on the 5.15 from Bury, phone ahead and get the paper to do the pick-up from the guard's van at Liverpool Street.

Later, when it's finished and everyone's gone and the house is quiet, I get to reflect on the events of the last few hours. We're on the cusp of great social change and I want to be part of it. I'm not simply aiming to be an aviator, I tell myself, I'm more than that.

Next morning the cold compress has done its work on my foot and at last the big day has arrived, the moment I've been praying for all these years, the occasion of my first flying lesson – weather permitting. The swelling's gone down, so I'll be able to use the left foot to its fullest extent on the control pedals without distraction. Now, at last, to catch up with Brother Dear!

Scott picks me up in his Bentley (eyes agog at all the windows) and we motor down to Broadlands. I have my pride. I'm going to pay him back for getting me out of that awful courthouse. And now I feel the need to impress, so put on the blouse and skirt combination that's becoming increasingly popular. The top is white muslin with a lace Valenciennes collar and whitework embroidery at the front. At the clubhouse

I insist on the use of a changing cubicle to get into something fit for flying. I'm grinning to myself. The last time I was in Guildhall Street I invaded my brother's room and liberated a pair of his overalls. He's a skinny kid, unlike his sister, and the strides are tight and short and as scratchy as hell but better than wearing pantaloons.

Out on the apron I can hardly contain myself while the Avro is fuelled up and checked over. At last I get to approach the fuselage from behind the wings and head for the observer's seat – that's the one in front of the pilot's – and there are more instructions about where to put my feet when climbing in, lest some clumsy soul (not me, of course) should put his size twelves through the flimsy fabric of the wing. When I'm in, the position feels tight and cramped, like sitting in a miniature bathtub, but once I wriggle about it feels better, almost snug and safe, with much more protection than the exposed position on the Farman.

Scottie's behind me, talking me through all the instruments of control: stick, rudder bar, altimeter, rev counter. When he starts up the Gnome the ear-splitting racket at such close proximity is even more hellish than I'd anticipated and it's a struggle to hear his commentary on the moves he's making. We trundle over the grass, position ourselves to face into the wind, then let rip and after a few hairy bumps on wheels that could definitely do with better springs a floaty sensation announces that we're up. I peer over the side, fascinated as we soar into the sky, quite forgetting I'm supposed to be an aviator and looking ahead. Hey, this is better than climbing a tree, trumps the tallest tower I've ever climbed. Higher and higher we go. Instead, I act the passenger and marvel at how the countryside looks from above. It has a strange map-like quality. At first, I can't quite equate what I see with what I know, then I pick out the river and finally in the distance our town which looks so small amid the vast green countryside.

At 500 feet instructions come over my shoulder that I should take control: 'Keep straight and level,' he yells, 'eye ahead level with the horizon, don't do anything crazy, just get the feel of her.'

'Right-ho! I have control.'

What a gas! I have our lives literally at my fingertips. After a while, however, it begins to seem a bit lame, like riding a bicycle up the High Street, so I reckon on pulling a right turn, but in the process I haul the stick back as well as over to the side and the nose of the aircraft shoots up.

'Stick forward' is the cry from behind.

A sudden rush of panic. Stick forward! But it's too far, and the nose goes down into a dive angle, so I pull up again, aghast at the wallowing feeling I've created, my heart rate thumping, my stomach disappearing somewhere to the west.

'Try and keep her level,' he shouts. 'And next time, look where you're going. You didn't check to make sure the space was clear of other aircraft.'

Other aircraft? Up here? But I nod and veer back on to a straight course, and after another minute try a left. Looking first this time and keeping a slightly better angle.

'Doing okay,' says the voice from behind, 'but try some more gentle turns, say a wide circuit and a figure of eight.'

This is it. I need to perfect some graceful and smooth turns, not jerky stunt turns like my brother, so I give it my best effort. Circuits, figures of eight, an S-formation... it's a strange blend of opposites up here. On the one hand I feel great exhilaration, on the other hand, fear. Excitement and adrenaline versus panic and dread. This, I guess, is the intoxicating mix that's going to be my future.

'You've done well,' he shouts, before adding firmly: 'I have control.' Time to come into land, and he's not fool enough to let me try that.

Once on the ground my sense of joy is unbounded. The release of tension is simply huge. I feel drained, as if I've just run a marathon, but ecstatic. Then comes the slap in the face.

'Just got news of your brother,' he says.

'Oh?'

'You know the military. Wheels within wheels, news travels fast.'

I say nothing.

'Provided he passes for the pilot's licence, he's been provisionally accepted for the Flying Corps.'

I nod and look away to hide my frustration, then demand through barely open lips: 'How long before I can take the test?'

CHAPTER SEVEN

I worry about my landlady Katie, how she's getting on in jail, hoping her wounds are being properly treated. They must have a treatment room, surely? And when visiting day comes around I'm there, with ointment and balming cream in my pockets, just in case, hoping to hand them over.

Mooseface has been worried too, moping about, hardly saying a word and not so much as a thank you or acknowledgement when I give him his breakfast these past few mornings.

That old prison is a forbidding place. I've always avoided it. Well out of town on the Sudbury road, it has a vast flat frontage and looks like a Napoleonic fort. Never been inside before, of course, and when I enter through a nasty little gate with wobbly hinges and a greasy handle I can feel my feet slipping on a yard bespattered with mud and debris. There's a long queue ahead of me, lots of weeping and wailing, filth on the stairs, everyone waiting to be searched. It suddenly comes to me that this is an almost exclusively female zone with lots of tear-stained faces and tatty shawls. On the wall is a chalkboard containing a peremptory notice. No touching, no gifts, no handing objects over, no changes of clothing, no this and no that. Everything's forbidden, it seems, except breathing. Any infraction of the rule results in a penalty of six months on the wrong side of the bars.

At the top of the steps is a man sitting behind a table. He has a rough blue serge uniform, a sour expression and warts all over his face. Bluebottles, that's what the turnkeys are called. I pick up this much from the queue and he's none too gentle with his search and curt with a demand to record the personal details of every visitor – name, address, age, occupation, relationship to the prisoner.

I say *sister*, producing borrowed documentary identification, to wit, Katie's rent book.

Then another queue.

'How long is this going to take?'

He doesn't answer. I look around at the visitors and realise that in my peach silk day dress I'm probably the best-attired person in the place. All women and mostly poor. Dowdy dresses, stringy shawls, ragged footwear.

Another notice orders silence but there's a low murmur of complaint and plaintive stories of hardship and poverty made worse by incarceration. After fearing that this is going to use up my whole day, I'm finally beckoned forward by another turnkey with a long list and a voice that belongs on an army parade ground.

'Three minutes. Not a second more.'

I take a stone seat in front of a grille, hold my breath and wait. Eventually, a door opens somewhere on the other side and finally Katie's blanched features appear in front of me. She looks terrible. She limps, has no shoes and there's still a bruise on her face. 'Treatment?'

Katie shakes her head. 'No. They just don't care,' she says. 'Their attitude is just total hostility. Rats and cockroaches everywhere, a bucket in the corner of a crowded cell, no privacy, murderers and prostitutes and other awful people...' Her voice trails off into a silent misery.

In London there's talk of a class system within the jails in which the suffragettes are given privileged status, but this doesn't seem to operate in Bury. No recognition has been given to her status as a protester. She had to scramble like all the rest for something to wear among a heap of stained, patched and discarded prison garb dumped in a yard.

'Please, Charlotte,' she says, 'get me out of this awful place.'

'Don't worry, I will.'

Suddenly that voice is a blast in my left ear. 'Time's up!' and I can feel a rough hand on my shoulder.

'But I haven't had three minutes,' I protest, equally loudly and turning to confront.

'Oh yes you have.'

'No I haven't.'

'Next!'

He's a cheat. I recognise his type. He wants to get rid of the queue as quickly as possible so he can get back to doing whatever turnkeys do when they're not bullying visitors. I stand my ground, directly in his eyeline.

'You're a bully but you don't frighten me.'

'Just watch your lip, young lady.'

I shove my face next to his. This must be a new experience for him, someone biting back, because I register a sudden flicker of uncertainty in his eyes before he yells 'Next!' once again.

I demand to speak to the governor to complain about the conditions in which my 'sister' has been kept. That's when I notice all the buttons missing from the turnkey's tunic. Not an encouraging sign.

The governor, when he eventually answers the call, is not exactly an upstanding town official. He has a stubble head, a boxer's nose and fingers like joints of meat. My eyes automatically register these details but I don't feel like drawing them, not just at the moment.

'I want to get my sister out of here,' I tell him. 'The conditions are appalling.'

He puffs himself up like a bedraggled peacock past his prime. 'I'll have you know, this is a model prison, specially designed for the purpose.'

Then God help the others – but I just stop myself saying this. His gaze doesn't flicker and I recognise that a jailbreak from this fortress is not on – if it ever was. Finding the money to pay the fine seems the only way.

'Fines must be paid at the courthouse.'

'She has no shoes, how can she be released without footwear? She can't go barefoot through the streets.'

'Not our concern.'

'I would like to know when the release happens so I can meet her with a new pair of shoes and better clothing. She's in rags.'

'Release takes place after court payment. If not, she'll serve her full sentence.'

'When is release likely?'

'In due course. When we're good and ready.' Then he gives me a baleful glare. 'Perhaps next time you people will think twice about causing the authorities so much trouble.'

No point in going direct to the courthouse. I don't have the money. I consider the problem. Sell the bicycle? Never, it's my lifeline. The gramophone? Pity, we really enjoy the syncopated rhythms of the ragtime bands. I used to drive Mother mad foot tapping to honky-tonk and the blues. But, like the bike, the old machine won't raise enough. A painting then? There's my favourite landscape, of course, the cathedral with its snoutish little tower, the one they couldn't afford to finish all those centuries ago. That might do, even if I'm rather fond of it. And I know just the man.

'I might be interested.' It's the town magistrate, Jonathan Cowper, belittled by local nobility 'as merely trade', but the wealthy owner of the Cowper and Jelling department store. Last year I sold him one of my paintings, a landscape of the Abbey rose gardens, and his wife Rose loves the yellows of my sunflowers which she has adorning her dining-room wall.

'Come round to the judges' lodgings tonight,' Cowper says. 'I'm visiting at eight o'clock and you might find a buyer there.'

I rush back to get to my wardrobe in Guildhall Street. This calls for some serious dressing up: a tweed check costume trimmed with velvet, my very best. And the judges' house is normally forbidden territory, of course, to anyone without a full bottomed wig. Empty for most of the year until the assizes are held, the touring judges then arrive to lodge at this enormous palatial building, three storeys high and as wide as a block.

Cowper answers the side door and ushers me in. The contrast is daunting. Outside, just around the corner, is a line of artisan cottages dating from the 16th century, still in use, crammed full of families in tiny dungeon-like rooms and cellars, without running water. Here are luxuriant carpets, velvet walls, the finest mahogany furniture and showcases full of precious porcelain. Don't even look at the billiard room bigger than a row of houses, a kitchen large enough to feed an army, the exquisitely laid dining table and a vast living room adorned with wig stands, desks, bookcases, armchairs and a large fireplace.

I hold my breath as I stand by the door of the billiard room, fearful that my appearance may still fall short of expectation, but no one is at the table. In one corner are two stands on which are draped full-length robes in red, black and purple. In another is a large sofa on which a male figure is sprawled in a pose of petulant indolence reminiscent of some 17th century regent just back from losing a fortune at the card table.

'My Lord, this young lady is a talented local artist,' says Cowper, 'and offers you this wonderful view of the town.'

His Lordship doesn't rise. He rubs a bulbous nose and scratches his great bald dome of a head. Perhaps I'm meant to be intimidated by this strange mix of opulence and threat and an inner voice warns me to be careful how I conduct myself. This man has an awesome power to impose draconian punishment. Erasmus Lockwood is known in Bury as the hanging judge. For a second I wonder how Kate, the woman on whose behalf I'm here, might cope with this scene. No doubt she'd be petrified, the details of his fine garments imprinted on her mind. Not me. I'm fixated on the extraordinary physiognomy; the warty nose amid a mosaic of bumps and scratches that look as if he's had an argument with a rose bush. This time my fingers itch to get to my sketchbook.

'Is this the woman who was arrested in the riot?' A scratchy, imperious voice.

'A misunderstanding, My Lord, an unfortunate moment in a melee with one of the horses. No action required.'

The judge snorts. 'Don't hold with all these protesters. No compunction about sending damned suffragettes to the cells.'

Cowper is manoeuvring my painting into the best position for viewing but the man ignores him and gives me full beam disapproval while wagging a finger. 'Make sure you don't cross my path again,' he says, 'and no, I won't buy your darned painting. Pretty pictures?' A splutter. 'Hunt trophies are what I want on my wall.'

Outside on the staircase the magistrate is all apologies for no-deal. 'Never mind, my dear,' he says in a hushed tone, 'I'll take it for four guineas, will that suit?'

It certainly will. Pays the fine for Katie and payback to Scottie for my own.

Someone from the jailhouse queue has given me a helpful hint – the sort of forbidden advice that comes from the side of the mouth and is delivered with a wink. It seems they release prisoners every morning at 6.30, so I'm outside the prison at that time every day with shoes, a warm coat and some tasty biscuits. On the third morning she is pushed roughly from that nasty little gate. I toot and she limps over to the cab I've hired. We embrace and I whisk her back to Tenement Row where we send Mooseface on his way before getting out the old tin bath. I heat up some water on the range while she rips ravenously into bread and jam, then it's a good rub down, soothing ointments and off to bed.

'Don't get up and start on the house,' I tell her. 'Let him do that.'

I realise, but don't say, that the chances of Mooseface cleaning the fire irons, polishing the brasses, wiping windowsills and washing the steps is probably a remote possibility. She makes a face. She's relieved to be out of that dreadful place – but not joyous. An ominous-looking official letter has been waiting for her on the kitchen table – they don't have a mantelpiece. When she opens it, my fears for her are confirmed: she's been dismissed by the hospital for joining the march and getting arrested. 'Conduct unbecoming of the traditions of the service' was how they put it. How they love to kick you when you're down.

She says: 'Now all I've got coming in is your rent money and what my Rufus can make doing his fence work. When he's got any work.'

What can I say? There are no comforting words for the sudden impact of losing a job. Unemployment round here is the norm. It's a disease. Eventually, I tell her: 'You'll find a way, I know you will.'

She shakes her head. 'I don't have registration, I went into nursing before all that, and now it's all getting much more difficult, very official. Will I ever get back in?'

'Well, if you don't have a registration you can't be struck off, can you?'

Always best to look for the positive is my motto – but realise I need to do more than just commiserate. 'Tell you what,' I say in my most encouraging tone, 'I'll get my mother to put the word out among all the other shopkeepers in town. A bright young assistant is offering her services.'

I have to admit that right now she isn't looking too bright – but then I tell her about the pretty close call I had myself just the other day. The principal of the adult college where I teach three language sessions a week called me into his office.

'Miss Dovedale,' Jeremiah Laudenham says, fixing me with a glaucous eye, 'it has come to my notice that you took part in that disgraceful business in the square.'

I'm momentarily thrown until I realise he's talking about the Votes for Women rally.

'Arrested and fined!' he says in tones of vastly exaggerated shock.

'A misunderstanding,' I insist. 'Trampled by a police horse. Released when it emerged it was one of theirs.'

He sighs and looks at the ceiling. 'Not the sort of behaviour I expect of my tutors. You must realise, your position here is in jeopardy. I have the reputation of the college to consider.'

I look down at my hat which is placed on the table before me and my fingers curl around the hatpin with the needle-sharp point. Suffragettes have stabbed people for less than this. That's why we're banned from the top deck of London buses.

'Please,' I say. 'On ice?'

'No further public statements, actions or wearing of the suffrage colours,' he stipulates. 'No more demonstrations, marches or mention of the subject.'

I can't afford to be brave and, swallowing considerable resentment, give him a compliant nod.

It seems both Katie and I have paid a high price for our suffragist campaigning.

CHAPTER EIGHT

I t feels like yet another stab in the back. Like the world is out to get me. I'd been looking forward to my next flight as compensation for all the nastiness over the past few days. The Nieuport is an ace fighter from across the Channel; it represents a challenge, a delight, another potential notch on my upward curve to a flying career.

But not now!

Before Scott and I even arrive at the apron we know something is wrong. The Nieuport is already up, doing loops and circuits above the course and when Scott demands an explanation the Broadlands mechanic shrugs. 'Orders.'

'From whom?'

'Mr Quedgeley.'

I haven't seen Scott this angry before. 'We'll see about this,' he says. 'Someone up in MY aircraft!' He's already started towards the office when the mechanic calls after him.

'He's in the club.'

A loud snort of disgust. The Aero Club is an institution we both avoid. A den of raucous enthusiasts and drunken hangers-on, Scott says, as we march at a furious pace towards the door.

He's angry and I'm frustrated. I'd been anticipating another flying challenge to fight off all my doubts and disappointments over the past few days. I swallow, more uncertain now than ever before. I'm beginning to wonder if I can ever win through against all this inbuilt prejudice. Am I doomed, despite all my efforts, always to be excluded or relegated to second place?

We find the clerk of the course at the bar with a half-full beer glass in his hand. No preliminaries. Scott had a one-word question. 'Why?'

'Sorry,' Quedgeley says, looking anything but apologetic, 'had to give the flight to Jackson Forbes.'

I nearly spit. My place has been taken by that jeering Judas from across 'The Avenue'.

'Forbes?' Scott is incredulous. I haven't seen him this demonstrative before. He's normally so cool and restrained. I feel immense warmth towards him for his unflinching support.

He says: 'It's my aircraft, dammit, well, borrowed actually, but all down to me. In my care and I flew it here.'

Quedgeley shakes his head. 'We've had complaints.'

'Complaints, what complaints?'

'We understand your pupil is a suffragette.'

'So what, she's my guest.'

'Look, it's one thing for us to allow women to fly, but we're not having any damned suffragettes here. We draw the line at that. We don't want any trouble.'

'What trouble?'

'Their sort of trouble.' At this the jug-eared Quedgeley sighs deeply as if stricken by oceans of concern and regret. He's not my favourite person and I can't help noticing the stubbly chin.

'We really can't understand why you're indulging such a person,' he adds, as if he hasn't noticed that I'm standing just three feet away.

'Several very good reasons,' Scott says. 'She's tops. As a pilot and as a person. So, are you now going to ban Ruth Law and Harriet Quimby as well?'

'They're not suffragettes.'

'Perhaps Hilda Hewlett or Blanche Scott?'

'Don't be absurd. We welcome acclaimed aviators. We just don't want any troublemakers at Broadlands.'

Scott has the look of a man who'll brook no more contradiction. 'When Forbes gets down I'm taking immediate possession of that aircraft. And when my father hears about this, I'm not sure if he'll be ready to continue to sponsor your next motor race to the tune of... tell me again, how much is it?'

At this I place a restraining hand on Scott's arm. 'Don't drag your father into this,' I say quietly, so that only he can hear, fearing that Fanshawe Senior may easily turn out to be on the wrong side of the argument and anyway, I'm feeling distinctly uncomfortable with being the object of such heated controversy.

'I must say I also object.'

A new voice. We all turn to see a red-faced stranger in flying gear addressing us, fearing another opponent, feeling even more under siege than before.

'I see no trouble here,' says the stranger. 'I object to the objection and I see no reason why this lady should not fly.'

I smile broadly and nod my thanks to this new and surprising ally and decide it's time to make myself heard. 'Who is this person who has made a complaint against me?'

Quedgeley can't decide whether to answer or ignore.

'Yes,' says Scott, 'who?'

'As it happens, I believe he is the lady's employer.'

'Huh!' I snort. 'Laudenham, the snake. And how does a college principal have any sway at an aerodrome? Hardly a complainant of substance.'

At this point I sense Quedgeley's suffragette ban, if it had any force, is beginning to wither and die, but that doesn't help me. The daylight is already beginning to fade and when the Nieuport finally puts down Scott has no alternative but to fly straight back to wherever he borrowed this fantastic machine.

No flight for me in the Nieuport; another blow to my esteem. I do a quick calculation: three up – the B2, Avro and Bristol – but one down, the Nieuport.

Will I get another chance?

CHAPTER NINE

W e should be talking about aircraft, about three-point landings, stalls, glides and spirals, but we're not. We're talking fathers. Scott and I are in his bungalow, the rain is beating a tattoo on the roof and once again we're watching the windsock and praying for the rain to stop and the wind to drop.

'I guess we're two of a kind,' he says, tea in hand. 'We're outsiders.'

He, of course, is the youngest of three sons, the odd one out in a family of military high-flyers and I want to know how the family dynamic works.

'Father cuts the big figure,' he says, 'but Mother wields the real power indoors.'

One part familiar, one part not. This talk of fathers makes me angry. I've never known mine. Often searched but never found a clue. Christmas, New Year, birthdays... there was always something missing. As a child I recall writing letters to this mysteriously absent figure, yearning for the day he would get in touch. 'If you're reading this...' And then I'd hold imaginary conversations and I would answer for him, in the best way I could, thinking how he would reply, fantasising reasons why he never made himself known. Why? Was he a seriously bad man? And if so, what does that make me? Who am I, exactly? Perhaps these urges to push myself to greater feats of achievement are to find out exactly what I'm made of. It's this black hole in my life that puts acid on the end of my tongue. 'And your father – is he getting anywhere on my behalf,' I demand of Scott. 'On women flyers? On our behalf,' I add quickly. 'Moved any mountains in Whitehall yet?'

Scott, who'd suggested this possibility, makes a non-committal face.

I turn away and glare out of the window. 'Can't bear this waiting around, this delay is intolerable.' I know that even if the weather breaks, the Avro is in pieces on Tom's bench. His young mechanic is out there even now in his little hut, rebuilding the engine. I know because I've been out there with him, getting my hands oily to prove a point, and now I'm impatient and bang a fist on the table, making the teacups rattle. 'I've simply got to get up. Can't you find me another aircraft, Scott, I know you can.'

'I thought you liked working on the engines...'

'I'm getting twitchy. I want to be up. Up, up, up. Being grounded is driving me mad.' I put my head on one side and give him a look. 'I want to fly another type of aircraft. Something further on from the Avro. I want to be an all-rounder. Able to handle anything.'

I tug a strand of hair, suddenly a little guilty at this outburst, regretting my display of petulance.

He grins. 'All right!' A chuckle. 'Okay, you've asked for it!'

I look up, pensive.

'It's true, you've done extraordinarily well, so I'm going to give you a challenge – a big, big challenge – much earlier than I really should. Much earlier than anyone else is ever likely to.'

Now this sounds like progress.

'To be frank, your next aircraft will be a very difficult one, a wild bird. Some people even call her the Killer Bird.' He looks stern. 'But if you can conquer her... if you can manage this machine... you'll be able to fly absolutely anything.'

I can't wait. The Killer Bird. To think my brother Marcus is still lumbering around in his 2c... and, by the way, a word about three-point landings; they're getting your wheels and the tail skid down at exactly the same moment. When you can do that nine times out of ten, then you can say you're a pilot.

Call it an ambush! That's what it feels like when I walk into the shop next day to be confronted by my mother waving a copy of *The Planet* right in front of my eyeline. She's hitting it with the back of her hand, like she was beating the dust out of an old rug. 'What do you think you're doing, Charlotte? Seeing your name in this... this paper, really!'

Oh dear. She's just spotted my latest contribution in print. It features a sketch of my friend Jonathan Cowper driving the new motoring sensation, a gleaming Bullnose Morris complete with acetylene headlights, three oil lamps and shiny hooter, down a horsecart-cluttered street in Bury. Clearly this is a shock for her, and perhaps I should have anticipated her reaction, but still manage a smile of innocence. 'What's so especially dreadful about that?' I ask.

'Yes, dreadful. Really awful. In this publication, of all places. The poor people's rag.'

'There are a lot of us about.'

She gives me that look which I pretend not to notice.

'You, poor?' A loud snort.

'And it's on the side of women, unlike the rest of the papers,' I say. 'That's the big plus in its favour. And, of course, all those lovely pictures.'

She exhales loudly and looks away and for a while there's peace in the world as I meander around the shop, running a practised eye over the sable watercolour brushes and the racks of artists' oil tubes on the Winsor and Newton stand: the Prussian greens, Antwerp blues, lemon yellows, burnt umbers and flesh tints. Then I approach the cash till with the three 4B pencils and a sketch pad selected from another shelf and offer my money across the counter. I'm familiar with the prices.

Mother takes the cash, attacks the keys on the till, the machine chimes up my nine pence, the coins crash into the money drawer and the machine clangs shut. She looks up. I eye her. She eyes me back.

'And what about Brother Dear? Any news?' I inquire.

'I'm surprised you've remembered.'

With that she delves into her bag and produces a letter with RFC stamped all over the envelope. I read through my brother's words, written from some military camp in Scotland, headed by the salutation Dear Mama. Marcus, the eager recruit, is in the pink and on a fast track to officer status. Just tickety-boo for him.

'What's this about a car?' I ask, pointing at a reference on the second page.

She purses her lips. 'I won't have him placed at a social disadvantage to all those rich fellows he'll soon be mixing with,' she says.

'So?'

'He gets a car.'

There's a long silence before the details are revealed: a 1912 Crossley T5, a quite huge brute, the same model that did the London to Monte Carlo rally. Then she smiles. 'You too. I won't have it said you're being treated any differently. You can pay me back in weekly instalments.'

I'm momentarily floored by this announcement until she adds: 'Of course, there's a condition.'

'Oh?'

'You give up flying.'

I snort. 'In that case, no car. And Marcus... is he paying you back in weekly instalments?'

'He has Mess bills to think about.'

You may have noticed: Mother and I are snap quick into a fight. The other day, wandering around the house, it strikes me once again as particularly strange that there isn't a single photo anywhere of the man who was my father. The subject has simmered between us for years. Never seen his photo, nor any letters, a complete blank. I raise the subject again.

'Why don't you ever talk about my father?'

'There's nothing to know.'

'I'm entitled to know. I'm his daughter.'

'Nothing to know,' she says again.

'Why do you keep repeating that?'

'Because it's true. He has no part in our lives. He doesn't exist.'

Just then I spy my least favourite person in the kitchen: Nowak, the Dovedale School flying instructor. 'What's he doing here?' I demand.

'Come to collect his pay.'

'Don't you go to the aerodrome anymore?'

No answer.

'I don't like him,' I say.

'You don't have to. He doesn't like you.'

'He's a lousy instructor.'

'He'll do.'

I put my hands on my hips and say: 'I can't understand why you settle for second best.' Then I'm back stalking around the house in a rage, glaring at the pictures that are on display: Mother pictured with her many cars – her first, the sit-up-and-beg

Clement, the Model T, a Prince Henry Vauxhall racer and now the Fiat; Mother on a boat, Mother by her shop, Mother posed against an aeroplane – and there, skulking in a corner of the last photo is the detested figure of Nowak. I search drawers and cupboards for signs of certificates, letters or documents about my father but there are none. Not a single keepsake, not a badge, hat, walking stick or even an old harmonica. The man has been wiped clean and his very existence erased. Maybe I'll ransack her bureau when she's out and blame the busted lock on a burglar, but somehow that seems an underhand step too far, even for this.

Then I think again about my absent parent. I even feel sorry for him – whoever he is, wherever he is now – given Mother's unforgiving, hard-boiled outlook on life. Difficult to imagine a loving relationship there. Perhaps he felt like me: the outsider of the family.

It's the strangest-looking beast I've ever seen. Not a biplane but a single wing set high above the body of the fuselage. And the body looks like a big fat stump.

'The Morane Parasol,' Scott announces, 'an ideal aircraft for looking down. You've got a much better view than any of the others because the wing is above you. Great for gunnery spotters, for observing what's going on down on the ground.'

'Hmmm,' I say, fingering the ugly snout.

'Has a bad reputation. Dangerous to fly, a deathtrap, according to some.'

'And this is my challenge?'

'This is your challenge. Master this and everyone will be mightily impressed.'

I climb into the observer seat as he talks me through the

controls. 'If you want to prove yourself worthy, you've got to be better than just good.'

'I know that.'

'Breaking into the military, a strictly male preserve...' He shrugs. 'You're pitching against the impossible.'

'I know that too.'

'To have any chance, you need to be brilliant. In fact, you need to fly something others can't. Something they're actually frightened of.' He taps the top of the fuselage, which buckles under finger pressure. 'This,' he says, and levers himself up a foothold and into the hot seat.

'Feeling brave?'

I smile and nod, not trusting my voice, as he runs up the 80-hp Le Rhône engine, leaning forward from his position as he continues. 'The stick – never take your hand off it.'

'Oh?'

'The 2c may fly hands-off, but not this one.' The BE2c is the Army's basic model used for photography and artillery spotting, stable but slow. 'If you're daft enough to let go of this one,' Scott says, 'the stick will fall forward and send us straight into a nosedive. Never, never,' he repeats, 'relax for a second.'

I swallow, anxiety rising. 'Anything else?'

'It's a big step up from the 2c. This machine needs the greatest possible care, skill, lightness of touch and accurate judgement.'

I shrug. What have I got to be frightened of? I have the very best instructor and all I need to do is master the controls. The real test will come on my first solo. By then I'll know all the Parasol's little tricks and foibles.

I endeavour to watch Scott's actions as he takes her up, climbing and then levelling out at seventy-five before setting the aircraft down again like the accomplished flyer he is.

'Now you,' he says. 'And don't forget. If the engine fails on take-off don't turn. Keep on straight and find a field.'

'Anything else?'

'Don't do any turns anyway until you reach 500 feet.'

I give him a quizzical look.

'This is not the stable aerial platform you've been used to.'

Mindful of all the warnings about not relaxing a second and sticking strictly to instructions, I grasp the shooting-stick handle. It's tiny and doesn't even come up to my knees. Deep breath, swallow, then open up the engine, race the plane across the grass strip and push the stick forward.

I expect the tail to lift.

In a flash, it shoots right up over my head.

Panic! I jerk the stick back and the aircraft slumps down to the ground with a nasty crack while still racing over the grass.

Swallow and try again, pushing the stick forward. Up comes the tail once more. Repeat – and the tail descends. By this time the aircraft is at flying speed and the machine lifts itself into the air. I let out a long sigh of relief, not sure how much I had to do with the take-off. The thing has a mind of its own.

'Not my greatest,' I shout.

'Don't turn under 500 feet,' he repeats, but above that height I begin tentatively to regain a little confidence, making gentle turns and playing with the controls, noting how the rudder and ailerons are sluggish and slow to react. I'm breathless with fright and excitement but in the same instant buoyed by the joy of achievement. This is an emotion that began in childhood up a tree at twenty feet, now repeating itself at several hundred feet.

'Time to get her down,' calls the voice behind.

I float carefully back towards the aerodrome looking for the right spot on the grass, tensing at the prospect of my first landing in this unpredictable bird. Then comes a shout from behind.

'I have control.'

Landing, Scott tells me once we're down, is for another day. The Morane has a notoriously weak undercarriage and tends to flip over. 'The aircraft can always be put back together, but you, on the other hand, might be a much more difficult repair job.'

I'm back in my cramped room at Tenement Row, using the corner of the washstand as a desk, writing a letter to my friend Marguerite in Belgium. There's hardly room to move in here with all my things jammed in one corner, but I had to bring at least a few clothes with me. Katie and Rufus don't have that problem. They seem to wear the same clothes day after day.

I tread carefully around this couple. Downstairs I can hear voices. Sounds carry easily in these tiny places and I rather fear my friend and her husband are having words, but I try not to listen and concentrate instead on my letter and memories of childhood holidays with Marguerite. I recall all those warm summer days riding ponies and walking the hills near the big house at Freys, but it's no use, I can't concentrate. The voices from downstairs are becoming so loud and the words so clear. Katie is upbraiding Mooseface for breaking a vase, of blundering about and being clumsy after visiting the Rose and Crown. I also get full volume on his declaration that 'if it wasn't for her upstairs we'd both have space to breathe'.

I know their problem, another taboo subject: no babies. But she's a nurse, she should talk to a doctor, except, of course, she no longer has her job.

I sigh. Regretfully, their argument makes my continued stay in Tenement Row untenable. I won't come between husband and wife. Next morning – a decent interval, hopefully, when tempers have cooled and the said gentleman has gone off to repair some defective reed fence – I broach the subject with Katie, but she won't hear of my moving out. 'Just ignore him,' she says. 'He's crotchety sometimes, specially when the work dries up, but look, I love having you here, you're my true friend.'

She doesn't say it, of course, but she also needs the rent money.

So, much later, I'm trying to finish my letter to Marguerite when a note is slipped under the door of No.4 and Katie races upstairs with it. Her eyes dance. She can tell it's important.

And it is. A note from Scott to tell me that the day for taking the test for my pilot's licence is this Friday.

At last! What joy... and strangely, it turns out to be the same day that my brother Marcus is taking his test.

Now this should be interesting.

CHAPTER TEN

The great day approaches and my excitement soars at the prospect of final recognition. At last, I'm getting somewhere. The test will dispel all doubters. I nod to myself, but for some reason I can't repress a small voice from somewhere far off at the back of my head which keeps asking: Are you really that good?

Of course I am! I feel superbly confident. Who wouldn't, after the Morane Parasol and other aircraft I've now flown. Getting back into the Avro for the test should be simplicity itself.

I go to bed on Thursday night with an anticipatory smile – but what if the inspector has some hidden trick up his sleeve? Some way into the twilight hours strange images swim unbidden into mind: the controls won't respond, the machine flips over on take-off, Marcus emerges from the mist laughing and the inspector's pad shows the enormous word *Failure.* I wake with a pain in the gut, sweat on the brow. Massive relief! The Marcus dream. It's only five and not yet dawn but I get dressed in my big boots and new jodhpurs and go downstairs for a brew.

Getting fitted out in the jodhpurs – now that was a hoot – and the thought lifts my mood. As soon as I'd stepped into Septimus Salter's dark and gloomy old habit-maker's shop on The Traverse last week he was all of a lather. 'Putting women in trousers? I'll be run out of town,' he objects... until I tell him about all the orders he's going to get from the Emergency Corps and the Voluntary Aid Detachments.

Yesterday I did my nails, keeping them short for maximum finger control, and now I sit staring out of the window at the gloomy backyard which, touched by a half-moon, is just visible in all its black brick shabbiness. After a while there's a rumbling upstairs – you can't turn over in bed in this house without the neighbours knowing – and Katie emerges in a tattered dressing gown ripped at the back.

'Nervous?'

I shake my head. Never admit it!

Katie, though barely educated and the victim of a life plagued by poverty and deprivation, is anything but a simple soul. She knows what's required: diversionary conversation. We start to talk about men; specifically her Mooseface, whose increasingly detached behaviour includes laughing when I place a tiny mirror by the front door to check my appearance. He seems to think this demonstrates arrogance. Wrong! I'm simply on a mission to achieve – to make something of my life. These days you're considered an old maid at twenty-five and time is marching on. I vow not to waste these years, I have to make my mark in aviation while I still have all the vigour of youth.

The mood of the moment improves immeasurably with a knock at the door from a telegraph boy. It's still early and it's for me – causing quite a stir. Every motor car in Tenement Row rates a stare.

Mystified, I rip it open and read: *Good luck, best*

wishes for your test today. I look in vain for an attribution.

'Who's it from?' Katie is eager to know.

'Doesn't say.'

She makes a swooning gesture. 'Mysterious well-wisher... you've got a secret admirer. Now who's that, do you reckon?'

I wonder if it's Scott, but when he calls to collect me he denies it. 'You don't need luck,' he says, and it's true, I shouldn't. The Avro should be a piece of cake, I tell myself, blotting out all memory of the Marcus dream, repressing any lingering doubt.

When I get to the aerodrome we sit and wait on the veranda of Scott's bungalow, fuelled by more coffee and cakes, courtesy of his man Tom, keeping the champagne on ice for later. Is such complacency a bad sign? I ask myself.

The aviation authorities have decided that with two test candidates ready at the same aerodrome on the same day they will detail just one inspector to take both tests. Marcus is on first, at ten, and I know they're down there, Mother and he, just a hundred yards away in that stinky little shed, awaiting the hour. We've already had our words on the subject. She, of course, is ablaze with indignation. 'Is there nothing you won't do to rival your brother? Won't you give him a free run at anything?'

I told her days ago my participation will spur him on, make him try harder. Hot up the pace. Competition's good for him, I say, we've always done it since we were kids.

Now, in more reflective mood, I feel an unexpected twinge of guilt, an outbreak of sympathy for Brother Dear. I know him of old, he'll be nervous, especially with everyone looking on. Especially me, fearing I'll make him appear foolish. For a brief moment an astonishing thought flashes into my mind. Should I back off today, and give him what Mother describes as a clear run?

Then I shake my head. I'm damned if I will! I've worked too hard for this to let it go. He'll cope.

In good time we stroll down to the grass circle outside the control tower while Marcus is still in the air, passing Mother and her instructor standing rigid on the grassy edge. No words are exchanged. If eyes could kill... and the feeling is mutual as far as Nowak is concerned. The ill-concealed lover, such an unprepossessing little runt. Really! How could she?

We look up to watch progress in the air. Marcus is following to the letter the prescribed test format: take-off to 500 feet, two circles, a figure of eight and land and, I'm relieved to say, he doesn't make a hash of it when he gets the 2c back on the grass. That should be good for a couple of pips on his epaulettes.

Suddenly Mother is approaching, all smiles. Her boy has passed 'with flying colours' and we speak for the first time this day. 'And now I suppose I should wish you good luck,' she says.

This is a breakthrough. She feels this is what is required of her, but it's all front – she doesn't mean it, she'd love me to fail – it would restore things to their natural order, according to the terms of her world.

The inspector approaches. A tall, lugubrious man in a dark suit and wearing a scowl which accentuates the scar across his forehead. An old mishap, I ask myself, thinking how I might sketch this: Frankenstein forehead, razor-slash chin? Mr Grump gives me an unforgiving glare. 'This is a waste,' he says, 'a woman at this time. Don't you know there's a war coming?'

I ignore this and resist the temptation for a suitable reply. Instead, I say: 'How nice of you to devote your time to do this for me, kind sir, please may we proceed?'

I can see my mother's astonished expression from the corner of my vision as the inspector levers himself with great difficulty into the Avro. I'm surprised he can squeeze his six feet of misery into my passenger seat. Best physique for a pilot is five foot nothing. As I start up I can see Scottie's face and his expression is telling me to behave myself and not to overdo the flying, so I endeavour to give the inspector no excuse to fail me. Up, turn, circle, do the necessary and get down again, nice and gently, with a three-point landing, wheels and skid touching at the same time, like every accomplished pilot should.

The inspector struggles from his tiny pit, takes out his pad and writes on the pink slip. A pass. Hooray!

'As I say, a waste of time,' he repeats, but I don't listen and sprint back to the cockpit. Now to give 'em something to gawp at! I want to put on a bit of style, make it a show to celebrate with a flourish. First, a roll, then a dive, finally I buzz the tower in inverted order – that's upside down, to the uninitiated.

The tower, another fine piece of Broadlands flamboyance. Two storeys high, wide windows and a huge white scoreboard for the racetrack.

'Damned show-off!' says my brother, walking away when I get down. Then I see a tiny figure with a clipboard marching purposefully from the tower in my direction. His expression says he isn't pleased. Perhaps I gave him an earache buzzing the tower. The martinet finally arrives, pointing a finger and I recognise my jug-eared bête noire. It's Quedgeley, the clerk of the course. 'All flying must cease this very moment,' he barks. 'Perhaps you're blissfully unaware, but war is about to break out any day now.'

I take a step back. Ridiculous! How can he possibly know that?

But the bucolic little man is a blown-up bubble of officiousness. In reply to my sceptical responses, he says: 'Haven't you been following the news? Plain for all to see. Only a matter of time, so you won't be doing any more silly stunts like the one you just performed here, I can assure you of that, young lady.'

Surely the diplomats will have sorted out this ridiculous hiatus by now! I fervently hope this is just an outburst of official alarmism. 'Surely, just talk?' I venture hopefully.

'The government don't think so and I'm under orders. As from now, at this very moment, all private flying ceases immediately.'

I'm rocked back by this. 'But why?'

He sighs and waves his wad of papers. 'The War Office has telegraphed instructions to all civilian aerodromes. No more flying and most of the aircraft here are liable to be commandeered for use by the military. And another thing...'

He jabs another accusing finger in my direction. 'All women are banned from the air. For the duration.'

I stare back at him defiantly.

'From now on, leave it to the Army Flying Corps.' Then he adds, with a nasty little grin, 'Just leave it to the men, deary.'

He turns and stalks off, leaving me clenching and unclenching both fists.

CHAPTER ELEVEN

I've blocked off the outside world. My head is in my hands, eyes downcast and staring at the grainy texture of Katie's kitchen table. I've hardly spoken to Katie, whose tone this morning was sympathetic but her words went unregistered. I didn't even notice Mooseface moving about, despite the tiny spaces of Tenement Row, and I don't want to go out of the house, certainly nowhere near Guildhall Street or the shop or the college.

I sigh. I'm not often downcast, but what's bright about today? It's the first day of August and the war drums are beating their doleful tattoo. We've just heard news shouted down the street: the Germans have declared war on Russia, and the whole of Europe now looks set to join in. So where does that leave me?

I examine the knots, swirls and grooves, running a desultory finger around the edges of this great teak table and feel as if my whole life has been overtaken by events. Forces beyond my control have moved with sudden and brutal effect to smash up my hopes. What chance now for a career in aviation? I'm overwhelmed by a sense of unfairness. 'All women are banned from the air' ... that pronouncement by the detested Broadlands martinet sounds like a death knell. Reliving it, I've even neglected my coffee routine. Instead, I begin to flick my desultory way through the pages of *The Planet* to learn the details of this new world of aerial prohibition and the serpentine trail of the diplomatic gaffes which have brought us to this crisis. The Austrians, I gather, have been given a blank cheque by their allies, the Germans, to do what they like in the Balkans, and Austria has promptly declared war on Serbia, which has stirred up the Russians who've begun mobilisation, followed by objections from the Germans.

I splutter at the sheer madness of it all.

'Have you heard the latest?' It's Mooseface, grinning, a rare event, and he's looking down at me. 'Your Mrs Pankhurst has chucked it in.'

'Never!'

'She has. No longer at war with the government. Given up bombing Lloyd George's place. All of a sudden they're best pals. She's going to call off you girls, ditch all that equality stuff and show everyone how hard you can work for the war effort.'

He walks off chuckling and I turn back to the paper. Women, *The Planet* says, are forming huge queues at labour exchanges to volunteer, and women doctors are defying opposition from the War Office to set up their own hospitals. It's this last piece of defiance that brings me out of my paralytic gloom and begins to fire me up when I next see Scott for one of our many meetings at the Angel Hotel.

The Angel is now our home from home, neutral territory for us both, protection from the inevitable social awkwardness of meeting in Guildhall Street or Tenement Row or – perish the thought – Scott's parents' place. We two happily straddle the class divide, but they do not. We declare ourselves above it, but it has the capacity to cause acute embarrassment. The maître d' welcomes us as honoured guests, though I worry we might suffer some embarrassment due to my arrest, brief though it was, at the Pankhurst rally on the hotel steps. But no such social hiccup occurs, probably due to Scott's impeccable social status rather than any blemished reputation of mine.

'They're doing it all over again,' I say as soon as we're seated in the carpeted lounge, 'no vote for women and now no proper role either. How long can half the country's population be treated in this disdainful way?' I take a huge deep breath. 'So unjust. I'm going to fight it.'

Scott screws up a doubtful face and says: 'Have you really thought this through, Charlotte?'

'What do you mean?' For a moment I fear for the loyalty of my closest supporter.

'I mean,' he says, 'certainly, there's no doubt you can fly – but are you really a fighter?'

'Of course I am.'

'Sure. Lots of spirit in the cause, but my question is: are you truly aggressive?' He looks at me closely. 'In the air or on the ground, you need to be ruthless in war. No appeal, no quarter given.'

How can he doubt me? I try to persuade him to drive me to the nearest aerodrome to talk my way into the Flying Corps but he administers a cold douche of reality. 'They won't allow you within shouting distance of an aircraft,' he says, 'they'll only refer you up the chain of command.'

'So?'

'Difficult.' He sighs. 'We're both outsiders here.'

He looks away, his deep sigh of resignation a form of chastisement to me. It suddenly strikes home that I've been overly self-obsessed about my own future. 'So what about you?' I manage.

Scott is also desperate to serve but has the problem of his lame leg. He has a built-up shoe but still can't run or walk at any pace and that makes him a dead duck for marching. This ranks him as an outcast in the midst of a status-conscious military family. He sees himself as a failure next to two high-achieving brothers. He screws up his face. 'I'm also banking on persuasion,' he says. 'Pilots sit, pilots don't run. I have to find a way. I need contacts. Maybe we both do.'

He's contemplative for a moment, then says, 'What you need is the chance to explain your point of view to someone with the authority to make decisions and change policies. To explain to them just how you and other women can make a difference.'

I gesture assent. 'That's exactly what I need.'

He considers for another long moment before saying, 'Father's mantra is stand on your own two feet... but I'm still going to ask for his help. Ex-Foreign Office, ex-government, contacts in the right places.'

It doesn't add up to much. A hint, a slight chink of light. I'm just trying to weigh up the prospects of Fanshawe Senior turning out to be a doughty fighter in the cause of women when there's a hubbub across the big room. A crowd of guests are getting to their feet in some haste and making for the door. Scott calls across the waiter, a tall, nervous fellow with a protruding top lip who says, 'They're going to the square for the latest news.'

I take a look out of the window. The street is full of people moving in one direction – towards the Buttermarket and I can guess why. The newspaper office has a telegraph. The only place to get hot news.

Scott looks across at me. 'Shall we?'

When we strike up the sharp incline of Abbeygate Street and reach the big square, the crowd is building, though there are gaps in this vast cobbled arena. People are standing in groups but the spaces fill up fast, more figures flow in from the four corners, from Cornhill and Brentgovel, in a great tide of concern, excitement and trepidation. There's a chill in the air and I'm glad I'm wearing this hand-knitted sports coat I bought from Debenham and Freebody. We're all looking in one direction, up at the first-floor veranda of the Bury *Tribune* office where public announcements are expected. Shop girls stand in doorways and faces are pressed against windows at the legal offices of Bryce and Bryce, at the Victorian post office and the upper storeys of the Moyse's Museum. A low monotone of murmured conversations suggests a general mood of expectancy, a sense of the dramatic, of being a witness to the eruption of some huge and unquantifiable event coming over the horizon. 'It's as we feared,' says Scott, 'events are taking a turn for the worst in Europe.'

I turn to him as he talks about a chain of inescapable consequences. Once Austria declares war on Serbia, the Russians are immediately dragged in because of their Slavic connections, he says, and if there's fighting involving Russia then France is treaty-pledged to come to her aid. I sigh at this tangled web and then recognise some familiar faces in the crowd, the Smiths and the Jenkinses from Guildhall Street, others from the town and even a couple from our tenement. Close by are men in their working clothes, fresh from workshops, factories and the brewery; women too, clutching shawls and looking lost.

Suddenly the general clamour ceases, becoming an eerie hush, as a door opens on the first floor of the *Tribune* office and a boy – he can't be more than fourteen and dressed in starched white collar and brown knickerbockers – steps out on to the veranda. All eyes are on the piece of paper clutched in his hand, but he doesn't need to consult it. He clearly knows its contents by heart and calls out in a clear voice, all the more starkly poignant for its tone of innocence and youth: 'Germany has demanded right of passage through Belgium.'

This news is received in a kind of silent trance.

He glances down briefly before adding: 'Belgium has refused.'

I'm dumbfounded at an outbreak of cheering from the front of the crowd. Are they mad?

A voice hails me from another part of the square and then I see her, pushing her way through the crowd. It's a breathless Mel. 'So you've made it! I reckon half the town is out here, trying to find out what's going to happen.'

She eyes me and Scott and points to the barred front door of the *Tribune* office. 'I think we should get in there for an insider's view, don't you? Take a look at their telegraph.'

I'm dubious. 'Will they let us in?'

'I own a tiny corner, a cubbyhole office in there,' she says, 'so I'm entitled and you are my guests.'

She waves us forward and we push roughly through the press of bodies. I'm hanging on to my hat. I don't want to lose another! Mel taps a sharp tattoo on the office glass, mouthing silent recognition signals to figures inside. After some reluctance, the door is edged slightly ajar and she grabs both of us by the sleeve and drags us inside. More bodies clutter the foyer. I feel hot and clammy in my new coat and I'm amazed that we've actually been allowed in. I can't resist a grin. Only Mel would have had the gall.

We clamber hastily up some steep steps. I grab the handrail. Hobble skirts are on my prohibition list but still, even with these wide pleats, it's hard to keep up with the eager people in front of me. Now, it seems, we're part of Mel's special party, allowed into the teleprinter room to witness the arrival of news of impending mayhem from across the Channel. It spills out in a noisy clatter from a battery of printer machines, sounding like the work of an office full of hidden typists, but of course, there's no one on the keyboards. The typists are all at the other end, the inputting end.

A tall man with a bobbing Adam's apple and wearing elasticated armbands to keep his shirtsleeves taut gives us the guided tour. 'You see here the very latest equipment from America,' he says, beaming.

I wonder if his buttons will pop with pride.

'We're very up to date at the *Tribune*, as you can see. These are the Morkrum printing telegraph typewriter page printers.'

That's a bit of a mouthful, I'm just about to say, but Scott gets in first. 'Where's all this coming from?' he wants to know.

'America, Europe, around the world, from the bureaux of Associated Press news agency.'

The telegraph boy with the big white collar appears on the scene. His job, apart from being the public voice of impending apocalypse, is to tear off the reams of paper spilling out from Morkrum's new gadget and arrange it into page-sized sheets before delivering to another desk across the room. Here there is a maze of wire baskets and a huge metal spike. This latter is already filling up.

'Over there,' says Adam's Apple, pointing to a figure seated behind this paper barricade, 'is the foreign copytaster. He decides which item to submit to the editor. And to alert everyone to the latest rushes. The rushes are the instant flashes of breaking news.'

By now I'm taking a keen professional interest, anxious to crack the code of how the process works, given that I've already submitted several hopeful half-guinea sketches to the *Tribune*'s big daily sister in Fleet Street. One of my contributions has

already made it big: how No.2 Squadron of the Royal Flying
Corps is forming up ready to support any British Expeditionary
Force that is likely to be sent to France. I loved that gaggle of
2cs on the grass 'drome near Dover; proud that my country has
at last taken aviation seriously but wishing I could be in the
cockpit with the flyers. A bitter taste in the mouth as, with
difficulty, I drag my attention back to the man with the big
spike. Yes, a man. No woman beyond Mel sets foot in this
territory. I note the dress code. Copy-man's head is an
enormous bald dome which shines and reflects the light from a
nearby hissing gas light. Tiny spectacles are perched above
bushy grey eyebrows and he sports a red-spotted bow tie. And
yes, just like an actor in an American film Scott and I saw in the
West End several days back, he's fitted out with a green eye
shade.

A sudden thought comes to me: if I'm going to be banned
from the air then at the very least I need another passion to take
into this coming war. And now it hits me. Perhaps this is where
I should be.

There's a discernible stir; the latest 'rush' from Associated
Press has it that the British government cannot allow the
Germans to invade Belgium, whose neutrality we've promised
to protect. 'If the Germans go into Belgium,' says Scott, 'we'll be
dragged in, no doubt about it.'

I look around, taking in the desks and the ambience of this
place and my insistent feeling grows. If they won't let me back
as a pilot, I could at least be in the thick of the news action at
this most dramatic moment in the life of my country. I grab
Adam's Apple after one of his long explanatory lectures and
give him the benefit of my new line of thinking. He stifles his
surprise. 'A woman on the staff? Never happened before.'

'But there may be a war,' I tell him, making the most of the
situation. 'A crisis calls for change.'

He nods uncertainly when I press into his hand my hastily scribbled address details.

'We'll have to consider it,' he says.

I take a deep breath. Fine! But I still haven't given up on my fight to get into the air.

CHAPTER TWELVE

There's a kind of limbo, war but no war, and everyone wondering what's just over the horizon. I'm aghast at what some people are describing as an outbreak of 'August madness'. In capitals across Europe crowds are gathering in jubilant excitement, chanting nationalist slogans, beating the drums for war.

What is this craziness? I recall our own foolish people, mostly young men, in Bury's square cheering at the announcement of the first move towards all-out conflict. What is the matter with these people? This isn't going to be some great adventure, an extended boys' outing. We're in danger of being led into a period of dark destruction in which much blood will flow. I have it on the good authority of Mel who has made it her business to be well-informed. Her insight into the current state of military science tells us that it is now more powerful, more terrifying and more murderous than ever before. I hear again the words of Emmeline Pankhurst – 'a great male evil that will drench the world in blood' – even though the arch-suffrage campaigner herself has now buttoned her lip and thrown in her lot with Lloyd George.

I sigh in frustration at all this. It's two days since we studied the telegraphs in the *Tribune* office and I wonder if we will ever again have the pleasure of trips to the London galleries, the National and the Portrait. Will they close? Perhaps for ever?

In the meantime Scottie and I try to maintain some normality in our lives and indulge the joy of looking into each other's worlds, the pleasure of seeing life through the eyes of the other. We walk the length of Cornhill while he expands on the architectural features of Bury's town hall, the Corn Exchange and the extraordinarily elaborate facade of the Post building. We visit the Garland Street Gallery to study portraits of other familiar landmarks: a church surrounded by trees, a lighthouse, a windmill, a cottage, a weeping willow in full bloom, Moyse's Hall and the lounging soldier statue that dominates the market square. I allow myself to think of better days when the world will be at peace and we can tour the concert halls and galleries of Europe. A special dream is to sample the golden splendour of Vienna's Musikverein, though I seek no romantic entanglements that would inhibit a future filled with the ecstasy of flight.

Finally, reality intrudes. I'm horrified to see recruits in khaki using bales of hay for bayonet practice in the street. This, in full view of everyone, women and children included. Grinning, agile men enjoying what they seem to regard as sport.

'Military training,' Scott says. 'They're anxious to do their bit.'

I snort. 'Those bales of straw represent some mother's son, someone's husband. As a public display, it's an unthinking obscenity.'

More reality on Wednesday August the 3rd, a prophetic date. We're drawn by shouts from the crowd to approach the square once again, just in time to hear the latest announcement from the piping tape-room boy on the *Tribune* office balcony.

A moment of great trepidation. And now we learn the

worst: Germany has declared war on France; it has sent its troops into Belgium and the British government has reacted by giving Berlin an ultimatum: *withdraw your soldiers immediately*.

There's a deadline for compliance.

It expires at midnight.

CHAPTER THIRTEEN

D awn breaks over August 4th and, of course, there's no reply to the ultimatum and consequently we're now at war with Germany. The lights, they say, are going out all over Europe and the Kaiser's troops are pressing on towards Paris. For the moment my own hopes are pinned on Scott's diplomatic skills with his father, but the delay is frustrating. Waiting for something to happen has never been my way. I want to get on, I'm angry at being shut out of the action, and I won't delay long before considering alternatives.

There are other avenues. I could press my case with Mel, get her to use her contacts. Or, despite Scott counselling against rash displays of impetuosity, I might still gatecrash the Flying Corps on their home turf. Mrs Pankhurst may have called off the suffrage campaign, exhorting women to go to war on the home front, but the home front doesn't interest me. I want to fly. Like my brother.

I sigh and think afresh. I'm feeling divided by this war. It's still a form of madness, yet I refuse to sit quietly on the sidelines in some passive role. I have the talent and skill to contribute.

Finally, my luck turns and I get the message I've been waiting for from Scott. *They* will see me.

Contact! My engines are all fired up, figuratively speaking, as I exit the Tube at Trafalgar Square and pace as fast as my costume will allow down Whitehall, building up a steam of righteous indignation. I'm taking my cause to the top. I'm not letting this absurd and unjust ban on women flyers pass without a fight.

80 Pall Mall, my target for the day. Confront the beast in his lair, that's my motto and the huge seven-storey stone edifice facing Horse Guards Parade is where my enemies reside. I take back everything I said about old man Fanshawe who's proved his willingness to reach the right people.

By now I'm standing on the corner of Horse Guards looking up at this monumental granite heap – the two miles of corridors, the 1,000 rooms and the grand balconies that make up the War Office.

Fifteen minutes to go. I slide out a tiny mirror to check my hat and my appearance. Something very conservative, I've decided, for a very conventional place: a smart costume with velvet lapels and lots of buttons.

How can they refuse me after fifty flying hours on a succession of aircraft, the B2, the Avro, the Bristol and a Parasol? After turns, spirals, dives, stalls, glides and practised forced landings? I smile, recalling Scott's appreciative accolade: 'An absolute natural.'

It's time! I climb the War Office steps to Reception and produce my letter of introduction, hoping this will open doors to someone of rank and stature. If not the Minister of War, then I'll settle for the head of recruitment.

Instead, I get an officer from Section 1(2b) for policy and support. I'm sitting outside his office, waiting. I can hear typing, telephones and hushed voices. Male voices. While I wait my mind is cast back to the animated discussion we had last night around Katie's kitchen table. 'I'll fight it,' I say, 'I won't let them beat me,' and Katie is all sympathy, though her expression clouds when she asks, 'But why d'you want this so much? Where does all this anger come from?'

'If my brother can do it, then I can too!'

And there the exchange ended, though I'm sufficiently self-aware to acknowledge this isn't the whole story. In truth, I'm not cut out for cooking, scrubbing, marching, nursing or driving ambulances. So, I'm different! I don't want the usual stuff: husband, home, wealth, babies. Not for me. Just let me fly!

A long, lanky person is at my side, asking me to follow him down another corridor. It has an elaborately decorated ceiling. There are pillars and porticoes and mosaic-effect floors. How these people love to surround themselves with the pompous artefacts of empire. Inside an equally elaborate room I'm greeted by a tweedy, rather balding fellow.

'Now, Miss Dovedale, do have a seat, what is it you think I can do for you?'

He's a Mr Brown and he has maps, books and trays for 'in' and trays for 'out' covering a remarkably plain green metal desk that doesn't seem to fit with the rest of the ornate decor. And when I look at him closely, at the fawn jumper, the dull eyes, the weak chin and the fidgety hands, I'm not impressed. Only later do I discover he's so far down the chain of command he only rates standard issue War Office furniture.

Some say I'm too outspoken but I don't care, I won't play the compliant female. This is a new age, the age of modernity, so I make my prepared speech. However, the shock, anger and outrage I endeavour to communicate doesn't seem to register.

'Quite impossible,' he says, 'there's simply no question of you flying. Pretty obvious, I would have thought.'

'Where is it stated in King's Regulations,' I demand, 'that women cannot take part?'

He shrugs, a gesture of exasperation. 'Just isn't done! Simply not on, I'm afraid.' Then he sits forward in an attempt at sweet reasonableness. 'Look, I admire your spirit. Jolly good show and all that, but I have to say I've only agreed to see you out of respect for your brother.'

'My brother?'

'Indeed, the War Office has already learned from the Admiralty about the exploits of your brother. While you were waiting I had the necessary papers brought up.' He shuffles some documents. Those hands again. Playing with the paper. 'He's already come to our notice, has Marcus Dovedale. Doing great things in the naval service. Already sent an enemy trawler to the bottom with an aerial bomb. A great achievement. You should be proud of him.'

I take a moment to control my emotions, then say: 'That only proves my point.'

'Whatever do you mean?'

'If he can achieve such feats, then so can I. I could chalk up such victories. Decisive achievements. Because, without any disrespect to my brother, I know that I'm much the better pilot.'

This does not go down well. He gives me a blank look, tidies the sheets on his desk into another neat pattern. He clears his throat as if to speak but I can feel a great heat rising. 'I don't want some tame domestic job,' I insist. 'Washing and cleaning or feeding the troops. Why should women be expected simply to fill the shoes of men sent off to war? Little more than drudges in dull jobs and on half the pay? I have talent. I'm an accomplished flyer. Better than most. I demand to be used.'

This last sentence is delivered with a slightly louder tenor. Following this there's a long silence and a deep sigh from the other side of the desk. And then he says in tones of finality and dismissal: 'Miss Dovedale, I strongly advise you to devise a way to make your contribution to the war effort by confining yourself entirely to the home front and keeping both feet firmly on the ground. Like every other woman in the country.'

I don't accept this rejection. I sit, glaring at him, incredulous at his insistent stupidity.

'Dear lady,' he says in an exasperated tone, 'go home, sit quietly for half an hour and then take tea.'

CHAPTER FOURTEEN

I won't give up, I won't. I told him that. As I left the office of the almost anonymous Mr Brown I insisted: 'I don't accept this rejection for a moment, I'll be back, you'll see.'

Whether he ever does see is a moot point, but I forget him and return to the Tube station, back to that great bland brown-tiled exterior on the street that's so depressing it precisely matches my mood. Then I take the only avenue left to me; I meet up again with Mel, my motorcycling friend on *The Planet* and give full volume to my feelings on the situation. 'Your paper's the woman's friend, right? What are you going to do about it? Shrug and accept that our sex gets all the dirty jobs, making drudges out of a whole generation of women, without any of the power, or without being able to penetrate into any of the male preserves? What happened to equality? Did we give that up with Mrs Pankhurst's quick fix?'

'I can see you've lost none of your passion,' she says, thinks a moment, then says, 'I'll talk to the ed about it.'

After that, there's no choice but to cool off around Katie's kitchen table, getting out my pencils and pad and forming caustic shapes from the events of yesterday: Mr Brown as a seven-headed serpent stuck in a box labelled 'Men Only' with monstrous eyebrows shooting off into the far distance.

Disasters, it seems, come not singly but in droves and my prospects take a further dive for the deep when the postman delivers another bombshell to the Snows' doormat. It's addressed to me and is a letter from the *Tribune* regretfully informing me that they are unable to accept my kind offer to join their all-male band of scribes, citing, as have others, my 'participation in suffragette protest activity' which they consider to be inconsistent with their 'reputation for rectitude and objectivity'.

I tear it into strips and stick them on the nail in the lavatory.

Everything now depends on the attitude of *The Planet*.

Over the next few days, when I call at the shop, Mother is predictably talking down my flying ambitions. She's still raw over any perceived challenge to dear Marcus's aviation halo and has been issuing threats to 'write to the authorities' about me. I dismiss this as silly talk designed merely to unsettle me. But it seems she meant every word.

Several days on, when I make another brief duty call at the Artists' Emporium, she has a dangerously smug look. She's waving a piece of paper, demanding I read it. 'This will be interesting for you,' she says and warily I take possession of another letter and this only increases my sense of foreboding. My brow furrows deeper as I see the big War Office letter heading and her name as the addressee. I skim to the bottom to find the signature is a scrawl for someone signing himself H.T. Steadman, Private Secretary to Field Marshal, the Right Hon. Earl Kitchener of Khartoum KG, His Britannic Majesty's Secretary of State for War.

What! Why are the big noises writing to my mother? Worse is to come as I stare in alarm at the words of the message.

```
In  answer  to  your  letter  of  the  10th,
concerning  the  future  activities  of  your
daughter,  the  field  marshal  is  pleased
to  confirm  that  during  the  period  of  the
present   conflict   until   its   final
cessation  there  will  be  no  exceptions
made  to  the  general  bar  on  female
combatants.
```

I look up open-mouthed. What have I done to deserve such venomous familial disloyalty?

'Told you, didn't I,' she says. 'Warned you.'

'Why have you done this?' Yelled at a high decibel count.

Silly question.

I slink back to the tenement and experience a shiver of fear. The cold sweat of rejection. Everyone is against me. I'm buffeted by bullies, imprisoned by insurmountable barriers, betrayed by my own family. I feel alone with a secret dread of failure. That my life is void, that whatever I do, I shall never overcome.

My low spirits give vent to a further bout of introspection about all the other things that have gone wrong over the years. About the big hole in my life. About a missing father. About the hint and stigma of illegitimacy, the suspicion that my parents were never married, though my mother has always denied it. Once I tried tackling Lomax on this subject. She's Mother's assistant, has been around for ever but is the most enigmatic soul I have ever known. No result. Insistently tight-lipped. Only old George, my favourite among the artists, was any help and when I mentioned that she never seemed to go out in the evenings even though her wardrobe was stuffed full of elegant evening dresses, many with the price tags still attached, he surprised me. I recall the conversation.

'Oh, but she used to,' he said, 'when her husband was around.'

I leapt on this clue. 'Tell me more!'

'Can't remember his name, but they went out often. Liked to go dancing, to the theatre and dining with friends. Moved to London years back.'

'What was he like, this man?' I swallowed. 'My father?'

He gave me a wan smile. 'Tall, distinguished, well-spoken, slightly bald, had a red birthmark on the neck.'

'And?'

'They were all very smart, done up to the nines, big car, serious faces, not many smiles.'

'What happened?'

A reluctant sigh from George. 'The word was... vanished... left high and dry.'

I let this sink in, then insisted: 'There must be more.'

A shake of the head. 'Long time ago, Charlotte. Not in my social circle.'

I recall the state of old George – ragged jumper, stubbly chin, crumpled features – and sigh at this continuing blank wall, then try to lose myself in routine. I've brought some essentials over from home: a comb, a metal hatpin stand and a selection of Adie and Lovekin's agate, turquoise and serpentine pins, a tub of Rubinstein's Valaze cream, a bar of Old English lavender soap and a tiny mirror. I break the soap in half and leave one portion in the kitchen for Katie, then begin brushing out my hair. When I was feeling better about myself I was tempted to get one of the new bob cuts, but didn't want to be labelled a brazen hussy. Sticking with long hair, however, means drying it in front of the range and Mooseface has been complaining about the smell of singed hair, especially after that time I let the curling tongs get too hot. In the old days, of course, Maisy, our maid, would help out, but goodbye to all that.

I sigh and after a while begin to feel hungry and look around for a snack. Only chance is a small slice of chocolate left over from yesterday's journey. This points up the paucity of diet and bleak life prospects borne by Katie and Mooseface. Recognising this, I feel guilty and admonish myself for self-obsession. An inner voice insists that I stop feeling sorry for myself; that there's always someone worse off. My gloomy mood lifts a little. Of course, I knew what I was doing when I left home to lodge here, taking several steps down the menu ladder to dine nightly on devilled fish, corned beef rissoles, mock duck and prune pudding. All these tenements perpetually reek of fish, this being one of the cheapest dishes, and worst of all, for me, is coley – 'coalfish fit only for the dog,' according to my mother. Somehow, we've managed to avoid tripe and onions – the most sick-making odour you can possibly imagine.

Unlike many of my college colleagues I don't look the other way and pretend not to notice the class divide and the poverty it sustains. I know from talking to Maisy what it feels like being forced to pawn a treasured overcoat to buy a much-needed hundred weight of coal; the desperation of five people crowded into one icy stinking room with no hot water and the baby sleeping in the top cupboard drawer to avoid the rats; life in a six-storey tenement with the smell of unwashed bedding, sour food, small washbasins, relentless grime, a lavatory between twenty-three families...

When Katie's back from a fruitless trip looking for work, I buck up and get straight into a sharp discussion about Votes for Women – this is the hot topic between us. It's not just about voting, she insists, but a much wider push for women's rights. I say it should go hand in hand with a way out of poverty, then we start to disagree.

'Mrs Pankhurst should never have called a halt to the campaign,' she says. 'Should have carried on.'

'More militant tactics?' I ask. 'More arson, more broken windows, bombings, assaults, more arrests?'

She nods. 'The war was our opportunity.'

I shake my head. 'That's just antagonising the general public. Most people hate it. I know, I hear all the complaints from my mother, in the market and down the college. People are losing sympathy with the suffragettes.'

'We can't expect popularity, we must fight!'

'If you carry on fighting, people will say it's unpatriotic in a war.'

'Aren't you a suffragette anymore then?' she demands and the discussion would probably have continued with some heat had not the quiet street outside been blasted by the sound of a very noisy motor. My focus instantly changes. I recognise the sound as Mel's Douglas motorbike and I'm hoping she has good news from *The Planet*. Besides, I console myself on the way to the front door, I'm still a suffragette; I just happen to be advancing the cause of women by getting into aviation.

Mel's bodily presence in Katie's tiny room is all-consuming: the big hat, the gloves, the trousers. She dominates the space. A strong smell of leather, petrol and her perspiration obscures the pervading vegetable-and-fish odour that's our norm.

'Discussions about your case are still going on,' she says, sitting at the table, capturing Katie's favourite chair and accepting a mug of tea. 'All very secretive, not sure where it's going, and no outcome – but you do realise it's going to be an uphill struggle. The military will fight you all the way, but if you win, you'll be a first.'

'Hurrah to that,' I say. What greater incentive could I have? It would be my validation.

'Times are changing,' Mel says, 'but slowly, very slowly.' This prompts talk on the troubled state of the nation. As a correspondent she's been an eyewitness to its most dramatic recent moments: the coal strike, lockouts and riots in the docks, calls for a general strike by railwaymen, engineers and shipbuilders, the unions becoming ever stronger. 'The most frightening stuff I've seen,' she says, shaking her head, 'food wagons looted, fires started, clashes with police – and the children, that's horrible.' Her eyes water at the memory. 'The strike leader calling on God to strike dead the head of the dock employers, damning him for murder by starvation of children, women and men.'

We're all silent at this, each consumed with our own thoughts on this exalted country and its vast empire, a land torn by a gulf in class and wealth.

Mel looks up and eyes me. 'By the way, Charlotte, good sketches for *The Planet*, they particularly liked the Pankhurst arrest.' That was the one I drew of the huge policeman carrying a diminutive and fragile Emmeline away from the gates of Buckingham Palace. Better than the photograph that appeared in the paper on the day. I've gone wider with the Palace gates and balcony and a placard draped across the railings. Mel smiles. 'Went down well.'

Two days later Mother sends a message to say there's an official-looking envelope addressed to me on her mantelpiece. This time she has high hopes of 'a prestigious position making use of your languages'.

Instead, it's from an official whose role and line of business are vague in the extreme: a Charles Waterman at the Department of Information. Such is the sense of mystery at his request for an interview that I suspect he's from some cloak-and-dagger set-up. With the spy scare sparked off by the outbreak of war still in full flow, anything is possible.

'For goodness' sake, wear something suitable,' my mother decrees, but the tweed check has been damned in my eyes by rejection at the War Office. Something slightly less formal, ever so slightly theatrical? Like French designer Paul Poiret who mixes tactile fabrics such as velvet with exotic furs and jewel-coloured silks? Yes, my blue velvet – even though I feel a momentary tinge of guilt at making use of a wardrobe funded by my mother.

The interview requires another journey to London – but this time with a difference: before, I was the one pressing hard for an assignment; now someone is issuing an invitation. However, such an official is unlikely to have any aeroplanes at his disposal and I certainly won't be a party to any skulduggery. The current public frenzy over German spies is all hysterical nonsense. I still have a picture in mind of Mr Leishmann's shop with the windows stove in. I vow to be cautious at this meeting; I have the college principal Laudenham as a prize example of deceit. And my doubts continue when I realise I have to retrace my steps almost to the same place, just a few doors along at Whitehall Court. Same building, different entrance. This time, however, there's a more kindly reception from an old soldier, wheezily cheery with his clanking set of badges, as he escorts me across a marble foyer and past doors marked Typing Pool, Conference Room and Registry until we reach one marked Director.

Waterman turns out to be a most unmilitary person, an ageing but upright and benign figure who, I glean later, is the son of a distinguished journalist on the *Morning Post*. I'm met with smiles and old-world courtesy as if visiting an aged relative, and the room is set out with chintz-covered armchairs and a magazine-strewn coffee table, as if this man does his business chatting over teacups rather than at formal interviews. I notice a desk, located in a corner, rather as an afterthought. I'm holding a cup of Earl Grey while he continues his beaming welcome, saying how he likes to make all his people feel at home. 'This is a new department,' he says, 'nothing has been done like this before.'

Still on my guard, I say: 'Doing what, exactly?'

'Information,' he says – and goes into an obviously prepared script: 'This war needs to be properly explained to the general public. Its aims, requirements and duties. We need to keep everyone supportive. An informed public is most desirable.'

At this I almost laugh. I see through it in an instant. After the first flush of enthusiasm, recruitment of men into the Army is tailing off. The great adventure that would be over by Christmas has turned into a filthy, squalid trench stalemate that's leaking men at a rate faster than the supply of replacements. And the government is hesitating, fearing that to impose conscription will be unpopular. Hence this propaganda exercise.

'Your work has come to our notice,' Waterman adds. 'We've been following your contributions to the daily press.'

I note that he doesn't say the penny press, penny dreadfuls or any of the other sniffy put-downs routinely trotted out by the upper classes. He exhibits no scorn for writers with a popular readership. It's a signal as clear as a chime from Big Ben. He wants something from me. I adopt a quizzical expression, put my head on one side and ask: 'Do you get along with your colleagues?'

'I beg your pardon?'

'Your colleagues along the corridor – or should I say, along that labyrinth of rooms and passageways over there.' I point in the direction of the War Office. He looks confused. Are we playing a game here? After a nonchalant shrug I add: 'I've had my troubles with them.'

Waterman shakes his head. 'Whatever has been said in the past is quite immaterial. This is a new department and it has its own quite considerable powers.' The tone is one of injury. Offence has been taken that his authority had been questioned. 'We have backing from the very top. The War Office cannot stand in our way. This operation is something the government is very keen on.'

I do the sceptical stare.

'At the very top,' he says. 'Can't say more.'

I don't respond. After my experience with Mr Brown, I won't be manipulated by any Whitehall functionary. He continues his preamble about an informed public and I recognise some significant phrasing about 'our people in the air' needing public acclamation. He looks closely at me. 'A flyer,' he says, 'someone knowledgeable about aviation, a talented artist, a writer, you have all the skills we're looking for.'

Not so fast. I won't be an apologist for a war that's turning out to be brutal and nasty. 'I've been studying the papers,' I say, 'examining some of the despatches. Several of them I regard with distaste. Smacks of putting a gloss on misery.'

He draws in a deep breath, moves his chair closer and looks at me with an earnest face. There's a distinctly journalistic slant to his response. 'I'm looking for a writer ready to tell it like it is. What the men at the front are experiencing. How our troops are holding up to the demands of trench warfare. How the brave men of the air are succeeding.'

I study him intensely. Is this man a Judas? I like to think I can judge people and there's not a trace of the oily salesman here, no artful deceiver at work. I decide to believe in his sincerity.

'Would you be prepared,' he asks, 'to visit our aerodromes in France and send back news of how the flyers are faring? In your own words and sketches, still using your connection at *The Planet*?'

I breathe in deeply and contain the urge to grin, amazed by this sudden turnaround in fortunes. It's my rule never to be passive. When you see a door ajar, fling it wide open. 'As well as the men you mention, I know for a fact there are also women serving abroad,' I say. 'They're not supposed to be there – but many have made it on their own initiative.'

'Indeed.'

'And on the flying stations.'

'So I understand.'

'Naturally, having been active in the suffrage movement, I'm focused on the female view of what's happening... is that also on the agenda?'

'Certainly. Part of the new policy.'

'How our women recruits are facing up to the rigours of war?'

'You've got it. The female perspective is an important part of this process. Does all this engage your interest?'

I look down to cover my astonishment and swallow. I play with the buttons on my costume and brush a hair from my collar. Don't appear too keen, I tell myself, giving him a slow, considered nod.

An hour later I leave the department having seen a handsome letter of authority which states:

> This is to certify that the above-named
> person has been appointed as an official
> war artist and newspaper correspondent,
> accredited under the Department of
> Information art and information scheme
> attached to the British armies in
> France, and is now engaged in making
> drawings and writing reports under
> conditions approved by the above named
> department. Your active co-operation is
> requested in this endeavour.

It's signed by Charles Waterman, head of department, and the signature is a florid set of initials: CFGW, the man's full name, I presume. Don't ask, just be grateful!

Then I'm sent on my way with the heavy suggestion that I should 'trot along to Fetter Lane to fix things with your *Planet* friends'.

I'm so triumphant I eschew the idea of taking a bus. I just want to walk the pavements and enjoy my moment of victory; buoyant, excited, light of step. I reason that even if I cannot actually fly in this war, I can at least get close to those who do. Close to the action. And who knows what other possibilities that might bring? A light drizzle ceases and sunlight catches the tops of the buildings, mirroring my mood. How do I assess my sudden change of fortunes? It can only be down to the chaos and contradictions of war, I decide, but I have one reservation: I will not pump out lying propaganda. I pledge to myself at all times to maintain personal integrity and honesty in the search for the truth. I take my cue from Mel, a person who doesn't give a fig for convention and stays true to herself. I vow to follow in her footsteps and to resign rather than compromise.

By now I'm turning into Fetter Lane, full of anticipation.

Most probably I'll learn even more advanced telegraph wizardry, better even than my impressive experience with the *Tribune* in Bury. And despite my many contributions, I've never actually visited the *Planet* offices, nor met an editor. What will he be like? Is Mel anything to go by? Dynamic, a whirlwind, forceful, fearsome? I draw up a mental list of questions to ask, anxious not to appear a tongue-tied, clueless country hick.

Planet House reveals itself to be a crumbling, ageing dark building full of twisting corridors, creaky lifts and constant vibration. Not the slick outfit I expected. When I get to the second floor I'm seen by Ed Brewster, the deputy. He has big specs, tufts of hair around the ears on an otherwise bald head and smokes a pipe. He doesn't use the desk, instead sits on a big radiator as if he's perpetually cold. I can see black scuff marks on the wall where his shoes have beaten a tattoo.

'Sorry you can't see the ed,' he says. 'He's away at present. Actually...' He looks forlornly out of the window at a rain-specked roof and finishes: 'He's probably with the proprietor right now, teeing off on some sunny golf course, lucky blighter, but he'd have liked to have seen you.'

Finally, he gets off the radiator and rummages on the desk. A tall man in a scraggy brown pullover barges into the room with an armful of long pieces of paper on which I can see narrow columns of type. 'Sunday's feature on the factory girls of Lancashire,' he says, dumping them on the desk.

Brewster ignores him. The telephone rings. He ignores that too. Instead, he picks up some cuttings. 'Been looking at some of your stuff,' he says, 'back numbers. And I must say they're very good indeed. And...' A pause here while he looks for his matches. The pipe has apparently gone out and all conversation ceases in favour of the tortuous process of refilling. This involves an extensive performance of tapping, cleaning, digging about with a penknife and refilling from a large round pink tin labelled Franklyn's Fine Shagg. Lighting up takes just as long with a string of flared matches followed by an eye-watering billow of smoke. I do my best not to cough and feel like the unseen spectator at some exclusive private ritual until he looks up with an expression that seems to suggest he's surprised I'm still here. Then he sighs. 'So, it has been suggested to us that you would be the ideal person for this job the ministry has in mind.'

'Department,' I correct.

'Yes, yes. We like your stuff, we like your commentary, we think you'll do a fine job, so I take it you're agreeable?'

Finally, we get down to brass tacks – in this case paper, silver and copper – and agree on a rate of a guinea a piece, plus the details of the method of transmission. And since it's obvious this has all been settled before I even set foot in this gloomy place, I take the opportunity to bang my particular drum. The paper, I say, should be challenging the *Daily Mail* on its coverage of aviation. The *Mail* sponsors races – London to Manchester, London to Paris and so on – but *The Planet* should also get in on this. Aviation is the coming thing, I press him. Never mind the war, it's the future.

'And how do we do that?'

'Sponsor women flyers,' I say. 'Run a contest for the first woman to fly the Channel and back in one continuous flight.' The American, Harriet Quimby, the lady in the purple pantaloons, has already done the one-way ticket, I remind him, and I'm ready with a pocket biography of other leading contenders: Hilda Hewlett, Britain's first woman licence holder now running an aircraft factory turning out warplanes; Katherine Wright, silent partner of the Wright Brothers; daredevil stunt pilot Blanche Scott and a host of American pioneers including Bessica Raiche and Matrilde Moisant.

He looks at me through the fug and mumbles: 'Maybe, but not until after the war.'

When I leave Planet House, despite its decrepitude, I'm exultant about my new role. But there's a nagging doubt about such a fast turnaround in fortunes. It's almost as if my way is being smoothed by some unseen hand. That my strings are being pulled.

But whoever it is, I'm damned if I'm going to dance to anyone's tune.

CHAPTER FIFTEEN

I'm waiting for my departure date and in the meantime I've gone home to Guildhall Street to prepare: cold weather clothing, sketchpads, pencils, stationery – all the tools I'm going to need in France. Contact with Mother is minimal as I stay in my old room, thinking about long-gone days, revisiting my childhood, remembering other kids' fathers if not my own. I'm surprised to bump into Marcus while brewing up tea in the kitchen. He's on a short leave and to begin with we're icily polite, holding back the latent animosity of two siblings who've grown country miles apart.

'You're hardly ever home these days,' he says, 'you've become quite remote. Why are you living with that peculiar woman? Surely, this is your natural home.'

I shrug. 'What do you expect?'

I can read him. How he resents me and my passion for flying. He thinks it's an infringement on what he regards as his own special field. Feels threatened by it. By me, the bossy one, the intelligent one, the competent one of our youth who led the pack. That's not how it should be now in his adult world.

'Why keep chasing my tail?' he suddenly demands. 'Isn't teaching enough for you? And womanly things?'

I can't resist a dig. 'Am I chasing your tail, or are you chasing mine?'

He gives me a long stare. 'You should know, I now have a direct line to a career in flying... but you don't.'

'Well, we'll just have to see about that, won't we?'

'Don't kid yourself, you haven't got a chance, the RFC? They'll never let a mere girl in. Never ever.'

I recognise that he's no longer the gawky, tentative and nervous kid I once knew. There's a new swagger about him, evidence of his exploits over the sea. He's itching for me to ask... and I might have done, had he not come out with that reference to a 'mere' girl. 'You haven't been keeping up with the times,' I tell him. 'Things are changing. Soon we *girls* will be getting the vote and then...'

'No chance!'

'You won't be able to keep us out. After all, flying isn't an exclusively male thing. You don't need brute strength in the air, do you?' I grin. 'Just intelligence, aptitude and sensitivity at the controls.'

'And guts,' he says, storming off up the stairs.

The contrast between life in Guildhall Street and the tenement is quite startling. Mad Mary has a house full of cats and a dog called Disraeli and surfs the bins to feed them. Across the way there's an old circus clown who keeps a tiger cub in his bathtub. The grinding noise of a cartwheel out in the street announces the arrival of the rag and bone man. 'He'll be lucky,' Katie says, 'we've long since flogged anything of value.'

Three doors hence is a little ferret of a man in a flat cap who constantly touches his forelock and repeats 'thank you, sir, thank you, sir' over and over to anyone who'll listen, like the words have got stuck on my mother's spanking new Edison Fireside wind-up gramophone. And you can bet, if there's anything of interest occurring, a crowd of urchins turn up looking for spectacle, hoping for mischief.

Walking back from the centre of town I stop to chat to old Morty, my favourite street person, sitting like a squaw in the doorway of No.1. He'll miss me when I've gone. Over the past few weeks I've adopted him, supplying cheese sandwiches, repartee and a handful of copper dropped in his hat.

Our conversation is interrupted by Ronnie and Harry, two ragged kids with perpetually runny noses who live at No.2, kicking a pathetically deflated football from one side of the street to the other. They're belting this bit of old leather with such gusto it's rebounding off the brickwork to the accompaniment of resounding echoes and rattling against a parked handcart. An aproned figure with arms crossed glares at them from an open doorway. I make a mental note to find them something better the next time I'm near the shops.

I retreat into No.4, thinking about my next meeting with Scott at the Abbey Hotel. We're drawn to one another. Scott's company is great. I borrow his camera, drive his car, fly his plane. Some may mistake this for manipulation but you have to understand that someone in my position has to grasp every opportunity to feed an ambition as large as mine. Despite every rebuff, I vow never to stop until I've lit up my name in aviation. He understands.

At last the weekend arrives but when I get to the hotel there's no sign of Scott at our favourite table and the maître d' approaches with a grave and regretful expression.

'Mr Fanshawe sends his apologies,' he says, and hands me an envelope.

A sinking feeling. And the note inside doesn't make me feel any better:

Dear Charlotte, No time to cancel, had to grab this chance with both hands, Papa's wangled me an interview. You can guess the rest!

Oh sure I can. What it is to have influence in the right places! He'll now be on some remote Flying Corps aerodrome, Day One on the route finally to joining the military. What happened to the gammy leg, I ask myself, and reckon the authorities must be relenting under the strain of dealing with the high-powered father. Maybe, also an urgent need for pilots. After all, you don't have to be a marching man to sit in a cockpit. I only hope Scott can fit his tall frame into whatever aircraft they give him to fly. Best fit for a pilot, we're always being told, is five feet nothing.

I retreat from the Abbey Hotel, all anticipation of treats wiped clean, and return to the tenement feeling bereft, a sense of hurt at the abruptness of it all, even a little betrayed. I'm pleased for him, really I am, knowing that only in the air can Scott finally reach validation, recognition from the family that he's now inside the big Fanshawe tent and not outside it.

But I also realise I've just lost my most ardent ally and supporter. For him, the big chance; for me, an empty space. No longer will I be the centre of his attention. His focus will be entirely elsewhere.

I sit alone in my tiny room and for a long while wonder where our friendship goes from here.

I'm back at Guildhall Street for a change of clothes. The place still stinks of lily of the valley – mother's favourite which she puts everywhere, festooned around the house in vases, the smell of which I can't stand, rather like her appalling taste in covering everything in purple paint, but there are also benefits in maintaining a link to home and one of these is that she's recently installed one of the new telephone machines. And finally, this is how it happens. I take a call from Waterman to say he has my documents and a sailing date. We fix up another meeting for the handover, this time at the Hyde Park Hotel.

'Much more pleasant than Whitehall Court,' he says, and I smile at the avuncular tone, thinking I've struck lucky with this new department.

Same costume? I'm momentarily thrown into a state of uncertainty: formal wear or not? Then I decide. No, I'm on the staff, a correspondent bound for a war zone, so look the part in a Norfolk jacket and ignore the raised eyebrows. Perhaps I'll even tell him what's in my trunk.

At Hyde Park comfortable armchairs await in the Knightsbridge Suite, with tasty tartlets and other delicate snacks displayed on doily-covered tables and English Breakfast ready and waiting. Waterman is already ensconced in a discreet alcove. He gives me a welcoming smile and says how pleased he is to see me. Like he really means it. 'Shall I pour?' he asks, and goes ahead anyway without waiting for my agreement. Obviously, this man has style, clout and a lavish expense account.

Then we get to the detail: passport, accreditation document in an impressive official folder, movement order for trains and troopship, stationery for despatch of my work and – another surprise – a War Department-issue camera.

'Can't give you a map,' he says. 'Security and all that, in case it falls into the wrong hands.' He shrugs apologetically. 'You'll be attached to No.22 Squadron of the Flying Corps at a place called Vert Galant, that's near Amiens.' He smiles again. 'If you get the chance, visit the city, well worthwhile.'

I can't help feeling he sounds like my holiday guide. 'Just make sure you're at Victoria Station by eight o'clock on the 9th, okay?'

But then there's a subtle change to the meeting and I look out for trouble as soon as he utters the words: 'Thought I'd take this opportunity to give you a few words of advice.'

So this is where they try and box me in. I say quickly – before he can get started: 'I only accepted this assignment on the assumption I'll have freedom of expression, that I won't be censored.'

He throws up a placating hand. 'Heaven forbid,' he says. 'I'd never try any such thing, though of course you do realise you'll be subject to the usual military censorship imposed at aerodrome level.' He shrugs. 'Over that, I have no control. But it's only the normal stuff about not giving away military secrets. Given your subject matter, you should have no trouble.'

There's a short silence before he resumes his 'advice'.

'Some people,' he says, 'have a glamorised view of the air war and I just wanted to put you wise on the reality of the situation.'

'Won't I discover this when I get there?'

'You might, and you might also encounter the reserve of the military establishment who may, shall we say, be less than forthcoming. Just as well for you to be prepared.'

I fold my arms, adopting an attitude of undisguised scepticism, expecting another attempt to clip my wings before I've even got started.

'Right now, the Flying Corps are going through a sticky patch,' he says. 'To be frank, the aviation situation is quite critical.'

I gather from all this that the Germans have some wonder plane, the Eindecker, that's shooting down all our aircraft. It fires a machine gun through the propeller without blowing itself to pieces. Instead, it blows our flyers to pieces and we have no answer until our boffins can come up with the answer.

'You write well,' Waterman says. 'Nice turns of phrase, aware and sensitive to the female perspective. The folks back home want to know how their people are managing but they don't need to hear anything too dispiriting,' he says. 'Don't forget, the audience back home will be reading your words but so too will the enemy.' He shrugs and smiles. 'That's all I wanted to say.'

Dispiriting? Yes, but without any of the suffocating restrictions I'd feared. The atmosphere is relaxed and friendly. Not at all the sharp businesslike tone I was expecting, almost as if he's inclined to linger now that his formal instructions have been delivered. He smiles at me, folds his arms. 'I admire your indomitable spirit,' he says, 'in many ways it mirrors what I hope for in my own daughters.'

It appears that Waterman has three of them and they've been talking up the age of liberation to their papa. 'I've already made the point to the people in my department,' he says. 'Very useful to have the feminine perspective on any given situation. We should encourage our young ladies to widen their horizons. This world of ours, it's changing fast.'

Not just refreshing, I decide. Revolutionary! An official in Whitehall who sees the future? I'm at ease in this man's company and don't take it amiss when he gives me an obvious propaganda line justifying the war. 'We're not just fighting for ourselves,' he says, 'we're fighting for all the oppressed peoples.'

This is perhaps not the time and place to voice my reservations, so I say nothing and he lowers his voice. 'As you know, I'm in what you might call the information trade and all sorts of material comes across my desk.' He grimaces. 'And let me tell you it's no joke for those poor people living on the other side of the front line. The civilians, the French and the Belgians. We should all be grateful we're not living under the heel of the invader.'

I lean forward to pick up my teacup which is still half full. Minton, I notice, as I sip. 'I'll probably hear all about it when I get over there,' I say.

He nods. 'Those poor souls. Enough to make you weep. A tyranny. Terrible threats for non-cooperation. Threats to put them in jail, levy huge fines or even burn down their villages.'

'Truly dreadful!'

'Do you know? They have to hand over their guns, bicycles and pigeons or face being shot.' He's clearly been shocked by something he's been reading. 'And then, every week, they must supply the troops with eggs, chickens, wheat, pigs, horses and wine. The Germans even specify – would you believe? – that each hen must lay two eggs per day.'

I shake my head. 'Almost laughable! Hens required to lay to order? Barbarity etched with clinical precision.'

'Well put!' He bows his head in a form of salute and begins to gather his things, bringing our meeting to a close. 'I have to think about the well-being of my correspondents,' he says, 'so you just be very careful about your security. I know you're an adventurous soul...' Here he grins at me, then adds, 'But don't do anything to place yourself in danger.'

'I won't,' I assure him, touched by his concern for my welfare. And when he wishes me 'all the best' at our parting I'm still impressed but a little puzzled. Once again, I have the worrying feeling that someone, somewhere is pulling strings and smoothing my path.

CHAPTER SIXTEEN

M y big day arrives and I set out on the great adventure full of hope and anticipation. I see myself as a pioneer. Charlotte Dovedale, first woman correspondent on the front line. And maybe, just possibly, Charlotte Dovedale, first woman to fly in the war... well, maybe, perhaps, if I get the chance. You never know!

At any rate, it's some victory to be given a correspondent role attached to an RFC aerodrome, so I dress conventionally to fit in. What I keep secret is what I have packed in my case.

Some of my bounce, however, is deflated at Victoria Station. There's a fight to get past the military police cordon at the platform barrier where they do their best to be unconvinced by my documentation. When I finally make it on to the troop train bound for Dover I decide to set about my new task with journalistic vigour. What are the men thinking? What is their mood, now that they're on their way to the Front?

'You can't interview other ranks,' insists some snotty chap with an armband stating Movement Control. 'You'll have to ask the War Office for things like that.'

I flash my impressive official accreditation in front of him, expecting him to crumple, but he still goes off to fetch higher authority, forbidding me to open my mouth.

He should wish.

I'm in one of the new corridor coaches and sitting in a seat immediately made available to me by a whole compartment full of grinning fellows. One of them is telling me about his former life in a Lancashire cotton mill when Movement Control reappears with a deeply frowning subaltern. He announces loudly that he cannot allow the release of military information.

'For goodness' sake,' I protest, 'I don't want any military secrets. I just want to ask about your feelings, what you're thinking, the spirit of the men going off to face danger and war.'

He looks at me as if to say other ranks don't have feelings. It's then I notice the veil of bum fluff curtaining his upper lip and I can quite easily visualise this man giving the loyal toast at a Mess dinner, hear the scraping of chairs and the thunderous chorus of 'the King'. The subaltern clears his throat and decides instead to take on the mantle of military spokesman, answering on behalf of the men. 'Simple enough,' he says. 'We're all in very high spirits. Jolly keen, in fact. Our one wish is to serve King and country and cover ourselves in glory.'

I twist a stray skein of hair around my finger. Can I get this man to climb out of his pit of clichés? 'Anything else?' I ask, giving him an inviting smile.

'To send the Hun packing, of course, what else?'

If this stuff is a foretaste of what I can expect at the aerodrome, I know I'm in for a difficult time as a writer. However, I reckon I'll have chalked up my first win simply by getting to the war zone. In the meantime I make a mental pact with the Tommies and the Katies of this world to tell the unvarnished truth; to tell it like it is. I visualise my readers as the sort of people who do not always feel compelled to say the right thing or to 'play the game'.

The Channel crossing is a horror. Stacks of kit are stowed in every recess and corner of the troopship, which rolls in the swell and hundreds of men jammed in the aisles groan and retch. It's an ugly brute of a boat. The wind whistles above the throbbing vibrations of the engines and somewhere an unlatched door bangs furiously in the gale. Seasick effluent runs in rivers down the gutters and across the floor. I tiptoe around holding my nose. Never before have I had to endure such a stink.

Somewhat shamefacedly I escape to the refuge of the first-class lounge and join the officers as hundreds of young men leaving their country for the first time look back at the receding image of the white cliffs and wonder if they will ever see Dover again.

'You should have taken the civvy ferry,' advises a uniformed figure from deep in an armchair. How can a twenty-mile stretch of water produce such a ghastly introduction to mainland Europe?

The train journey from the docks is less of an ordeal but tortuously slow. That, I decide, is the inevitable condition of war. The khaki company is loud and brash but I don't do ladylike stand-offishness and join in the chorus on its way to Tipperary, sending tuneless goodbye-ees to Blighty and noisy greetings to a certain mademoiselle from Armentières.

However, my arrival at the nearest station to Vert Galant is a shock. I ask myself: is this a studied insult? A donkey cart waits in the yard with a peasant farmer holding aloft a scrap of paper bearing my name misspelled as Dovecote. Is the RFC trying to put me in my place, demonstrating that I'm on the bottom rung in their concept of status?

'How far?' I ask the bundled-up, unshaven figure – a man, I notice, with horse dung on his boots. He simply shrugs.

We jog joltingly over the cobbles and I get my first close-up of the real France: houses flush to the narrow street, walls of small red bricks picked out with stark white pointing and elaborate lintels. The road leads out of the town and across a vast wide expanse of rolling French countryside. It's a painfully vibrating ride along a straight, narrow and rutted stretch which bears the scars of the recent passing of many vehicles. Indeed, soon the creaking, unforgiving cart is making way for a succession of khaki-coloured Crossleys and Fords heading in the opposite direction. At least I get cheery waves from uniformed figures once they spot my precarious perch and the big trunk. Progress is so slow I think I could walk faster and there seems no end to the arrow-straight line that stretches out in the direction of Amiens.

It's strange. This country seems so different, looks different, smells different. By comparison, England is a crowded place, but France appears asleep, almost de-populated. It's like a small slice of Britain is being dropped into an empty piece of territory and the locals haven't noticed because there's no one actually here.

I clock a distant ridge and anticipation rises with the faint sound of aero engines. Then, abruptly with a complete absence of announcement or preliminary, I'm there, atop the ridge, the roadway flanked on each side by low farm buildings. Soldiers in familiar British battledress are going in and out of rough wooden doorways. Through an archway I can spot a courtyard full of horses and several thin strip notices in English indicate that this is indeed the administrative hub of the aerodrome.

The cart stops and the man nods. He doesn't offer to help.

I struggle the trunk down and drag it across the muddy road, waving in response to several loud honks from a Model T and wolf whistles sounding from its retreating tailgate. That's when I spot a sight that makes my heart leap. I dump the trunk by the side of the road and find myself drawn like a magnet to the slope on the far side of the ridge. And there, alongside the road like a set of soldiers ready for inspection is a fantastic line-up of the squadron's aircraft. Dozens of them, squared off, exactly in line. I'm near enough to feel the hot breath of recent exhaust, smell the oil, hot metal and the tang of fuel. Even, I think, the sweat of human endeavour.

I'd anticipated this moment of arrival; that I would love it; that I'd be excited and eager at being in such close proximity to the flyers. And it's impressive, sure. There's a swelling of pride that we as a nation have at last taken aviation sufficiently seriously to put on a display of such strength and numbers. But no, there is no joy. My eyes cloud over. There's a pain in my chest and a constriction in the throat. I pick out two Avro 504s – my first love – a Farman looking eerily out of sorts and a gaggle of the RFC's basic standard BE2s. Aircraft I have flown, aircraft in which I first took to the air.

I can hardly contain myself. This is where I was meant to be – flying, not reporting! All the bitterness and resentment at the injustice of the female flying ban flares up and threatens to overwhelm me. I'm raging inside. I want to let rip, to tear someone to shreds. Can I trust myself to keep my temper when I announce myself at the squadron office? I might easily wreck the whole mission in a flash of emotional lightning and be sent packing back across the Channel.

I drag my eyes away, turn and begin pacing grimly back to the farmhouse buildings. Concentrate! Control! Distraction! Look at the detail, examine the artefacts. That's when I notice: the doors are a mess but the white wooden shutters latched back from the windows are a different class. Think architecture, I tell myself, immerse in the quaintness of this place. I run inquisitive fingers down the marble smoothness of the shutters. Such smartness contrasts with the gritty exterior of the red brick.

Still floundering in the mud, I locate the correct entrance for 'Commanding Officer, 22 Sqn', prop open the door and haul my burden into an outer office occupied by a man displaying a sergeant's three stripes.

'Charlotte Dovedale,' I intone loudly, adding: 'Dovedale, not Dovecote, I'm not a damned pigeon.'

He mumbles into a telephone, then rises from his desk, a wide grin in place, and marches the few steps to another door marked 'CO'. He's signalling to me to follow while rapping deferentially in the manner of all efficient factotums.

'Come!'

I'm ushered in. The person inside isn't sitting behind a desk. He's standing next to the window, immobile to the point of becoming statuesque. I've done my homework, I can read the badge on his epaulettes and I've read the notice on the door. Major The Hon. Crispin Wycliffe is surprisingly young – hardly older than me – with a lithe body encased in the tailored battledress and tight breeches of the RFC. But the face gives him away. He has a grey visage, the look of a man old before his time. He watches me, a cold-eyed gaze following my movement as if he might be gauging a likely target in the sky. Probably just turned twenty-one, I guess, but note the pipe parked unlit on an ashtray and the walking cane hooked over a chair.

I stop in front of the desk and say nothing. He doesn't invite me to sit. No ladies' man this. Finally, he takes a step toward me, pointing.

'You,' he says in a strident if slightly boyish tone, 'are a problem.'

———

I give Major Iceberg one of my special melting smiles. I know how to do charming when I have to. 'I don't see how I can possibly be a problem for you,' I say.

He splutters and bangs a fist on the desk. 'Don't be

ridiculous! A woman in a hothouse of men? A menace, a distraction! I won't tolerate trouble from you. I won't have my men distracted from their task. This is no place for the fripperies of women.'

Fripperies? I bridle. I've already clocked the presence of women on station, but he clearly sees them as 'menials' who don't count as members of the same species. 'You think I come here in the spirit of idle distraction?' I say. 'Absolutely not.'

His eyes don't leave me. 'You realise this is a very dark place. We're dealing here with death on a daily basis. A pilot here lasts a max of eleven days. Eleven days!'

'I know the score,' I say, 'I'm on your wavelength. I'm a pilot myself. That's why I'm here – because I know what I'm talking about.'

He snorts. 'A pilot – what have you flown?'

'BE2s, Avros, the Morane Parasol.'

This last silences him.

'You know about the Fokker scourge?' he asks.

'I do.'

I take the opportunity to lay out my bona fides, though he shows no inclination to examine the documents. I fan out the big buff pouches that Waterman has given me, addressed prominently in big bold black sans serif type, the word *URGENT* standing above the address, *Department of Information, Whitehall*. I point to the folder. 'That gives me all the authority I need to talk to the men and the girls' – yes, I've already clocked them at Vert – 'and to write and sketch about their everyday lives, their feelings, their welfare, how they're getting on.'

He's not impressed. 'I'm not interested in this kind of tittle-tattle. My job is to kill Germans. Knock their planes out of the sky.'

I nod at him. 'I know about the Fokkers, I know we're having a very difficult time.'

At last he sits and opens the principal folder. No flicker of enlightenment, no softening of attitude. 'Go and talk to the women, if you wish, but you will be confined to the female barracks and you will submit all your writings to me.'

I smile at him again. 'So sorry, but you can't do that. You see, if you read the wording, I can talk to everyone. To report on the work of the aerodrome I need total access. You can't wrap me in cotton wool if I'm to do my job, the department is expecting a constant stream of despatches and sketches.'

'I forbid it.'

I point to the folder. 'It requires your full co-operation.'

He glances down. 'It's only a request.'

'Believe me, I didn't come all this way with all this equipment and with the Minister's specific instructions to be confined to one barrack.' I pause and give him one of my accommodating smiles. 'I don't want to get off on the wrong foot, really I don't, but you must realise the word *co-operation* is a relative term, a word loaded with official politeness. If necessary, it can be adjusted.'

At this the Hon. Crispin buckles with a sullen face. 'You will stay out of the aircraft staging areas, the hangars... and the Officers' Mess,' he adds, as an afterthought.

'I need to speak to everyone. To write about the brave men of the air.'

'I can't have you wandering around the station just as you like. Interfering, asking inappropriate questions, getting in people's way. You'll have an escort. A conducting officer.' At this he yells for the sergeant. 'Get Lieutenant Swallow over here.'

I'm tempted to object but then he's off on a long rant on a predictable subject – purdah. I've been warned to expect it. The

Royal Flying Corps is fearful of any sexual scandals being reported back home.

'We maintain a strict division between males and females on this station,' he says, 'and we don't allow any misbehaviour. The reputation of the corps is at stake here. I will not have it known that there is any lax behaviour or any relaxation of our high moral standards.'

At this point I decide to act the outraged Edwardian Miss. 'I strongly object to any implication of doubt about my own moral character or behaviour.' Delivered in a strident tone.

'I'm not casting any aspersions on your reputation,' he interjects quickly.

But I'm not letting him off lightly. 'Furthermore, I have to say that I expect to be treated by all the people on this station with the respect due to my sex.'

The major doesn't cave in easily to displays of indignation. He's probably heard it all before. 'Quite so, you will be, but I must insist that nothing is written that might suggest otherwise.'

I nod gravely. Sparring over. 'I'll reflect the correct situation in my first despatch,' I say, and he appears mollified by this. He even nods. Perhaps he thinks I'm an acquiescent female after all. In the absence of any further objection I decide this amounts to a grudging form of acceptance. Apart, that is, from the presence of a gangling young lieutenant who I know has just arrived in the outer office.

CHAPTER SEVENTEEN

We head off on a tour of the far-flung extremities of this vast piece of military territory. It's strung out on both sides of the main road and we march off at a fast pace to visit the fuel store and the ammo dump. I'm introduced to the men, pleased with my welcome, confident they'll remember my face. When they see me tomorrow I won't be wearing the long skirt and jacket. I steer well clear of the hangars and aircraft apron as I don't want the lieutenant censoring my questions to the pilots.

Vert Galant, once a temporary establishment, has now achieved permanent status along with the static front line. It even rates a brick-built bomb store to guard against enemy air raids. No roof, of course – just in case!

We also visit the laundry hut, a first-aid post and a dope hut. Here a group of women belonging to the Voluntary Aid Detachment repair damaged aircraft using dope to stretch and join the best Irish linen across the wooden framework. However, the dopers are quick to tell me they work with poisonous compounds and can only last for two hours at a time before having to quit and drink a glass of milk.

There are so many women on this station it occurs to me

that it's not just on the home front that the female workforce is an essential part of the war effort. It's here and it's obvious. The country couldn't fight a war without us. I take a moment to think back to the suffragette battles and decide this is how we'll get the vote – not smashing windows or bombing houses. All the marching in the world won't rival this.

Swallow has gone to lunch at the Officers' Mess and I'm billeted with the volunteer nurses staffing the sick bay, orderlies for the Mess and the many women who've managed by one means or another to squeeze past the absurd official ban on female service overseas. Of course, they're my first writing subject. I've been given a bed and a locker and join them in the cookhouse for dinner, meeting a kindred spirit, known to all as Enfield Annie, a despatch rider in daily contact with base camp at St Omer and of course, we're soon talking bikes. Hers, naturally, is a Royal Enfield, the model that raced successfully at the Isle of Man TT and the bike most favoured by the War Office.

There's plenty of plain fair: beef tea, mutton broth, potato pie and duff pudding – that's boiled suet and dried plums to the uninitiated. I splash on the tomato sauce which goes some way to pep up the stodgy pie. 'Some days there's curried cod or a bloater,' she says. Again, one of the delicacies of my new lodgings: smoked and salted herring.

Gradually I work around to why I'm here: searching for 'raw copy' on the female contribution to the war effort and find myself soft-pedalling the patriotic line. It seems duty to King and Country didn't have much to do with the motivation of the average recruit. Couldn't wait to join up, Annie says. Living in a tenement, sharing a bedroom with two brothers and a sister, no running water and a stinky backyard; Ma and Pa looking worn out and drawn; working in an awful factory fourteen hours a day for a few pence...

'Why wouldn't I join up?' she says. 'Now I get proper pay, my very own bed, three meals a day, time off in the evening, respect for who I am. Give me the Service every time. Please, don't stop the war, I don't want to go back to what we had before.'

Not quite what the Department of Information had in mind.

Next morning I'm out in the field, sitting on an empty ammunition box, shivering in the early morning chill. The aircraft are lined up at the edge of the field. Between them and the adjoining road is a narrow curtain of trees. The mechanics have brought the Crossley station wagons, parked them on the road and offloaded the tools of the trade on the grass below the drooping branches. Boxloads of .303 ammunition are being fed into drums and belts ready for the expected dogfights of the day. A hum of easy chatter takes place between armourers and ground crew. These men will not be risking their necks at 10,000 feet.

'Women in trousers, whatever next?' says one, looking in my direction.

'Had your eyes shut? I'm one of many on this station.'

'Yeah, but you're hardly one of the skivvies.'

'It's the coming thing. Get used to it.'

I approach a lean, leathery man with a hangdog expression and a toothbrush moustache. John Porter looks up mid-conversation.

'Happy in your work?' I ask, giving him a grin. This is still my beat, getting under the skin of reality.

'Why not?' Porter looks belligerent. 'Beats Civvy Street every time. Three meals a day, clothing all found, regular pay, a comfy billet...'

This story is beginning to repeat itself. 'And before?' I ask.

'Flea-pit house, working all hours, drunken missy, stinking

cesspit. Know my first job?' He doesn't wait for an answer. 'Chopping firewood. Skin used to hang off me fingers like damp wallpaper.' He shrugs. 'What life is that, eh? This...' He points in the direction of the aircraft. 'This is easy street. God bless the war, that's what I say. Don't let 'em finish it. No way do I want to go back.'

Hardly fitting the preconceived picture of heroic warriors putting their lives on the line to defend a beloved homeland. Not a message the War Office or the Department of Information want to hear.

The sound of aero engines and hammers is an immediate draw and I wander into one of the strange big black beasts they call the Bessonneau hangar – a huge canvas cover over a wooden frame invented by the French – and find the source of my interest at a workbench. I recall Saturday afternoons back at Broadlands, flying and tinkering with all things aviation. 'What's this job precisely?' I ask a young kid in overalls.

'Stripping down a Gypsy. Want to have a go?'

'Sure,' I say, and grab his spanner.

'No, no,' he objects, 'you'll get me shot.' Lots of laughter, talk about engines, talk about flying. 'Rumour is,' says the kid – his name is Earnshaw and he looks about fourteen – 'that you're a flyer, that you reckon you can fly a Parasol.'

'Done a bit.'

He looks sceptical. 'That's a killer bird. Everyone knows it. You don't want to be touching that.'

'I'll prove it to you one day,' I say.

My talk with the major must have left its mark. I know the Flying Corps hate the Parasol. They've lost more than their fair share of pilots to its unpredictable flying characteristics. Most RFC men think they've got more chance of beating up the Red Baron than surviving ten minutes in this dodgy bird.

Still, I'm much taken with this kid, small and stunted but

with a big grin and a wild mop of ginger hair, so I fetch my sketchpad and begin to draw his outline, playing down the sledgehammer chin.

'Finished?' he asks after a while, and when I show him my work he's impressed and persuades me to set up easel in the Other Ranks Mess after dinner to sketch his companions. They crowd around, all grins and anticipation, as I make a show of it and pick on a likely subject, Percy, poor fellow, whose features lend themselves to exaggeration: big eyebrows, bulbous nose, pouty lips, double chins, 'electric' hair. An absurd caricature, accompanied by screams of laughter. He becomes a local celebrity and they're clapping and cheering and patting me on the back. I realise I'm enjoying this acclaim, feeling at home in the warm glow of their approval. Perhaps, I reflect, I have need of this.

Later, I turn the original of Earnshaw at the workbench into a pen-and-ink drawing and write a short accompanying commentary. It's my discreet first despatch containing nothing the censorious major can take exception to, but the real story won't be going off to the commander's office for onward transmission through official channels. An unofficial and non-attributed piece of social commentary drawing on my interview material will instead go in a letter to a Mr and Mrs K.A. Arbuthnot of 29A Acacia Avenue, Sidcup. The 'Mr' just happens to work at *The Planet* and the next airmen bound for home leave in dear old Blighty will be better off by several bars of canteen chocolate in exchange for posting my letter when he reaches Dover.

There's no flies on Arbuthnot-aka-Brewster.

One of the most intimidating places to visit at Galant is the Chateau Picardie, lodging for visiting dignitaries and home to the Officers' Mess. A strange mix of braggadocio and humility, peopled by men knowing their lives are hanging by a string. I'm introduced by my gangling conductor, Lieutenant Swallow, amid some predictable ribaldry about my jodhpur get-up and I'm savvy enough to know that women don't wear trousers in the Mess.

The contrast to the camp is stark: here there are coal fires and carpets, elegant chandeliers, white linen tablecloths, fine china for tea and coffee and old masters on the wall. I'm hoping to interview top-scoring ace Major Albert Ball, but he's a retiring soul who doesn't want to talk, so I make do with Gambier, the non-flying adjutant with the gammy leg.

'When we get a kill,' he says, 'there's intense rivalry about who can claim it. Generally, several of our lot have all been having a go at the same Hun, but Ball – he's different. Happy to concede the kill to the other chap to boost his score.'

You're an ace, I discover, when you've downed five. And with the Fokkers currently in the ascendancy we haven't many aces.

I ponder Ball's strange attitude. A serious lack of rivalry. No such modesty, I reflect, would have been on display had it been between me and my brother.

But the adjutant's manner has become taut. He knows I've been suggesting the sergeant pilots should have better quarters. Officers are nicely situated at the chateau but the sergeants all live in rows of bell tents at the aerodrome – draughty and horrible on frosty mornings and easy meat for marauding enemy scouts with bombs to unload.

'The men are used to it,' he says. 'Expect it. Part of their station in life.'

I can feel my blood pressure rising. He's the natural product of his enclosed world, I tell myself – public school, Sandhurst, the regiment, them and us. He can't help it. It doesn't make him a bad person, and my job is to seek understanding.

Gambier comes closer, speaks more softly, making the message all the more menacing. 'I know you've been talking to some bolshie types on the field but I'd be very careful if I were you. Stirring the men up. Trouble-making, disaffection of the troops, that's a very serious offence. Could land you in a whole heap of trouble.'

It's been an uncomfortable voyage into military life for me: from the warm rooms of Guildhall Street via the cramped quarters in Tenement Row and now to a wooden hut, a cinder floor, draughty windows, frosty dawns and the smell of latrines and sweat-stained clothing.

Outside the hut is a separate ablution block with buckets of cold water, sinks and no roof – more than a tad chilly in the mornings. Still, this is what I wanted, I console myself, and take in the varied aspects of this strange installation: the muddy tracks, lumbering tenders and lines of aircraft contrasting with the former existence of what had once been a large farming community. This morning I'm back at the chateau, curious to know about an influx of replacements and peer down the list of names posted on the noticeboard hoping to find someone I know, perhaps Scottie or even the Broadlands braggart Dan Jackson Forbes. That's when I do a double-take. Here is a name I never expected to see: Nowak, Aleksander, flying officer, posted from the St Omer replacement pool.

When the bus draws in and Nowak appears through the door, looking in his RFC uniform a shade more kempt than during his time at Broadlands, the atmosphere between us is a little short on welcoming. For me, his arrival at Vert Galant is another twist in this chapter of injustice.

He grunts at me. 'Still a happy little bird, I see.'

'Why you?'

'I'm a replacement. Hadn't you noticed?'

They must be desperate – but I stop myself saying this. I still find it incredible my mother should take him as a lover. How did he worm his way into her affections? I swallow the acid taste on the end of my tongue and ask: 'What are you flying?'

'The 2c.'

'How many hours?'

'Fourteen.'

I try not to snort. With that amount of experience on the 2c he won't last five minutes over the lines. 'Maybe,' I say, 'you'll find it a little more challenging than the old Boxkite at Broadlands.'

At this point all pretence at politeness fades. He says: 'You think you're some hotshot,' then adds spitefully, 'Shame! You're grounded and I'm not.'

'The only reason for that,' I reply, trying not to spit, 'is you're male and I'm not. Don't you worry, I'll be in the air soon enough. Then we'll see who can really fly.'

'Says you.'

'Is that a dare? Want to put it to the test?'

'You can't.'

At this point a loud voice interrupts. 'So why don't you? Put it to the test?' Followed by a loud guffaw. 'I'd be most intrigued by the outcome.'

It's Captain Carstairs, the second in command who's been earwigging our little tiff from over by the fireplace. His lank figure uncurls from the sofa and approaches. 'Our dear leader is due some well-earned leave next week,' he says. 'Off to Paris for a rest. Nice for him. Which means, as his number two, I'm in charge. So, why don't you two make it pistols at dawn by the hangars on Monday morning?'

Duelling with His Majesty's highly prized aerial assets is, of course, strictly against all the regs in the book, but then Carstairs clearly isn't one for the book, so Nowak and I check out the spare kites not down for the Monday flying rota. He picks the 2c. Mine's a Bristol Scout.

I'm looking over the Scout, familiarising myself with the controls and trying to remember Scott's advice on the best technique for looping when an arm comes across mine and my antagonist from the Officers' Mess, the adjutant Gambier, is close-up and almost in my face.

'Don't you think we're losing enough pilots to the enemy without trying to do it ourselves?' he says.

I pretend bafflement. I'm up for this contest.

Gambier persists. 'If you go ahead with this silly stunt the CO will bounce you straight back to Blighty and there'll be no coming back.' He looks at me closely but on this occasion he doesn't seem to be in hostile mood. 'And besides,' he says, 'do you hate this man so much you want to risk his life in a stupid dare?'

I consider this point seriously. Would I like Nowak to look stupid? Yes. To crash and possibly kill himself? No.

'Besides,' Gambier says again, 'he's Polish, he didn't have to come, he volunteered, and that makes him an okay type in my eyes.'

'Why would he do that?' I ask, possibly a daft question, but I'm genuinely mystified.

'Because both the Germans and the Russians are marching

all over his country. Some Poles have been forced to fight for the Austrians. Some are with us. We should thank them, not confront them.'

I concede the point and relax. It's chilly out here in the open and I blow a reflective breath into my cold hands.

'And there's something else you should know,' the adjutant says and he's talking to me like my favourite uncle. He's no longer the man who riled me over sergeants in tents. 'We're not here to win personal points and clock up some sort of glory score for ourselves, we're here to score a victory over the enemy. You can take that competitive reflex of yours a little too far. Don't you see?'

I look into his eyes and don't recognise an opponent. Images instead of flyers sharing out their 'kills'; echoes of selfless comradeship in the face of danger. I sigh deeply, nod and turn away from the aircraft. 'Tell him I apologise and the contest is off.'

He gives me that avuncular look again, etched with the merest hint of a grin. 'Why don't you tell him yourself?'

Humility is offering a heartfelt apology to someone you'd rather drown in the nearest village pond. Try kissing an enemy, why don't you? Abasing yourself, inviting the ridicule of fools.

I find Nowak down by hangar No.1 and tap him on the shoulder. He whirls around. 'Forget it,' I say, 'I don't want you risking your neck for me. Sorry to have stirred you up. Keep all your venom for the Hun.'

I can't say he was gracious in response and I can't say it was my favourite experience, but it had to be done.

The world of aviation is really quite small, so it's more than a fair chance that any day now someone from my flying past will pitch up at Vert dressed in RFC garb sporting pips or crowns on his shoulder lapels. It would be no surprise to find – say – Jackson Forbes posted in as a replacement pilot. However, what has just happened is completely unexpected.

'You're wanted!' the orderly room messenger informs me when I'm halfway between the Voluntary Aid Detachment sick bay and the squadron office and I anticipate another hostile session with The Hon. Crispin.

'Hangar No.2,' the orderly says.

Big surprise. I expect to see Enfield Annie astride her machine but no, it's my good friend Katie Swift from Bury who appears beaming into the wintry sunlight outside the Bessonneau. And she's back in VAD nursing uniform, looking pristine smart.

'How did you get here?' I demand in the midst of a big hug.

'Got a ride on the replacements bus. Just a quick visit. Heard you were here. Must be back by five.'

'Want a tour?'

'Things to tell you.'

I can read that look. This isn't just an old friends' get-together. 'Let's go to the Mess,' I say, and we hurry off in pursuit of tea, bread, marmalade and a chat. I want to know all about her new life ministering to the wounded at a base hospital but there's something else on her mind.

'I've been approached,' she says, grinning. 'Must have been that piece you did on me in the paper. People have noticed.'

'More promotion, bigger hospital, up for matron?'

'No,' she says, 'politics.'

I do my best not to gape. Button my lip. Worried. She's my best friend, a treasure, and I can see her self-confidence has grown enormously since I last saw her, but she's a barely educated working-class girl from the slums and this has to be one of the most class-structured societies in the world.

Now she's in full flood. 'I hate this awful war and the endless queues of wounded men and all the suffering but eventually this horrible business has to end and there has to be an afterwards, hasn't there?'

This is not really a question.

'When the world puts itself back together again. And when that happens I want to be there. I want to be part of the process of putting it back together. Don't want to go back to what we had before.'

I'm impressed by this new fluency but anticipate the nightmare of her going up against the tokens of the Establishment: Eton, the Guards, grand houses, high society. They'll humiliate her and enjoy doing it.

'Where's all this leading?'

In low tones of excited conspiratorial whisper I learn the suffrage movement is still active behind the scenes; that Mrs Pankhurst has been assured by Lloyd George that women will get the vote the minute the fighting stops; that plans are being laid to have women stand for election as MPs.

'You?'

My expression must have given me away.

'Don't be daft, I'd be slaughtered.' She shakes her head and I breathe out in relief.

She says: 'Any woman MP has to be able to match up to them, she has to be one of them, ready to do battle on equal terms, and we're planning for each candidate to have a team of helpers. People like me. They want me on the team.'

'Who's *we*?'

'Your friend Mel.'

'Figures.' Now this all makes sense. Maggie Melrose is certainly the right person to have a go. Brave and implacable as a correspondent, well-informed and eloquent, even if a little eccentric.

'I'm there so the workers won't be forgotten,' says Katie.

I look at her and grin. Feeling much better. 'Who would have thought it? Back there in Bury, sitting in that little house...' She's talking about equal pay, job security, better wages, hygiene, housing, security of tenure. This last reference brings her up short and I detect a sense a sudden uncertainty. She's lost some of that earlier bounce. 'That's my bad news,' she says, and tells me she's been kicked out of Tenement Row. Now there are new tenants at No.4, a dreadful bunch of scruffs who've wrecked all her knick-knacks and dumped her possessions.

I'm puzzled. 'What happened to Mooseface?'

'Goodness knows, haven't heard from him for ages.' She sighs and looks at me. 'Don't say it.'

'I wasn't going to.'

Her eyelids flutter, a change of mood from ebullience to sadness. 'Couldn't keep up the rent. Probably couldn't find work.'

'Must make you feel awful, no home to go back to, all your things gone.' I cradle her shoulders. 'Don't worry, whatever happens, you'll never be out on your ear. Friends stick together. Friendship counts.'

There's a silence before she suddenly fishes in her pocket. 'Nearly forgot! Brought you some stuff.' She produces a bundle of letters and talk from home, principal of which is that Brother Dear has chalked up another gong, this time a naval Distinguished Service Cross, for catapulting his aircraft off the deck of HMS Illustrious. Then she's looking at her watch, collecting her things and talking about the journey back to base, when she asks: 'And romance? How's it going with that pilot of yours? Handsome devil in his uniform.'

'You've seen him?'

'Met him in the street. A quick word.'

She grins conspiratorially but I don't want to discuss Scott. 'Don't go building any romantic castles.'

'Why not?'

'Just not.'

She giggles. 'Asked after you. Devoted is the impression I got.' Now she's serious and wagging a finger. 'You don't know how to play it, do you?'

I bristle.

'Men are just competitors to you. Rivals. Why hold him off?'

'I'm not.'

'Keeping your distance. Putting up the barriers.'

Close friend for sure, but she's crossing a line. I make a move for the door. 'I think you're going to be late for your bus.'

CHAPTER EIGHTEEN

I can tell long before I reach the entrance. Something is afoot this morning. No chatter, no carefree atmosphere, instead a tense and worrying sense that everyone is holding their breath.

At the door to the commander's outer office the sergeant – I've dubbed him the Gatekeeper – bars the way. 'I wouldn't go in there, Miss,' he says, 'your presence won't be appreciated.'

But I didn't come all this way to be pushed around by a three-striper. My instinct for a news story is aroused; I need to find out what's going on. A major development in the offing? Perhaps a change of strategy; perhaps a big operation.

'I must attend,' I insist and step forward, daring him to get physical.

Instead, he steps aside and I see a ring of silent officers with their attention fixed on some object or person just out of sight at the far end of the room. I can hear him before I see him and immediately catch my breath at the message. 'There's been a series of very unfortunate and distasteful leaks from this station.' It's a loud, booming voice full of authority and angst. 'Stories bypassing the censor. Talk of poverty back home contrasting with too much comfort out here. Cushy billets! Would you believe? All sorts of unpatriotic stuff from our people in the corps talking out of turn.'

Perhaps it might be better if I retreated at this point but the voice goes on, 'These leaks must be plugged, we must not have the corps dragged into controversy or disrepute. There's only one message to go out: the glory and derring-do of our fighting men of the air.'

This diatribe is greeted with muted and polite murmurs of assent and faces turn in my direction. An about-turn from me is therefore out of the question and I advance into the room to see the author of this strident message. I recognise him immediately. It's not difficult, he's known to all. General Trenchard, the man who's not just head of flying in France but the very embodiment of the corps. He almost invented it all by himself.

He focuses on my entrance, stares hard, his features contorting. Then he demands, 'What's she doing here?'

I wonder if I should fill the ensuing silence and announce myself. Instead there's a cough from close by and I spot Crispin Wycliffe who's speaking in an unusually subdued and modulated tone. 'She's the press correspondent who's been assigned to us.'

Another flash of anger from Trenchard.

'Get her out of here.'

A further embarrassed cough from the CO. 'Her papers are all in order...'

'I don't care!' Trenchard is working himself into a fury. 'She's probably the source of all this mischief, all these damned leaks. What idiot thought it appropriate to send us a female correspondent?'

I step forward. 'My despatches go through the censor,' I say sweetly.

Well, true, as far as it goes.

'The Ministry...' Wycliffe tries again but doesn't get very far.

'Give her a scrubbing brush and escort her to the latrines.'

Without further ado I find myself ushered outside. 'Told you,' says the grinning Gatekeeper, 'the weather's so bad no one can get up, it's no wonder he's in a temper.'

It comes to me then; the cause of his anger is much more likely to be that last letter to Mr Arbuthnot–aka-Brewster of Acacia Avenue, Sidcup; some juicy quotes and trenchant reaction from the ground crew following a prolonged weather-induced lull in aerial activity.

I shrug off any potential escort and vanish into the labyrinthine back ways of Vert Galant and head for the women's block, there to lie low for a while and hope the CO puts Trenchard right.

If not, I may have to invoke higher authority, though how you do that without using their telephones may prove a little tricky.

———

Two days later I'm standing around in that tatty outer office once again waiting for the next confrontation with The Hon. Crispin. What's to be my fate? Trenchard's fury was visceral and I can imagine a history of behind–the-scenes clashes in Whitehall between the War Office and the Ministry of Information.

'Go in, please.'

I'm through the door and staring once again into the gaze of Major Iceberg. Strangely, I note immediately, he doesn't look angry. Not friendly, but not actually hostile. 'I've called you in because I have some information for you,' he says.

He's playing with some files on his desk, stacking and rearranging them, and it seems to me that the absence of any mention of the Trenchard incident would appear to show that my unlikely sponsor back in Whitehall trumps even the power of Trenchard himself.

'Some material has come into my possession that will doubtless be of great help to you in writing your despatches,' Wycliffe says.

Huh! Beware such gifts, I tell myself. Doubtless, this is a ploy.

'We're not blinkered flyers here,' he says. 'Concerned only with ourselves and unaware of the bigger picture. We are very aware of what's going on down below on the ground.'

I should certainly hope so – but I'm wary. I can see a propaganda exercise coming right at me but I will not play the willing dupe.

'You obviously know that things are hard for the troops on the front line but you may not be aware of the hardships of the civilian populations behind the front lines in the territory occupied by the enemy.' He looks down and is obviously about to push some document across the desk in my direction. 'The latest information on conditions in the zone immediately behind the front lines has been put together in this statement for your use and I've just taken a quick look at it.' He clears his throat and shakes his head and I get the impression that there's an altogether more humane if unexpected side to him. 'Makes for awful reading,' he says. 'I must say it gives me pause. This man Kruger would appear to be an absolute tyrant.'

'You mean, the German Kommandant?'

'Yes, him.'

He turns the file around so I can read the formal details: Kommandant von Kruger, Etappen-Commandant 12/X of the 3rd Etappen-Inspektion.

I recognise this now. It's what Waterman was talking about at the London hotel.

'A hateful system,' Wycliffe says. 'Intimidation plus the

worst kind of exploitation. Kruger's obsessed about enemy agents. The locals say he's a crazy man. Strutting around, fantastically drunk, pillaging everything they've got.'

He nods and pushes the document across the desk. This is what I suspected all along: a propaganda exercise along the lines of 'why we fight' and similar campaigns that are running at home. On the other hand, this would appear to be well-authenticated information and confirms what Waterman was talking about. I now have the document in my hand and after examining the details I decide it's something I can believe in and report truthfully.

Later, after writing up all the ghastly details, I'm really glad that I don't have to live and survive on the other side of those lines.

CHAPTER NINETEEN

'Charlotte!'

It's little Ernie Earnshaw, hailing me from outside his hangar on another fine morning and I've already clocked the 2c parked on the apron in front of the Bessonneau. I can smell the fuel and feel the heat of the motor where it's just been run up.

I look over her minutely and spot some work on the fuselage where bullet holes have been patched. I love being around these things, fiddling with them, sitting in them, checking out the controls, checking the tautness of the wires, talking shop.

I take a deep breath. I can feel the old resentment rising that I'm not allowed to fly, even though I know I'm better than most of these pilots. I feel the rising urge to zoom up into the sky. My hands are on the struts where a flyer would haul themselves up... but the lead weight of my promised good behaviour is pinning my feet to the ground.

Earnshaw strolls over. 'I can see it, you're dreaming that kite into the sky.' He grins.

'I'm interested in how this camera works.'

We discuss the big black beast strapped to the side of the fuselage. It's plate-operated and points downwards. That reminds me – I saw them yesterday – a little knot of officers poring over a table covered in photographic prints, assembling the jigsaw into the basis of a map. It's the method the engineers use to produce trench maps for the Army.

Earnshaw points out the diagrams and instructions in the cockpit and the plan for the next run over the trenches. Then, with a conspiratorial glance behind, adds: 'I didn't say this. She's not on today's flying roster but she's fuelled up and ready to go.'

I look at him, suddenly aware of the drumbeat echoing around my ribcage. This man is Satan. Has put temptation right up close in my face. He's teasing me beyond all toleration.

'I'll be looking the other way,' he says. 'Disclaiming all responsibility. Nothing to do with me.'

Suddenly I ask myself: does anyone round here really believe I'm a flyer? I've read their sceptical looks. They think I'm a fraud. The frustration of this is too much to bear. Being grounded, so close to the action and yet so far. I look Earnshaw in the eye and recognise a kindred spirit of defiance. The 2c is ready and waiting... how can I resist? A little voice somewhere at the back of my head is saying *No* to such an act of recklessness, that it will get me into all sorts of bother, probably have me ejected from France altogether and ditch my mission. But a much louder voice is yelling *yes, yes, yes!*

Earnshaw says: 'Now's your chance. What can they do? You're not service personnel, you're an outsider, you represent *The Planet*, a big-time newspaper correspondent, you can get away with it.'

I can't hold back. Can hardly speak. 'Solo?'

'Percy here wants to be an observer.'

Percy Stride is the fellow with the double chin and the electric hair. No resentments – and suddenly he's right next to me, grinning like we're both just a couple of very naughty schoolboys. 'I want to go up with you,' he says.

A fan. After the session with the sketchpad he's an eager co-conspirator. He's been taken off the observer rota because they're short of mechanics but wants back in. Two chancers together!

I look around. No one else is about. I can't pass up this chance. I may never get another. This is what I've worked for, dreamed about, longed for. I know I shouldn't. I know there'll be trouble. I'll probably get the sack.

But to hell with conformity.

CHAPTER TWENTY

A plumber needs his tools, a soldier his weapon, an airman protective clothing. It's cold up there, no fool would fly without the necessary buffer against an icy wind. Style flees out of the window as I step into the hangar and locate a spare set of kit; helmet, gloves, goggles and the big padded overalls. Looking like the incredible rubber man, I climb into the cockpit and caress the controls, feeling I'm back where I belong – a seat that's mine by right, listening to the engine warm up, listening out for trouble.

But everything sounds right. Completely right. And I'm confident of success. I recall Scottie's words: if you can fly the Parasol, you can fly anything, and this is just a 2c. This flight, a serious operational sortie, will be my revenge on stupid, purblind, bureaucratic authority. I repress a doubt that says this foray may also be my last.

Instead, I'm bubbling. This is a sheer tactile pleasure: the pliable feel to the fuselage, the stick in my fingers, my sense at being the centre of gravity. I check the tautness of the wires, work the connections, tense the control cables. I sense Percy watching me, enjoying his moment, amused by the sight of a crazed woman at work. The familiar mix of engine heat, noise and latent power shoots through the canvas frame and enters my soul, a precursor to the excitement and challenge to follow. My whole body seems to be vibrating in sympathy. I'm like the sailor with sea legs who rolls with the motion of the ship.

Can I really get away with this? I look around but no one, apart from Percy, seems to be taking note. Control is relaxed, having already despatched the day's patrols and now there are other air movements, ferry arrivals and test flights, mechanics swarming out of the hangers. I give the signal and we head off as if embarking on a practice hop over Amiens, well away from the Front. The earth falls away, the countryside one huge vibrant map made up of soft shades of light and colour, the dark brown of the woods merging with ploughed fields and the roads which seemed so definitive now inconsequential ribbons. I pull her round eastwards once out of sight of the aerodrome and feel myself grinning despite the wind slashing my face and mouth below the goggles, and quite soon the nature of the landscape below begins to turn ugly, pockmarked with shell holes, a watery wasteland as we climb to 7,000 feet near the zigzag pattern of the trenches. As I approach doubts begin to dim this sense of elation. The next few minutes will be the ultimate test – what I've been striving for since I first glimpsed the wonder of flight. Everything has been pointing to this moment: ambition, a competitive edge, implacable willpower. It's the first time I've deliberately placed myself in mortal danger and if I fail all will be lost in damnation and disgrace, not just for me but perhaps for all women flyers for years to come.

I recognise the peculiarly crooked section of enemy trenches that are marked down for the next photographic over-flight, finding a twisty bend in the river and a ruined church as landmarks. The greyish-brown earthworks scar an already desolate moonscape. Calm and steady, I tell myself. The job is to fly straight and level over the correct spot. Of course, I know that as a recce plane, the 2c is a joke. I can see some of the crooked shapes below but others are obscured by the mainplane. Percy, on the other hand, kneeling on his observer seat in front of me, can see almost nothing. He's wedged under the centre section. He has a Lewis gun but can't fire forwards because of the prop, only backwards, and even then struts, wires and tailplane get in the way. His task is to keep an eye out for the enemy. Mine is to operate the big black mahogany box that is our camera.

Keeping a steady course over the target area, I do my best to follow Earnshaw's instruction: sight the camera by leaning over the side of the machine and look through a ball-and-crosswire finder. Despite all the padding and headgear, looking into a seventy-mile-an-hour wind brings a shock reality to the task. Then I must fly the machine with the left hand, keeping over the required track, and reaching an arm out into the slipstream to push the camera lever back and forward. Changing the photographic plates means tugging on a lanyard between each operation.

At the first attempt I fluff it and drop a plate. I swear. The gloves are too clumsy for this work but when I remove one and use my fingers I scream out so loud Percy changes his position in alarm. The icy blast to bare flesh is like a knife to the bone. My thumb seems glued to the ice surface of the camera. Damnation! Another dropped plate. At this rate the great adventure is turning into a farce.

Then things take a turn for the worse. Several puffs of grey smoke appear to our left and my observer screams 'Archie!' The enemy is shooting at us from the ground. He has a good target since of necessity we're flying a steady course. Within a short while he gets our range and height and there's a sharp crack followed by a tearing sound. A lump of shrapnel from a shellburst close by rips open a hole in our fabric, followed by a momentary smell of acrid smoke.

I swallow and turn back to try again, mouth dry and fingers stiff with pain. This time I will work that damned big black box – but will they range us yet again?

'Got to make another pass,' I shout at Percy.

'We're really asking for it now,' calls a strained voice from the front seat and this time I pull the string and change the plates through sheer willpower, screeching through the shock, shedding skin in the process but getting at least half a dozen camera shots without dropping another plate. I plan one more turn – then Percy screams, cocks his gun and shouts: 'Fokker!'

A sharp crack and the 2c shudders. We've been caught unawares by the scourge of the skies, a German Eindecker, shooting through his own propeller, pointing his plane at his target, a highly effective method of attack. We're now the target. I pull the 2c round in a tight turn to avoid his fire and the sound of his gun is muffled by the roar of our engine. Percy is shooting off his Lewis gun right above my head, an ear-shredding racket, but our defensive fire is not enough and the Eindecker comes on again, eager for the kill. This time I dive and turn even tighter, veering one way and then another, working us closer and closer towards our own lines. The enemy is reluctant to follow and turns away. Later I learn their pilots are under orders not to venture over British lines lest they crash and inadvertently reveal to the Allies the secret of their interrupter gear.

By this time our engine is making a terrible din, clearly damaged in the encounter. We need to get down and fast. Percy is pointing out an advanced landing ground – a strip made ready for this kind of emergency – and we glide down, skimming some poles and rumble to a stop.

Percy is first out of the plane, walking around it, examining the damage. 'Good grief, Charlotte, I thought we were done for.'

I don't reply, just nod. Don't want him thinking I'm rattled.

'I don't know how we're still here, look at these holes,' he says, pointing at the chewed-up wing and fuselage, a neat tattoo around the wing stub, like the Eindecker had been using us for bullseye practice. 'More holes than the cookhouse colander,' he says. 'He wasn't a bad shot, so why did we survive?'

I shrug. 'My flying,' I suggest.

He looks at the sky. 'Maybe ran out of ammo.'

Then I consider the situation and how to retrieve it. I approach him, stand close and look him in the eye from a range of two feet.

'Look here, Percy, there's something we must do. We have to agree on our story and stick to it.'

He's startled. 'What do you mean?'

'We can't say I was flying, you know that, don't you? An unauthorised flight over enemy territory? If we tell them that they'll murder us both.'

He looks scared.

'We'll have to say you were piloting the plane and I was the observer.'

'Impossible!' he objects. 'I can't fly, I'm an observer.'

'Yes, but you've been taking lessons from your pilot friend and you know how to do it, you're quite confident and you thought this was your big chance. You mistook the rota and thought you were down for your first flight.'

'They'll never believe that...'

'It will limit the fallout when we get back to Vert. You'll probably get busted for a while but you'll be back. They need good flyers.'

'But I'm not a flyer!'

He looks over his shoulder and I follow his gaze across the fields to the distant road. The crash tender is already on its way.

'Witnesses,' I say, 'they'll clock us soon enough, so we'd better get our story straight right from the off.'

He looks doubtful.

'Now or never,' I say and he gradually, ever so slowly, nods agreement.

The recovery team are nearly on us, ready to retrieve the 2c and haul it back to Vert for repair.

I give him a final challenging stare and he nods agreement once more. Even so, I know there will be big trouble when we get back to the aerodrome and the uptight major will be holding my feet to the fire.

CHAPTER TWENTY-ONE

Major The Hon. Crispin Wycliffe is incandescent, as I knew he would be. I'm in front of the desk once more while he, as before, is by the window, this time ranting.

'Never heard the like of it,' he says, 'a rogue flight over enemy territory, against all the rules, endangering my aircraft, reducing my chances of taking the fight to the enemy, damaging His Majesty's property.' He pauses for breath. 'And you – I don't care about you – but placing one of my crew in peril...'

I don't interrupt. In a way he's right, of course. My first operational sortie is a disaster. No great victory to set against The Hon. Crispin and his no-woman diktat. To be fair to him, it's a War Office diktat. Actually, the ban on women flyers is an edict from the whole damned ruling class and the government, so don't let 'em cow you, Charlotte, I tell myself, ride the storm.

'Corporal Stride should have known better than to attempt such a foolish flight. He has to be made an example of.' Wycliffe is smacking his elegant thighs in agitated indignation. 'He'll be sent back home in disgrace on the next available transport.'

'Now wait a minute,' I object, 'you can't do that. It wasn't his fault, he thought he was doing right...'

'This is none of your concern.'

'It's unfair to blight his chances by sending him back,' I say. 'He wants to stay on operations, he's enthusiastic, he's a good man.'

He looks at me questioningly, as if puzzled by my concern. And I can't let it pass. Can't deflect all the blame and heap misery on poor pliant Percy. I swallow and breathe out. 'Okay,' I say, 'I have to admit to my part in all this. I haven't told you the full extent of it. Percy was just the observer. He wasn't flying. I was.'

This produces another icy blast from by the window. 'Then you too will ship out with Stride. Back to the UK with both of you.' Suddenly, he's across the office and in my face. 'And don't think that fancy booklet and letter will save you. After this episode, let me assure you beyond any last remaining doubt...' He's glaring, eyes bulging. This man carries an enormous burden. He's under severe pressure. Anyone over the age of twenty-one would be having a heart attack. Will he make it past thirty?

'You're finished!' He stamps a furious foot. 'Now get out of my sight.'

The price of confession is an uncomfortable and miserable ride to St Omer in a Crossley station wagon, accompanied by a gloomy and resentful Stride. I console myself. At least it's a motorised journey and not that damned donkey cart. 'Don't fret,' I tell Percy, 'I'll get this thing resolved, you'll see, you'll soon be back.'

He doesn't look as if he believes me.

When we reach Britain's main RFC base in France I'm pointedly led to the transport office ready for the next stage in my disgrace, another journey, this time to Calais and the troopship back to Dover, an itinerary I have no intention of completing.

I demand to see the transport major, produce my letter of authority and request the use of a telegram to inform my superiors in Whitehall about this 'current misunderstanding'. With reluctance, the request is granted and I send off a message to Waterman at the Department informing him of my present difficulties with the CO at Vert following a 'trial flight involving some slight damage to an aircraft'.

Then I tell Osbert Blackley-Jacket that my telegram to higher authority will shortly change the situation.

'I'm fully aware of the nature of the telegram,' he says.

'Then it shouldn't be a problem to wait for the reply,' I say.

'No problem, provided it arrives before the next transport to Calais,' he says with a smile. He's not a bad sort really and adds: 'Look, I have all the details and I can tell you now, they won't overlook an unauthorised flight over enemy territory, risking military property and needlessly imperilling the life of a serving soldier. That's far too serious.'

I shake my head. 'They will.'

He grins. 'Then I can only admire your chutzpah.'

He's still in a good mood when Waterman's response arrives. Relief! I'm being returned to Vert and Percy Stride gets a new posting at St Omer.

'Enjoy your reception back at Vert,' says Blackley-Jacket with another grin.

My best policy is to keep out of Wycliffe's way and adopt an unchallenging profile, at least for the time being, knowing that the CO will have received fresh instructions about co-operation.

Back at Vert I wander into the chateau only to find the place almost empty. The stick-thin gangling Tim Swallow, youngest subaltern on the station, is all alone, sitting on a stool at the bar. I notice some of my despatches to *The Planet* have been pinned to the noticeboard. That can't please a certain major.

However, Swallow is talkative. He's cock-a-hoop that he's scored his second 'kill' becoming lyrical about the purity of air combat, the chivalry of the air, like knights of old, this being so much better than the mud and blood of the trenches.

I'm not sure I share his enthusiasm.

'What better way in war than two men duelling to the death, the best man wins.'

I draw in a long breath preparatory to objection. I've already had this sort of discussion with Katie who demanded to know why I'm comfortable with people who shoot to kill. Flying for me is a vital part of my being; its denial is a wasted talent, a lost resource, like snatching the flame from the Olympic torch-bearer, but shooting is another matter, a purely defensive reflex. I know I have to be careful at this moment, not to stir up a controversy so soon after my problem with the CO, however, I will not let Swallow's attitude pass. 'Can't agree,' I say, 'I find fighter tactics rather...' I hesitate. I was going to say *sick*, instead I opt for *dubious*. 'Hanging around in the sky ready to pounce on some unsuspecting flyer in an inferior machine and killing him just for the sake of it...'

'Now steady on!'

But I drive on. 'Surely, it's enough to force the enemy away, enough simply to stop him photographing the trenches. That's the real object, is it not?'

'But the blighter will be back again in the morning.'

'So drive him off again. A duel to the death – that's ridiculous. A silly idea. I could never be part of that – but I'll do a job, I'll do the recce run.'

'Don't think they'll give you the chance.'

I don't like the obvious being pointed out, so I plunge on: 'Killing for the sake of it. Cruel, uncivilised, reptilian.'

'Tell that to the men down there in the trenches.'

'Not what I've heard. Soldiers fire over the top of enemy heads rather than at them.'

'A cop-out!'

'But human!'

There's a silence and I chalk this up as a victory. I've had the last word. Bad mistake! At this precise moment the more abrasive personality of Gambier enters the Mess and it doesn't take him long to rekindle the discussion. 'I can see what's going on here,' he says, eyeing me as if I'm some upstart come to spoil his day. 'I can read you. You see yourself as the advance guard for some legion of independent women.'

'I want to see women flyers, yes...'

'Then you and your kind will have to answer one very simple question. Can you kill?'

I restate my contention about fending off the opposition but this cuts no ice with Gambier. 'There you are, on your next recce mission, snapping away at the trenches again and you're not going to attack the Hun. But what happens when he comes in for an attack, your observer shoots back to drive him off and just happens to kill him in the process, shoots him down in flames, he burns to death while smashing himself into small pieces on the ground, what then?'

His chin is up, challenging. For the first time I notice the flushed appearance, the bulbous nose, the acne.

I sigh. 'I'd be mortified...'

'But you'd be alive and he'd be dead, where's your passivity now?' He looks at me almost sadly then. 'But of course, in reality, the chances are, the result would be the other way round, you realise that, don't you? You'd be dead.'

To which I have no answer.

He comes closer. 'There's something else. A warning.'

My hackles are already up but then I see he isn't being

confrontational. 'A word of advice to keep you out of trouble. Just so you don't go putting your foot in it and making a fool of yourself. And us.'

My hands are on my hips. Another attempt at censorship?

'This is an operational station.'

'I know that.'

'On certain occasions operations take place here which are strictly off-limits to the press. Not for public consumption. The people back in London will know this. Stuff that will never ever be allowed to be published and going anywhere near it could make you look very foolish indeed and land you in all sorts of deep hot water. Now do you understand?'

I look at him quizzically. 'You mean, hush-hush?'

There's the merest hint of a smile as he says: 'I'm trying to save you from yourself.'

Later that evening I'm still keeping myself invisible to The Hon. Explosive Crispin by staying in barracks, chatting to the girls and gazing out of a condensation-streaked window. I can afford to be relaxed and idle but the VADs can't. The place is all energy; attending to kit, washing, sewing, ironing, manicuring nails, writing home. The wind-up gramophone is blaring out 'Keep the Home Fires Burning' and the amenable company goes some way to compensate for the shortcomings of the place. I'm still suffering from the taut springs of the iron bedstead and the smelly stove which throws out an inefficient heat leaving pools of cold and damp, mainly in my direction. Still, the olive-green War Office decor has been livened up with calendars and newspaper cut-outs. And the first question asked in any barracks is: 'Where are you from?' That's something I'm learning; the Army is a great leveller with humour and asperity going hand in hand. The girl on the top bunk who's never been outside Glasgow is being caustic with her neighbour from the West Country and in the next bay a native of Hackney has trouble deciphering the Cornish accent. That's another discovery: everyone is irritated by the chirpy Cockney.

Penny, I'm buoyed to find, is from my own area of Suffolk, but there the similarity ends. I'm a townie, she's from the deep countryside. Life in a tiny cottage, no electricity, no running water, bread and marm for dinner, her father walking his sheep eleven miles to market... the plight of the rural poor is as foreign to me as if they lived a thousand miles away. This is the picture it's now my job to paint for the printed word: the gulf that divides Britain today.

There's a lull in the conversation and I return to my window gazing. I'm in a reflective mood. I should be glad to be back at Vert, still active despite my misdemeanours, but somehow it feels like an anticlimax. That's when I notice a new arrival dropping out of the sky and almost fall off my perch when I recognise the unmistakable profile of a Morane-Saulnier Type L, otherwise known as my dangerous friend the Parasol. Its presence is anathema to most of the flyers on this station. My intrigue is heightened when the aircraft moves away from the hangars to a small hut on the far side of the aerodrome. Two figures emerge and walk into the hut, a structure shrouded and made more mysterious by an encirclement of trees.

What can possibly account for such strange behaviour? Pilots who don't want to socialise?

It's almost dusk so I slip unnoticed out of the VAD barrack and sidle round the edges of the aerodrome to arrive outside the strange building. The way has been hard going; long grass, uneven ground. Not many people choose this path.

I hesitate at the door. Lord knows what's inside. My hand closes over the doorknob. It's wet from recent rainfall and rough to the skin. Will it squeal when I turn? No! It's military, well-oiled and doubtless the subject of regular inspection, so I ease the door open and pause on the step, peering in at the gloom. I can just glimpse a slumped male figure on a chair in an otherwise empty space and wonder why he's sitting in the dark. Are the curtains drawn? No, they appear to be tied back. The shutters then; they must be closed on the outside.

The penny drops. All those hints from the adjutant. Dark secrets, cloak and dagger, hush-hush, all the slightly humorous references to spying. Of course, this is what he meant. I'm looking into the secrets room and all those jocular references don't seem funny anymore. I breathe in deeply and intrigue keeps me rooted to the spot.

From somewhere in the interior another door opens and I'm confronted by a new figure. There's something familiar about the shape of it, and then it hits me like a slap in the face.

I gasp. It's Scott Fanshawe.

'What a surprise!'

He doesn't look pleased. 'I knew you were here.'

'But didn't seek me out.'

'I'm not allowed,' he says. 'This is a closed operation. You shouldn't be here and I shouldn't be talking to you.'

'But you are!'

'We're supposed to be strictly covert. No contact with anyone on the station. Complete seclusion. If Huckerbee finds you here...'

'Why the Parasol? What's it all about?'

'Can't say.'

'Yes you can.'

He gives me an exasperated look and I point to the figure in the corner. 'I get it, he's a spy, but what are we going to do with him?'

'What do you think?'

'Flying him across?'

He doesn't react.

'Landing him on the other side? Dropping him into enemy territory, behind the lines?'

Still no comment, no confirmation, but I see it now. Of course, why else would flyers be involved? I breathe out at the sheer effrontery of it. A ridiculous idea... putting down in the enemy's backyard and getting away with it? Crazy! I consider, take a few seconds more, then change my mind. No, not crazy, marvellous! I stare at him in sudden doubt. 'But what good's he doing over there?'

'You don't need to know.'

'Tell me.'

'Go!' he says, but I indicate that he should come with me. Outside in the gloom we can talk.

Little mental cogs are whirring. The Parasol, flying across the lines, landing and taking off again and finally returning in triumph... could there be another door opening for me? In the short walk to a quiet place out of earshot I formulate a plan and go to work on him. I know how to do it but strangely the discussion becomes heated and he exclaims, rather too loudly for my liking: 'No, Charlotte, absolutely not.'

I shush him and get him into another room, empty of anyone or anything except some old picnic tables and tell him: 'Scott, you have to do this for me, you know how much it means.'

He draws in a deep breath that speaks to conflicted feelings. 'Look,' he says, 'you know I'm willing to help, to back your cause, but this is really insane.'

'Sorry,' I say, 'I hate stealing your thunder.'

He snorts. 'It's not that. I'm no glory hunter.'

There's a silence at this. I suppose it means he thinks I am. I feel the wound of an unspoken barb. The selfless Ball and the supportive Scott both seem to be mocking me.

'This is a special operation,' Scott says. 'Absolutely secret. We can't change the arrangements just to suit ourselves. This is being run by the people upstairs. We'll have to consult them before we do anything.'

'That will kill my chances stone dead,' I say.

'Besides, it's crazy, there's nothing wrong with me, I've never felt better. I can't just feign a sudden illness, it would look suspicious. And I'd be very unhappy at such deception.'

'Scott, stop this! This is me,' I say urgently. 'I need your help as never before. I need to re-establish my reputation after my recce disaster.'

I know it's asking a lot. I don't want to deprive him of the satisfaction of delivering an agent into enemy territory, a vitally important and risky undertaking, not least because he's flying the Parasol. 'It's not about glory, it's about justice,' I insist. 'I want to break this ban on women flyers.'

'I know, I know,' he says, placing a placating hand on my arm, so I make my big speech: what a great feat it would be for a woman to fly in this spy; a feat of daring in the face of danger and performed in an aircraft few wish to fly; a dramatic gesture to turn the tide of public opinion. They wouldn't then be able to say women were not up to it.

'Hang on there a minute,' he objects. 'Public opinion? This is a secret operation and nobody, but nobody, will hear about it. It won't be a famous exploit – just the very real possibility of a bullet in the back. Amongst other things.'

I nod. Agreed! It's not about glory. But it is about impressing important figures of influence in government and the military. I want to change the minds of people like Lloyd George,

Churchill, even Asquith and perhaps even the tetchy Trenchard. They will certainly hear about it through official channels and they have the power of decision. And we women, I insist, we're here, ready and willing, soon to be more than fifty per cent of the national population, and we cannot be ignored and excluded from this great endeavour.

His expression changes and he nods. I go to him, close-up, touch his arm, run my hands down the softly ribbed barathea of his uniform, stand toe to toe, then pick up his hands. Both of them. I have to make him understand I need this chance more than anything in the world; he has to support my cause. Flying for me is a vital part of my being. Maybe I'm trembling, I'm not sure, but there's this physical connection, as if the message I'm sending him by word of mouth is actually being transmitted by touch. It's a tactile storm. I know he won't be able to resist.

'But it's damned dangerous!' he says. 'Flying across the lines, landing in enemy territory, ground fire, anything could happen. And if you were caught...' He doesn't finish.

Harsh images of what happens to a woman in enemy hands fill both our minds. We've all heard the tales of what they do. Shooting out of hand, torture, defilement. They even nailed one Tommy to a door, so the story goes. The heathen Hun and all that.

'Absolute ruthlessness on the ground, I couldn't bear it happening to you,' he says, giving me that look, but I brush all such notions from my mind. This operation now represents the supreme test I've set myself. Success will validate my sense of mission. Obsession conquers all.

I look at Scott and know he's being swept away by the irresistible force of my need.

There's a long silence and I can tell. His resistance is at an end. He's going to do it.

CHAPTER TWENTY-TWO

L et me explain about the moon. Bomber's moon, they call it – Charlotte's moon, I earnestly desire to rename it. Ever walked down an unlit path on a black night? Chances are you wouldn't try it, especially if you're a woman, but the survivor of such an experience would soon discover that after ten minutes they'd get their night vision in. Few nights are truly dark. Any bobby on the beat and night patrolman will attest to that. It certainly applies close to the ground.

Scale up the experience to an aeroplane, however, and taking off into a black void of nothingness is a truly terrifying experience. There's no navigational or directional help at all, nothing to tell a pilot if she's flying straight and level – or nose down into the ground. A suicide trip, a mission fit for those truly tired of life.

Except, of course, on a moonlit night. The soft silvery illumination unveils a beautiful if spooky landscape, and that's why this mission has to be tonight and only tonight. Miss it and there's a month's wait for the next decent moonlit date on the military calendar.

Just after my talk with Scott an angry individual dressed in civvies and with a pronounced Adam's apple barges into the room and demands to know what I'm doing there.

Scott, who's clutching his stomach most convincingly and looking more than a little wan, tries an introduction. 'Charlotte, my very good friend, an ace pilot, the only one who can fly the Morane...'

'Are you mad, Scott? Get her out of here.'

Adam's Apple has a blotchy face and would seem to be the aforementioned Huckerbee, Scott's conducting officer and the brains behind the operation. But from the manner of his haughty disdain I decide he must have a copy of King's Regs wedged somewhere quite uncomfortable. The security exclusion zone he's yelling about apparently includes all other persons apart from the funny little man I'd seen slumped in a corner, the object of all this night's angst.

So I'm just outside the hut, listening to strident voices shouting at each other. Secret or not, a few phrases float interestingly to me on the night air... *don't be such a pig... it has to be tonight... I've got to go to bed... no way, no way...*

The voices fade but I want to know what's going on. I'm the subject of this discussion, why should I be cut out of the picture? They've moved further into the hut, which is long and narrow, so I parallel their steps on the outside hoping for another chance to eavesdrop. After a few yards I get lucky with an open window, their voices loud and distinct. Huckerbee is still agitated. 'I'm going to get slaughtered for this,' he's saying in a distinctly whiny tone. 'When a certain person finds out I've sent a girl across enemy lines he's going to ask me if I've taken leave of my senses. What am I playing at? Putting a member of the fair sex in the line of fire. Just a slip of a girl...'

'She's not just a girl!' A sharp retort. It's Scott's voice. Good on him. 'She's a highly qualified pilot, probably one of the best, I should know, I trained her.'

'This is a job only for the top man. Maximum peril.'

'She is the best. Better than anyone in this station. I can vouch for her expertise.'

'A suffragette? You can't take her seriously.'

'You'd better take her seriously, she demands to be treated as an equal. And she's one of ours now.'

'You're getting above yourself, Fanshawe, this is right out of line...'

At this their voices fade and I hear no more. I breathe out a great bubble of stress, endeavouring to stay calm. This whole thing is on a cliff edge and I begin to think about what I've just promised to do. A little flutter of doubt begins to worm its way into my world. I think about capture and degradation and experience an involuntary tremor in my right hand, like I'm spinning out of control on my first solo flight.

Am I being foolish?

Shush! I stamp my feet, angry with these inner quavers. I'm the can-do person, the ultimate competitor, the one with the implacable will; this moment represents the greatest chance of my life.

Back in the shadows another door opens and the bundled-up little man appears from the gloom of the hut, sidles over and stands at my side. He looks even seedier standing up than he did lolling in the corner. His shapeless jacket which may once have been mulberry pink smells distinctly agricultural. Presumably the whiff is part of the disguise, a device to protect him from the close attention of the occupier.

'What are they arguing about?' he wants to know.

He has a pronounced accent – Belgian, I'm guessing – and doesn't look me in the eye. His focus is strangely just off to the left and disconcertingly somewhere over my shoulder. I resist the urge to turn around. Instead, I explain that he probably won't be going anywhere tonight because the pilot is incapacitated.

'But I must!' The man clasps his hands in anguish. 'I simply must. I have to get back tonight. Delaying is not possible.'

This is certainly an evening of meaty emotions, so I stoke the pot even further by telling him to get back in there and insist he flies tonight. When the door closes I anticipate all the arguments Scott will be using on Huckerbee: the month's delay, the spy's urgency and the complete lack of Morane Parasol flying competence among the station crew. Hopefully he will be building me up as the only possible solution, the ready-made stand-in with unrivalled expertise.

In a further act of anticipation, I hurry down to the No.2 hangar and find the kit room, selecting the same padded Parker overalls, gloves and scarf I used for the recce flight.

Time now to await events.

Owls hoot and strange rustlings fill the night until eventually Scott opens a door, beckons me in and says, 'I doubt you realise just what you're getting into.'

'Tell me.'

He adopts a somewhat enigmatic air, says archly: 'I know someone you think you know... only I know him somewhat better.'

I sigh. 'Don't tie me up in riddles.'

'Waterman,' he says.

'What about him?'

'He's not the simple soul you take him for. And since you're so keen to push your way in here you'd better realise what a viper's nest this is. The flight, that's just one of the dangers. There's a secret chapter to this war you're not allowed to know, it's dangerous and it's unforgiving, are you really sure you're ready for all this?'

I want in and nod vigorously.

'Look,' he says, 'I haven't told you any of this...' and then he delivers a double-quick briefing. We, that is, us Brits, need to know what the enemy is up to, when he'll attack and where he's strong and where he's weak. The brass hats back at the War Office in London are demanding a constant flow of updated information and for this we rely on networks of spies in occupied France and Belgium. Hundreds of civilians are involved: men, women and children. They watch trains, report troop movements, count the guns. All the networks have names. Ours? Reseau Cicero, a vast undertaking which has to be organised and the information retrieved – hence our strange little spy and his smelly wicker basket full of homing pigeons.

'However,' Scott says, 'we have a problem. My immediate boss is beside himself with anxiety. Has grave reservations about our man's mental state. I think Huck's right on the brink of cancelling this op but I don't think he dare go against his chief's wishes.'

I nod. Relief. Cancelling would ruin everything. 'So?'

'Press ahead, despite all hesitation, operational necessity and all that. So here's what you have to do...' He unfolds a large chart of the area and we get busy with the business of navigation. Scott has a stopwatch and a slide rule and shows me how the course has already been charted in daylight and timed ready for tonight. There are red circles at the turn points – recognisable features I have to look out for, such as the sharp twist in the trenches. Straight black lines run between the turns and scribbled figures indicate my flying time. My task is to fly the plane on the relevant heading for the precise time indicated, using the stopwatch. It's all been calculated based on air speed and the latest forecast for wind.

At this I suck in a deep breath and refuse to be daunted by the complexity of the plan – even when I learn the magnetic variation from true north in this part of the world is twelve degrees west. This means I'll have to allow for that when flying on the compass. And I'll also have to watch out for changes in wind direction.

'There's more,' he says. 'Taking this on means you're needed straight away. You have to babysit this chap. Sit it out until the appointed hour. Keep him company. Cheer him up, smokes and smiles. He's a miserable blighter and you'll have to forget any stuff he tells you; it's secret, just humour him, okay?'

'Sounds crazy to me.'

A waspish smile. 'It's a crazy game.' Then Scott is serious once more: 'Just you and only you. He has to be kept under wraps until 0200 hours. Nobody talks to him until take-off.'

I shrug. 'He may be a bit strange, but surely we must give credit where credit's due. A hero to be doing all this.'

Scott shakes his head. 'Frankly, I don't think he was ever a hero. He's always been flaky. A chancer, a liar, a cheat, your local spiv who'd sell you out for a quick quid, a small-time racketeer, how can you put your trust in such a man?'

'Then why?'

'Top brass decision. Obviously, in their wisdom, they've decided a devious personality is the perfect fit for the role he has to play.'

He hands me the chart and the stopwatch and shakes his head, as if puzzled by something. 'Talking of real heroes, Charlotte, you're truly amazing, you really are. I know you can do this. You've certainly got what it takes...'

I think he's about to wish me luck when he suddenly doubles up and retches, and for a moment I'm alarmed because I think he's genuine. Then I notice the figure behind.

Huckerbee remains when Scott has limped off to bed. He gives me the beady eye. Scott has done a good job on him but he still looks as if he might argue or call the whole thing off. I match his gaze.

'You realise this is all against my better judgement,' he says. 'Normally I wouldn't countenance this arrangement but... I've been forced into an impossible choice. You or disaster!'

This, I realise, is a man under extreme pressure. Time for me to exude supreme confidence.

He points an accusing finger: 'Are you really as good as he says you are?'

'None better. I'll do your job, don't you worry.'

'You should be signing the Official Secrets Act...'

'Forget it.' I break into this before he can begin some bureaucratic monologue. 'I'm first and foremost a pilot, not a correspondent. I'm not going to destroy my future by blabbing.'

He doesn't look happy, then says: 'There's something I have to tell you.' His expression is grim. 'If you abort across the lines there's nothing I can do for you, do you understand? There's absolutely no chance of a rescue. That's completely out of the question.'

I nod. I won't abort.

'The occupied area of France and Belgium is stuffed full of the German Army. Thousands of them. No quarter given. Any downed airman out of uniform is shot as a spy. No escape. There are roadblocks and patrols everywhere. You'd be a dead man walking... sorry, woman.'

My grin at this really puts him out of joint. He gives me another glare, the mandarin look that says I don't belong in his tidy, regulated world, and stomps off. Finally I'm left alone to babysit the spy. The little fellow and myself are sitting on uncomfortable wooden chairs in the gloomy room straining for conversation. And he has the same question. 'I hope you're a good pilot,' he says. 'I need a good pilot. I deserve a good pilot.'

'And you've got one,' I reassure him.

He's an odd fellow, with that evasive stare and sudden

voluble diatribes. 'I'm an important man, doing all this for England, so she should treat me with respect.'

In response to my puzzled glance he says: 'I've been to see your king, a guest at the Palace, and he's given me a medal.'

'That should make you proud.'

'So why are we hiding away in this horrid little hole, a room with no facilities, no drinks, no eats, no champagne. Now I'm on French soil I'm entitled to decent food and drink, not those ghastly English sandwiches.'

I look around the dingy room, finding it difficult to imagine either of us tucking into royal cuisine and sipping flutes of champagne, so turn away, confronting the task ahead. Am I ready? My hands are slippery with sweat and I'm conscious of a quickened heartbeat. Will I remember all the Parasol's little tricks? Don't forget, straight up, no turning and don't let it twist to the left. I breathe deeply and rhythmically to stay calm while acknowledging that this is my second, and probably last, chance to demonstrate my skills. I won't get a third. I have to do this, I tell myself – but it has to be a perfect operation, nothing less will suffice. Once again I silently repeat the mantra from my youth: you have to be first in this race, anything else is last.

CHAPTER TWENTY-THREE

I don't wait for the appointed hour. With twenty minutes still to go I nod to the agitated and still grumbling figure in the corner and walk out into the moonlit night. A lot more confident now, I run through my preflight checks: all control cables firmly fixed, no rips in the fabric, wing joints secure, wires taut. Carefully, watching where I put my feet because of the shadows and the fragile fabric, I climb into the seat. My introduction to this particular aeroplane three hours ago had been a shade nervous. Almost panic. It didn't seem comfortably familiar, as expected, but strange and unwelcoming. Perhaps I'd forgotten everything in the time-lapse since I'd last flown a Parasol but then it came to me: the dial positions were different, the seat hard and square.

Huckerbee dogs my footsteps, stands next to the cockpit and leans over the cowling to ask if I'm sure I'm still confident. He doesn't really believe in me but then I don't believe in him. A blinker and a nervous wreck. He's stuck between two impossible choices, unable to refer back, forced to make his own decision and giving the go-ahead with that annoying pronouncement 'against my better judgement'.

Now, twisting fingers around a strand of prematurely grey hair, he tells me this is my last chance to call it off, am I sure? Of course I am! My burning need for this operation overwhelms the risk. I've already worked out the odds. I envisage the fruits of success as a round of VIP visits to press home the cause of women flyers with those who have the power to enforce such a change. I can see an RFC bigwig lining up the eminent and the famous for me to meet. Perhaps even the Prime Minister.

Dear Scottie worries about the risk – but night interception by the enemy is unheard of. There won't be any Eindeckers about and Archie will be asleep or taken by surprise. Huckerbee turns his attention to the spy. More talk, more exhortation, then guiding the man into the observer seat and fussing with the basket of pigeons that we have to deliver.

Contact. The engine fires up and I listen intently. Sweet and true and no sign of trouble. Thumbs up and waving Huckerbee away, the revs run up and we start to move. The airflow announces that this is going to be cold – very cold – with only a tiny breath of engine heat for warmth. The Parasol waddles rather than bounds across the grass and I can feel rainwater suction trying to keep us grounded, but at last we lift off with no sign of corkscrewing to the left and climb evenly to 3,000 feet, the ghostly shape of Earth fading below, the sound and smell of fluttering pigeons a new and not entirely welcome distraction. Our route is key. There's talk in the Mess of new night navigation equipment that's supposedly on the way, but we don't have any. Just my ability to pick out the correct flightpath across the trench lines and fly the compass heading accurately against the stopwatch, making adjustments for changes in wind direction and speed. This is the only way I'm going to find the chosen landing site. It's been spied out in daylight with appropriate landmarks and tonight the Belgian spy network is putting out the agreed recognition signal.

Did you choose the site? It was a question I put to the spy while waiting in that gloomy little room. 'Next to my cousin's place,' he says and I begin to think about him and his strange conversation during the long wait. Doubts multiply. Huckerbee has been keen to talk up his achievements as the pivotal figure in an intelligence network, but there's something distinctly odd about the spy's see-sawing moods. His swagger over Westminster and Buckingham Palace seem like information he should keep to himself. Clearly, a troubled personality. Is this the right person to pit his wits and risk his safety against an all-powerful enemy?

I'm scanning the silvery landscape. More landmarks to fix my turns – a road, a church, a railway junction, all in ghostly outline. The biggest danger is getting lost and running out of fuel. We have just ninety minutes max. I'm tense but jubilant. My defiance has broken the pilot ban, albeit by devious means. It's my way of proving they're all so wrong about women flyers. And now the orders are simple: get this man and his pigeons down, then take off immediately and head back across the trenches to safety. My big gesture, my vindication.

The aircraft drone must have woken Fritz at the last compass point because searchlights spring up from the railway junction and sweep agitatedly around the sky. We're well clear of it but the junction was my last point of reference. I'm meant to be allowing for drift due to changes in the force of the wind, now that we're side-on to it, but I must have drifted too far because we've lost our track.

The landing signal is supposed to be a line of white sheets on a washing line but so far there's no sign. My future now depends on this housewife's nocturnal laundry. I'm counting on her pristine whites to show up clearly in the gloom. I zoom down to a low level to get a better view. Where are those darned bedsheets? My grip tightens on the stick. A clutch of near-panic, the nails digging into flesh, finger muscles fit to bust, a grip of excitement and fear. This is the key moment. It must not go wrong. My heart rate is racing, the pulse count off some imaginary doctor's dial. There's a taste of bile in my mouth and despite the blast of cold air across my face the heat inside this flying suit seems set to boil. They say your senses accelerate at moments of tension and I can smell those darned pigeons, the engine oil, the frantic whirring of steel in front of me, my own tortured breathing and even the spy's bodily signature.

He's now heaved himself half out of the front cockpit and is leaning over the side of the fuselage in the same desperate search.

'Where?' I reach over and tap his helmet.

He's peering down intently, then pointing.

I recognise nothing. No house, let alone laundry. I cut the motor at 2,000 feet and spiral down in the direction of the spy's arm signals, knowing this has to be a low-level approach, then turn downwind and still without engine glide closer, the altimeter down to fifty feet, bugged by a worrying tailwind. Still no sign of white sheets.

The spy is pointing to a field. Okay, it's his location, he should know his own backyard, so I turn back into the wind and come in hoping desperately we don't hit a ploughed field with the furrows pointing in the wrong direction.

At zero feet I get it. No furrows, just a strange-looking field. It gleams back at me like glass.

Ice!

I swallow. And that damned tailwind is going to kill us!

I spot what looks like an even track and the wheels and skid touch down together. But instead of the neat job I'm used to in training we bounce back into the air. A scream of horror! Scott's words flash back to me in an instant from that first Parasol flight: a weak undercarriage that buckles and tends to flip.

All in one long instant I pray, I swallow, I tense, gripping the stick like a lifeline and when the Parasol makes it down again we skid and slide in crazy circles like we're on a skiing trip gone wrong. Nothing prepared me for this! Nobody warned me about this... a vague and guilty recollection contradicts me, Scott talking about weathervaning, rotating into wind, sideways force exerted on the wheels, no grip with a skid...

She's out of control, the Parasol gone crazy. Any second I expect her to somersault or cartwheel. And then, crack! We smash down with a violent jolt. The undercart is smashed, the starboard wingtip bites the ice, the tail flips up, the nose dives down.

I'm open-mouthed, frozen and helpless, but amazingly we're still moving and still upright.

Still sliding, slowing, slowing and finally slithering to an ignominious stop.

CHAPTER TWENTY-FOUR

Dazed and amazed to be alive, we extricate ourselves from the wreckage physically unscathed, but I'm stricken by a potpourri of emotion: shock, surprise, confusion, anger. I turn and look at my lovely machine – this ugly pug that I've grown to love, its beautiful yellow paintwork ripped, splashed and battered. I go to the nose and run my fingers over the magnificent prop to examine the damage. There are several deep scratches with ragged tears despoiling the fine, smooth varnished edges. Its elegant shape is hidden by mud splashed up the full length, such an affront to my mental picture of it sitting tall and proud back at Vert reflecting the rays of the sun.

Then I stoop to examine the undercarriage, desperately hoping it can be made to work again, but view the broken wreckage with a sinking heart. I know I'm pretending to myself that the Parasol can fly again but I can't help it.

'Here!' I beckon to the spy.

I'm going to will this thing back into the air.

'Grab this,' I tell him, 'help me get the tail down.'

He shakes his head and looks at me as if I've just escaped

from the men in white coats, rather than a plane wreck. That's when my anger erupts.

'Where are the white sheets?' I demand.

No answer.

'Wrong place?'

No answer.

'This isn't where we're meant to be! You've messed up, haven't you?'

He doesn't seem ready to take the blame. 'It's no use,' he says, pointing at the wreck, 'we'll have to leave it.'

'Leave it?' A breathless and querulous – if stupid – question.

'Yes, leave it. This won't fly again, will it?'

I look down at this hopelessly battered machine, its struts smashed and splintered. My eyelids flicker, my breath exhales, my chest slumps. Finally, I have to face it. No, of course it won't fly. It's stuck – and so are we.

Suddenly, full realisation of my new situation hits me like a vicious blow to the head. I shrug in desperate hopelessness, feeling utterly bereft. Stare back at him wordlessly. Grounded. Stranded. Vulnerable. All that vaunting ambition now stuck in this icy corner of nowhere. Now no glory, no success, the worst possible outcome; total mission failure. And I'm stranded behind enemy lines.

'You numbskull,' I cry.

He's shushing me, making silence gestures with a finger over the mouth and looking in the direction of a distant line of trees. 'Can't you hear it?' he whispers, and on the next waspish breath of a tiny wind I think I can.

Voices.

'Les Boches,' he says, grimacing.

I'm sick. Grinding my teeth, clenching fists. The Parasol had got us here but now, because of a stupid mistake, we've landed in the wrong place. In my fury I absolve myself for any blame in this fiasco.

I look in the direction of the trees and unaccountably, for the first time, feel overcome by a sense of helpless vulnerability.

'We need to make a run for it,' he says, 'before they realise what's happening. We're in luck so far because you cut the motor.'

'No!'

'What?'

'Can't just leave it. They'll be all over it.'

He shrugs.

'I need to set fire to it.'

'Don't be a fool. Fire would be a beacon to them. They'll get us, then...' He makes a gizzard-cutting gesture.

For a moment I'm stalled, uncertain what to do, then memory returns in a burst of frantic energy. Instructions on abandoning an aircraft. I lean back inside to collect the charts and then rip open the emergency wire clippers. Snip, snip, snip. Cutting the bracers above the wings would cause them to flop noisily, alerting even a quiescent enemy, but the flying wires beneath the wings present the opportunity for silent and final destruction. He's grumbling, hustling, hurrying me. 'Let's go,' he says.

I shrug. 'Where? How?'

He stops to explain, as if to someone in shock – which perhaps I am. 'It's only a matter of time before they spot us. Dawn isn't far off. We've only got two or three hours before they raise the alarm. Much the best to move as far away from here as possible.'

My confusion induces him to say more. 'I know the area. I

know where I am. We can make it across country, hide up in the forest during the day, then meet up with my cousin tomorrow.'

I stare at him, paralysed. I'm closing down. Breath is stuck somewhere in my chest. Fear and helplessness in the face of danger, laid bare and open before all the perils that lurk close by. Fear, reaching right down to the pit of the stomach.

'I promise I'll get you out,' he says. 'Out of the country – and across the border.'

I look at him – a man I suspected of incompetence or worse. And now he's my best hope. My only hope.

CHAPTER TWENTY-FIVE

I hardly know what I'm doing, stumbling along a path slippery with mud while following the detestable human shape ahead. There's some sort of hedgerow on my left, just a shadow of blackness even in the silvery moonlight, and to the right an open field with the occasional tree shape passing my jaded gaze like telegraph poles on a slow-motion train journey. These sensations barely register. My mind is in turmoil and my fists clench. This numbskull, this stupid man who has set us down in the wrong place, has wrecked everything. My operation, my plans, my ambition, my whole life! Maybe, if I were closer, I'd pummel his wretched neck.

Now he's turning back to look at me, beckoning me to hurry, but I dare not utter a word for fear of what I might say. And a horrible realisation is gradually creeping over me, like some slippery reptile come to strangle my last breath. This man whom I despise for his incompetence is now my lifeline. I have no plan, nor any idea where I am. And some sizeable portion of the German Army is all around and will soon be on our trail.

I determine not to go to pieces but have never before given much thought to how I might handle failure. Now I realise with a cold shudder that all that stuff I had in my head about a glorious breakthrough to female emancipation in the air is just a tangle of broken dreams. This is reality. The imminent prospect of arrest and a harsh and possibly cruel incarceration as an enemy spy, followed by a bullet in the back of the head. If I'm lucky.

I recall talk in the Mess of the near impossibility of getting out of a country locked in by a network of roadblocks and of occupation forces in serious numbers operating a repressive regime of control.

What chance of survival now?

I swallow my pride and try to make conversation with the spy as we go, but his answers to every question – how far to the village, who are your relatives, are the Germans nearby – elicit only vague replies. Then more directly: why do you do this job?

He grins with a leer I find particularly annoying. 'They're all weasels, les Boches, I enjoy cheating them.'

Not an encouraging, patriotic or wise motivation, it strikes me; more a squalid rip-off of his own. Are we paying him for this? Perhaps he reads me, for he tries to justify: 'We count them, report on their activities and equipment.'

'What equipment?'

He shrugs. 'Not much. They're just an occupation force, just a bunch of weasels.'

His favourite word.

'How come you can be absent for so long without being missed?'

'Visiting an aunt.'

'Don't you have to have a permit to travel?' I ask, displaying my newly acquired knowledge of occupation law, courtesy of Scott.

He winks. 'Of course,' and taps his nose.

Is this a commendable act of operational security, I wonder, or simply part of his natural deviousness?

'Tell me about your family.'

'My old lady, she lives in the village...' and somehow that's all I get. The conversation dries and I decide to concentrate on the physical task of trekking through the night. We've been at it for an hour or more and the exertion of continuous walking in a padded flying suit is taking its toll. I'm beginning to boil. While a sharp wind whips around the head, ears and hands, the build-up of body heat inside the suit is causing serious overheating and I wish I could fling off some clothing.

What's worse is that I don't have much confidence in the spy's sense of direction. He's taken a sharp left and is urging me along a gravel track with rutted evidence of the passage of farm carts, but does he really know where he's going? There's no point in being fatalistic, of bowing down to fear or mentally hiding in a corner. That old childhood mantra about being first or last comes back to mind. Regard this as a race, I tell myself, with first prize a successful escape. For now I must suffer my fool gladly but maybe, in time, I can dump him.

A glimmer of hope brightens the night, already touched by the first hint of dawn when I remember my pen friend in Belgium. Dear Marguerite! So many letters and such happy childhood times with her brother Jules and their generous and loving parents. Images too of the big house at Freys. Are we within reach of that? I have only the vaguest idea, but if I could get there...

The spy, whose name I don't know and don't wish to know, is looking up and there's no doubt about it. Daylight is about to leave us naked to the eye. He points to a forest. 'Over there,' he says. 'We'll lie up during the day until we can continue tonight.'

We search everywhere for a hut, barn or some form of shelter but find none. No choice but to lie down under some trees. I'm still in my flight gear, so have an advantage of warmth over the spy. He has only a raincoat and pulls this high over his head. Dawn is chilly and daytime sleeping doesn't come naturally and after tossing uncomfortably about amid the mossy earth and twisted tree roots, I drop off into a deep sleep of exhaustion and devilish dreams. This is interrupted when the sun is at its highest, sending spotlights of rays through tiny gaps in the tree cover, at which point I stamp my feet and stomp around in an effort to walk off cramp and stiffness, then lie down to try again. An hour before dusk I can stand it no longer and move back to the edge of the forest to observe activity down in the valley, the spy claiming not to have slept at all. And here's the strange thing: I don't commiserate or feel a jot of sympathy. Does this mean I'm hardening up – or just that my distaste for this man has overcome all natural empathy?

Inevitably my mind goes back to our disastrous landing and I relive those horrific moments bouncing and skidding about on the ice. I'm still sick at having to abandon the Parasol. However, I refuse to blame myself. No way, I silently insist, could I have anticipated such a peril. The first pangs of hunger are making themselves felt but I try to keep my mind occupied by visualising a map of Belgium and realise that Brussels, never mind the house at Freys, is a very long way indeed by foot.

Look for a cheery thought, I tell myself Napoleon's and Wellington's soldiers did it, marching miles across this very part of France and Belgium before facing each other at Waterloo. True, but they had baggage trains, cook wagons, daylight hours, appropriate clothing and leaders who knew what they were doing.

I glance across at the spy sprawled beside me. Perhaps I should give him more credit because he's certainly right about hiding up during the day. Confirmation of this can soon be seen in the distance at the bottom of our slope. An enemy patrol arrives at a village and starts working the houses. The search proceeds methodically and it's obvious the Germans have discovered my aircraft and are now intent on running us to ground. They assume we must be in hiding with the local population and I feel guilty the villagers are going through the wringer because of us. We scramble about in the wood looking for something to eat but all the berry bushes have been picked clean and all I find are a couple of turnips tasting like old leather. I try quizzing the spy about his plan of action but suffer another demonstration of his strange personality. At first he's full of egotistical rants about how he fools the Germans every day. I learn that he runs the local garage and looks after the French and Belgian cars and vehicles they've commandeered. 'I know how to handle les Boches, they're not so clever...' And so on. Then, all of sudden, he breaks off and falls into a sullen silence. I get the impression there's something seriously adrift at the centre of this man's ego. Finally, he announces his intention: we're making for relatives in his home village of Bouillon.

Light fades and we decide it's safe to resume the journey. Back in the briefing room Scott and Huckerbee had assured me I'm in good hands. This man not only runs a highly successful network of Allied spies, they say, his local knowledge is of a very high order. However, I'm doubtful. He's stumbling about and blundering into objects – trees, posts, fences – and I realise that for all the high-flown talk he isn't used to finding his way about in the dark. True, last night's moonlight is now history and what ambient light remains is obscured by cloud. I soon realise I'm much better at this. Cue brief recall of teenage dares and night-time treks. The secret is to keep well away from artificial light until the eyes become properly attuned to the dark and then it's amazing what you can pick out. The human eye is, of course, nowhere near as good as the wildlife hereabouts. We trail alongside a field hedge to a ditch, which looms black and menacing, and are about to jump it when he decides on a complete change of direction. When eventually we stumble on a wide farm track I suggest 'this way' and he concurs. Outside a farmhouse we find a nameplate which he wants to read to identify our position.

'We need a torch,' he says.

'You don't need a torch,' I say testily – how does this man stay out of the clutches of the invader? – and kneel up close to read off the letters.

'L-e-g-r-a-n-d B-el...'

'Oh,' he says, 'that's where we are.'

This marks an element of progress and we set off more confidently along the little road beside the farm. There's no traffic, of course, because this is curfew and if you're found outside during the prescribed hours they'll simply shoot you. Which is why, when we hear the noise of an approaching vehicle, we hurl ourselves into some trees and watch from our impromptu hide as a Reichswehr military transport travels past, its occupants in joyous mood, singing at the tops of their voices.

When it's all clear I expect some reaction from him. A curse or two, or some biting quip, such as 'We'll give them something to sing about', but he makes no such comment. His only remark is that from the knocking sound he picked up there was something amiss with the truck's engine, reminding me of his daytime occupation at the garage. I marvel at this man's coolness. Perhaps such aplomb in action is his secret, but then I get to wonder, despite the fictional aunt story, how he convinces his dangerous customers that it's acceptable to spend so much time away from the job.

'We close when we run out,' he says with a shrug. 'Of parts or petrol.'

The good news is, we're getting close to the village. The bad news is his cousin's place is full of Germans. I hang back in the shadows while the spy discovers from whispered conversations at cottage doorways that his relative's house has become a billet.

I wait outside another darkened door and hear more subdued but fractious voices issuing from inside. Eventually I'm beckoned forward and pushed through the door of a run-down sort of place festooned with boxes and packages stacked against a wall.

'You'll have to stay with the postmistress tonight,' the spy tells me. 'There's nowhere to put you at the garage.'

A plump and rather elderly woman eyes me without enthusiasm. She has black hair tied back in a bun, wears a black dress, carpet slippers and smokes a broken sort of cigarette. From her attitude I gather she's been pressurised into this. She isn't happy and I can't blame her. Giving me shelter could put us both six feet under.

'Sorry!' I whisper but my effort at apology has no effect.

Her lips twist into a bitter expression. 'I don't want you here, I'm being put upon, he should not have done this to me.' I resist the temptation to turn on my heel at being spoken to in such a manner, but then the reality of my situation kicks in and I say: 'The idea is that no one will think of looking for me here.'

'You don't know them,' she says, and there isn't any doubt about who she is referring to. 'It's bad enough having them stomping about my place without being landed with you as well. Never mind! You'll be gone in the morning.'

I get a straw mattress in the basement and she looks contemptuously at me, clearly unconscious of her own image, and says: 'You look ridiculous, get that lot off.'

I shed the flying suit.

She points an accusing finger at my overalls. 'And that! Just what are you supposed to be doing here?'

'Do you really expect an answer?'

'No I don't!'

So, I wonder, when is a question not a question? And my idealised notion of a quaint village postie is receding fast.

'Now the boots,' she says.

The basement reeks of tallow candle wax and mice. No electricity here, nor running water, but in the corner of this tiny brick-lined pit are the artefacts of rural domesticity: a wringer, a sink, buckets, bowls and a washing line, plus a shelf full of bottles and tins containing I know not what. I'm trudge weary so the mattress is almost a blessed relief.

I'm woken to a new smell – burning. Then I see that the suit and overalls have disappeared.

When I climb the stairs the woman points to a raggedy sort of coat dress hanging over a chair. This, I'm informed without much grace, is to be the new me. If I'm to look like a village woman I can't be seen in my RFC flying gear. But what really does me in is that my boots have also gone on the fire. They're replaced by a sloppy pair of ill-fitting shoes hardly fit for the dustbin.

There's no offer of anything to eat or drink and she can't wait to get rid of me. 'He shouldn't have dumped you here,' the woman says again with some asperity. 'This is the post. They're in and out of here all the time.'

And finally I get my instructions. 'At eight o'clock go to the bakery. There'll be a message waiting for you there, but enter only if a blue scarf is showing in the side window.'

'So – who am I?'

'You are Maxime.'

The replacement shoes are a horror and the dress ill-fitting, musty and disgusting. I've been warned the enemy frequently drive through the village, sometimes stopping to confiscate anything that takes their fancy, and a sentry is posted at the far end of the street to make sure farmers comply with the supply of specified produce. Every morning the Mayor has to attend the town hall to be given his orders by The Vulture – the villagers' name for the Kommandant – and the demands multiply: more pigs, more sheep, more chickens, wheat and fruit.

With two hours to go before shop opening time, I retreat to the fourteenth-century church whose graveyard has long since been levelled and planted with yew trees. It's the sort of place that was once trimmed, preened and clipped to perfection, but now it's a neglected tangle of leaves and branches. Perhaps the priest and the gardener have been sent away for war work. All to the good for me. The green chaos makes great cover while I wait and my familiarity with it will later work greatly to my advantage.

At fifteen minutes past the hour I walk past the bakery, noting the blue scarf in the window and the absence of a queue at the counter, before doubling back and pushing open the door. The bell clangs and I expect to find a plentiful display of bread, but there's only two loaves on the counter and a mean-spirited display of some thin-looking cakes. A big man gives me a stern stare. I guess he may only be in his forties but he has lived-in features crafted with deep folds and generous lines, no doubt the legacy of getting up at three o'clock every morning to light the fires and feed white-hot ovens. Thankfully, we're alone.

'I'm Maxime.'

He walks to the end of a counter and holds ajar a curtain of floor-length beads. 'Come through.'

It's a tiny vestibule of a room sandwiched between the shop and the bakehouse. I can still feel the heat from the ovens, even though baking has ceased, and the atmosphere is heavy with the odours of yeast and dough. I glance across at a big wooden grip for handling hot trays and the stack of thin paper for wrapping the loaves. We're seated at two tall chairs.

'Who are you, Maxime?' he says and I know I have to prove myself and there's no point in holding back. 'A British flyer stranded this side of the Front two nights ago. Brought in last night by your Monsieur...' How do I describe the spy? 'The man with the cauliflower ears. I don't know his name. All I know is he runs the garage.'

'Ah! Our Monsieur Bernard,' he says. 'Where do you fly from?'

'Vert Galant.'

'Never heard of it.'

'It's a small place, a farm between Amiens and Albert. I had the job of flying in with this Bernard and got stuck.'

The baker, whose name I discover is Dufour, breaks off to have a mumbled conversation with someone I can neither see nor hear but turns out to be instructions to his wife to take over the counter.

I'm wishing I'd come earlier, before the shop opened when he was baking the bread. There's the comforting mix of amiable cottage industry at work and I salivate at the thought of his loaves singing as he pulls them from the ovens. He notices my reaction and pushes across the table a small croissant. The sinewy crusty taste is a boon to my senses.

'Sorry,' he says, 'not much to spare, dough in short supply.'

My eyes light on a big dough-mixing machine, all dull-grey steel with its voracious mouth concealed beneath an upturned bowl. 'Very modern,' I say, pointing.

He shrugs. 'Kaput!'

I notice the unconscious incursion of the German vernacular. In fact, the baker turns out to be a lot more conversational than his peers and he's curious as to why I, a woman, should be flying an aircraft. I indulge him with a long explanation and that's good because we are getting along just fine. He's probably putting all this down to the mad English. Meanwhile I'm learning what it's like to be a villager living under the Germans and coming face to face with the visceral fear of the people, the reality of day-to-day oppression. This isn't something abstract you vaguely glimpse in the flight hut back at Blighty or Vert, this is in-your-face personal.

'They've had a down on us for some time,' he says, 'because of those soldiers.'

And I'm pretty sick to learn the story of the three unfortunate Tommies left behind in the great retreat of 1914. They tried to blend in as French peasants, were discovered and put up against the churchyard wall. The bullet holes are still there.

'It was The Vulture,' Dufour says with feeling – the Kommandant they all hate. The very same, Etappen Kommandant von Kruger, whose details I had been shown on the publicity material at Vert. There are daily patrols through the village on the lookout for any more left-behinds. Occasionally the Germans swoop and search a house, intimidate the villagers and plunder whatever they can. Anyone back home in Blighty who doubts the justification for this war should come and live here and suffer the oppression.

We discuss this for a while, then he surprises me by asking what I think of Monsieur Bernard. I make a non-committal face, not knowing how to play this, fearing to express openly my doubts about the spy. Dufour has me even more intrigued by his next comment: 'I'd be very careful of him... if I were you.'

'You would?' This sparks a sudden sinking feeling.

His voice is quiet, his tone confiding. 'I've known him for years, since he was a boy. Truth be told, his family were always a little odd. Not people you'd too easily put your trust in, if you know what I mean.'

'Meaning what, exactly?'

'We've told him, again and again. He should be careful how he runs this information network. The news we're sending back to your side...' A Gallic shrug. 'It's dangerous work.'

'I know that,' I say, thinking of all the soldiers looking for us two nights ago.

'He needs to be discreet, very careful how he goes about it.'

'And he isn't?' I guess, having experienced some of the bragging homilies in the last forty-eight hours.

'He isn't. He takes risks. Talks too much, to too many people. He's overconfident.'

'And the garage?' I ask. 'That sounds risky.'

The baker nods. 'He mends their cars and makes fun of them. Says not to worry, he can fool them, they'll never guess what we're up to. Says they think he's one of them.'

'Walking a tightrope?' I suggest.

'He thinks he's cleverer than they are. He uses the cars he's supposed to be repairing. He steals the good bits and uses old parts that wear out quickly so they have to come back for more. Tells them he's a specialist, the only one who knows how to deal with Renaults and Peugeots.' Dufour rolls his eyes. 'He's too cocky by half – and les Boches, they're not that stupid. He's heading for a fall and if we're not very careful he'll take us all with him.'

I'm in a shed at the back of the bakery, waiting for nightfall. Hiding up in daytime looks like being my routine from now on.

The place stinks. Old cartons, piles of paper, general detritus from the bakehouse that should have been chucked, but I'm not complaining. From cracks in the planks I have a view of the street and can see why the bakery is a message centre for the network. An ancient leathery figure perched on a donkey cart grumbles into view. While he shambles into the bakery I study the jumbled contents of his cart and decide he must be the local ragman. Several women in headscarves and long black dresses also enter the bakery and two farm carts pass by on their way to the blacksmith.

With time on my hands I get to wonder why these amazing people give shelter. My safety and that of any resister is in their hands, but they take the greatest risk in doing so. The Germans have put up fearful notices in screaming black lettering threatening death to anyone who shelters Allied soldiers. What prompts a family man like the baker, who has two small children, a wife and a business, to ignore caution and become an active resister? Is it natural human empathy to help those in trouble, revenge for an imprisoned relative, or anger at a loved one sent away on forced labour?

In the case of Monsieur Dufour it's anger at what is happening in his country; trampled, exploited and repressed by an invader given easily to casual acts of injustice and cruelty.

I while away the time snacking on scraps from the bakery and when darkness approaches I make my way towards the churchyard. Monsieur Dufour has a message for me – an instruction from the spy. He's making arrangements to get me out of the country, says Dufour. 'Meet him in the church at midnight. He'll be in the crypt. He'll have all the necessary information to help you.'

I look closely into Dufour's eyes and he gives the faintest of shrugs.

On the way I'm acutely tuned to the first hint of danger.

During the day the Germans have been through the village on three occasions, mercifully without stopping, and there's no movement at night. However, I'm vulnerable out in the open after curfew.

I recall the spy's promise: 'Don't worry. Trust me, I'll look after you, I'll get you out of the country.' But then I get to question this instruction to meet in the church. Why there? Why not the bakery or the postmistress's cottage? Does the church offer sanctuary, or at least some kind of bogus legitimacy as a worshipper... but at midnight?

I circle the churchyard with its sprawling yew trees to check out the location and find nothing untoward. Gingerly, I try the church door, which is open, and peer inside. Completely empty. It's still several hours before the rendezvous, so I investigate the crypt. This is well down on the right side, past all the pews, with just one access point. Am I getting paranoid? Because it seems to me there would be no escape from the crypt if anything should go wrong. I'm beginning to get twitchy and leave the church with the distinct feeling that this place is anything but a sanctuary. It's so far out of Bouillon no one will know what events take place here. Is that why it's chosen? I realise I'm falling victim to the fear of the hunted and the mindset of the evader.

Midnight is a long way off and I resign myself to the need for patience. A new virtue. My position is well back from the entrance, concealed in the cover of one of the spreading yews. The main road is behind me and anyone approaching the church will have to pass a few yards from my position. I've reconnoitred and there's an escape route to the left leading to a footpath.

I study my watch, then think back over the past few catastrophic days. I still blame Bernard for our predicament but only now am I ready to own up to my own role in the fiasco. As a somewhat negligent navigator I realise I failed to allow for wind drift, contributing to our landing in the wrong place. And the ice? I shrug. It had been a very cold night. Perhaps I should have foreseen the problem and perhaps turned back?

Nothing happens as the hour approaches and I speculate that Bernard is simply going to abandon me, fail to show and leave me to my own devices.

Then, at twenty-five minutes to midnight, footsteps approach. I take a deep breath, hold it and will myself to remain absolutely still. I've no training for this; am I an amateur up against a professional? I can't see a face at this distance but I'll wager it's his tread. The figure vanishes inside the church.

Should I follow? I decide to hang back. When he discovers the crypt empty he's bound to return and I can tag him on the path.

Just then there's a distant rumble which grows louder. A lorry approaching, by the sound of it. It stops on the main road. Voices, feet hitting the ground, then the crunch of many steps on the gravel path. Some feet, I note, appear to be circling the graveyard. Not all enter the church.

I freeze and listen. The truck moves off, then silence. The midnight worshippers in big boots appear to be a very quiet lot. No singing, no talking. Everyone appears to be waiting. It's an eerie feeling. I'm waiting for them and I have the distinct feeling they're all waiting for me.

At ten past midnight their patience runs out. I hear a door open and subdued voices. One could be Bernard's, it's impossible to be sure. The church door closes once more. Another five minutes elapse before the door opens again. More voices, this time in tones of annoyance, followed by a collective trek back past my hide to the main road, this time with less attention to stealth. There's a sudden flare of a match. Someone is lighting a cigarette. Foolish mistake on their part. It illuminates the wearer's uniform and now there's no doubt about it, I'm looking at members of the Reichswehr. The enemy.

Then I hear the vehicle approaching once more, bodies climbing aboard, the drive-off and finally the quiet of the night restored.

It's quite clear. This was a trap. Laid for me by my erstwhile rescuer. A bitter pill!

Should I now wait for Bernard to come this way, tackle him and reveal my knowledge of these events? I'm beginning to key into the thinking behind pursuit and evasion. No, I will not reveal my true situation. Knowledge is power – my power and his state of ignorance. He doesn't yet know that I've discovered the truth of his duplicity.

My first instinct is to run, to get clean away from Bouillon or any place known to Bernard, the animal urge to flee in the presence of a predator.

Instead, I sit quietly in my hide considering the question: what's the next move of this turncoat spy? Having failed to betray me to his new friends in field grey, surely the rest of the network is in imminent danger. I can imagine the treacherous Bernard and the detestable Kommandant von Kruger in some urgent council of war right now.

CHAPTER TWENTY-SIX

Should I care about the villagers? Stop to warn them?

The competitor department of my brain urges haste. Get to the border, make it back home, raise the alarm. The Network Cicero is busted. London needs to know that. Why hang around?

But uncomfortable sentiments bubble unbidden into mind. Words spoken by Captain Gambier back at Vert: 'You can take that competitive reflex of yours a little too far.' I breathe in deeply. This is not, I acknowledge, the road to personal glory. Already I have felt the strength of fear in this village. These people are working, and soon to suffer, for our cause. This, for me, is a testing moment. Am I now to ignore the wreckage about to be visited upon the very people who've been helping me?

Carefully, I check the graveyard is once more silent, then make haste back toward the village, avoiding a car heading in the same direction, the driver too indistinct to identify. Back in Bouillon I stand in a deep shadow some distance from the bakery, observing the building and those around for signs of another trap. It's possible a von Kruger snatch squad may have already reacted, ensconced inside the bakery, the baker and his family under arrest, waiting for me to show myself.

All is quiet for what seems like an hour but is probably a few minutes. I cannot imagine the young members of the family remaining silent, even under duress, for this long, so I flick a stone up at the first-floor window.

Nothing.

I knock at the door and retreat behind a wall to see who answers.

No reaction.

I knock louder and a light comes on upstairs. Eventually, I hear footsteps coming down the stairs. They can't be this good at play-acting and my instinct on this point is borne out. Monsieur Dufour's pudgy face appears in a crack of the doorway, peering out.

I step forward. 'Let me in.'

He's shocked. 'What's happened? Why weren't you at the church?'

'What do you mean?' I demand, suddenly thinking the worst. 'What do you know about the church?'

'Bernard,' he says. 'He was just here, less than twenty minutes ago, asking for you. Wanting to know why you hadn't gone to the church.'

'I bet he did.'

'What happened?' he asks again.

'What do you think?' I glare at him, all the anger bubbling up. 'It was a trap, an ambush. He tried to dish me to the Germans.'

He pulls me in and shuts the door, switches off the light. 'You got away?'

'I did. I'm not that green, I didn't go inside, stayed on the outside and saw them arrive.'

'You're sure?'

'The bastard's turned, I tell you! He's a double agent, working for them, had a lorryload of soldiers waiting for me. You realise what this means?'

Even in the dark of the hallway I'm sure his pallid features grow pastier. I bang home my message: 'You're in danger. All of us are likely to be arrested. Everyone in the network. We have to run before they come for us. Lie low until we see how things are.'

He finds his voice, just a cracked whisper. 'But I'm the baker, I can't just leave the business untended.'

'If you're arrested you won't be baking much bread in jail, will you?'

He slumps against the wall.

I say: 'You have to think of the little ones and your wife. You must keep them safe. Is there anywhere you can take the family? Somewhere out of harm's way?'

He swallows, runs a tongue round cracked lips. 'Arnette's old Aunt Carrie, I suppose... she lives in a cottage out in the forest.'

'Does Bernard know that?'

He shakes his head.

'Then you'd better get them there quick, before dawn. That's the favourite time for grabbing people, isn't it? Dawn?'

He nods, stirs himself and comes to life, shaking off his sense of shock and inertia, thinking clearly for the first time. 'There are the others,' he says, 'the network. They should be told.'

We discuss those in danger. 'You don't have to tell me their names,' I say. 'I don't need to know.'

But with Bernard now the enemy he needs to confide. 'You know about the postie?'

'Of course.'

'Then there's Halbot. He gets messages to your people.'

'The man on the donkey cart?'

'That's him.' Louis Halbot is the Pigeon Man. He's a bargee on the canal. That's several miles the other side of the forest. He's like a ghost, no one knows exactly where he'll be at any one moment. And there's more: he keeps his carrier pigeons in different places close to the canal banks. He poaches, shoots rabbits, sells carcases to Laurent the butcher and hawks firewood around the village. 'That sort of life makes him a natural for us,' says Dufour.

'Can we get to him?'

'We could take the van. Warn him on the way.'

'Do it,' I say.

A voice from upstairs signals his wife is awake and we have a rapid parley, deciding that I'll go to warn the postmistress while Dufour gets his family dressed and ready to travel.

He halts halfway up the stairs, turns and says: 'Just remembered.'

'What?'

'Bernard, what he said. To tell you, if you showed up, to go to the garage first thing. At least by five.'

'Tonight?'

'No, this morning.'

I snort. 'Told you. Five am and if I don't show, they'll be round here by six.'

The postmistress is being difficult. 'I'm not going, leaving my cottage, not for anyone,' she says. For someone well aware of the dangers of her covert role she is remarkably reluctant to quit.

Time to be brutal. 'You're okay with being put up against a wall, are you?'

She gives me a look that suggests I should be the one

standing at the wall. 'I knew you were bad news as soon as you crossed my doorstep,' she says.

'Not my fault!' Do I have time for this? 'It's him,' I say, 'that damned garage man.'

'Stupid man!'

'Not just stupid, a damned traitor.'

'But why would he do that?'

'Who knows?'

Eventually I manage to convince her. She can't go far; she's too old and slow and has no transport, so she'll have to find a friend in the village.

Another objection: 'I can't go wandering about outside in the middle of the night.'

I sigh. 'Don't go back to bed. Get dressed, pack a bag and be ready to leave before dawn. At the latest five o'clock. Walk down to your friend and get out of sight nice and early.'

She's still havering about the injustice of it, so I try placating. 'If nothing happens, you can always come back.'

'And say what? It's unheard of for a postmistress to go missing. How do I explain my absence?'

'You were feeling unwell, or your friend had an emergency. You'll think of something. And it's a good thing if you're still in the village in case there's any prospect of resurrecting the network when this is all over.'

'I'll need some cash. Can't live on nothing.'

'I'll tell Monsieur Dufour.'

'And I'm not telling you where I'm going.'

'Don't. I don't want to know.'

Packing bags, two fractious young children and a wife into the bakery van is no easy task. I keep shushing them but they're making a dreadful commotion in the dead silence of the early hours and I'm getting frantic in case von Kruger decides he can't wait for five o'clock. I ask myself why I'm still standing here, looking at these bewildered children and their agonising slowness. What price these possessions – toys, clothing, a doll's pram – against the loss of freedom? Why have I not followed instinct and flown? And when I tell Dufour about the postmistress's request for extra funds, he splutters.

'Forget it,' he says, 'the old baggage has been putting money aside for years.'

'How do you know that?'

He rolls his eyes.

We take the back lane to avoid waking the sentry on the main road and in between shrieks and complaints from the rear of the vehicle we discuss our strategy. We have to locate the Pigeon Man, I say, not only to warn him but also to get off an urgent message to London.

'Why?' Dufour queries. 'Does it matter if they know about this?'

'Of course it does. Any messages they get after tonight are going to be bogus – from him and the Germans. London has to know it's bad information. It'll be lies.'

We cross the canal and head for the main basin where houseboats and narrow boats jostle for space, but there's a gap where Halbot used to tie up. It's a quiet place with no one about but with an increasing sense of urgency we spot the lazy haze of smoke from a chimney and knock on the door of the occupant of a large houseboat. It's a woman, a light sleeper still in her nightdress. She shakes her head, not having seen Halbot in days.

Dufour knows some of Halbot's other haunts – a café at a nearby lock and a hut where he keeps most of his pigeons. The coop is empty. We can't spend much more time on this; every minute out in the open is a risk and the discovery close by of a scatter of dead pigeons brings us to a sudden halt.

'He would never do this,' Dufour says. 'Kill his own birds? Never. Someone else has done this. Someone who wants no messages sent.'

The culprits are obvious. We're too late. They have reached Halbot before us.

The children are crying and Dufour's wife is getting anxious, so we're back on the road fast, headed for the forest. 'Bernard – he's been taking us out one by one,' I say. 'First Halbot, I was to be next, then you and the postie. Trying to maintain a pretence of his own innocence, that the arrests were nothing to do with him... but why?'

Dufour knows his man. 'So he can carry on with the business at the garage without anyone suspecting him. The pretence of normality.'

There's a silence as he concentrates on the road.

'Tell you what,' he murmurs after a while, 'if I'm still around when les Boches go home...'

The rest is left unsaid.

We spot headlights in the distance, dowse ours and turn off into the forest. A convoy of two lorries and a car approach at a fast pace. Have we been spotted? I listen intently to the engine noise, fearing a sudden cessation, but the high revs drone on and the vehicles swish past.

We press on and it's almost daylight when we make it to the forest cottage. The van pulls up on a patch of gravel outside and the children spill out. A window opens upstairs and a woman's face appears. Indistinct words are spoken. All I hear is Dufour's response: 'Trouble in the village!'

I leave him to enter. He has some difficult explanations to offer, some serious arrangements to make, and I wander around the grounds and eventually find the hut in the woods that will be Dufour's ultimate retreat.

Out on my own there's time for a cool assessment. And I now know I'm the only person left who can raise the alarm. There's an even greater urgency than before to get out of this country. With Halbot and his pigeons out of action I must get back to warn our people that the Cicero network is destroyed, that any further messages received by pigeon will be bogus, emanating from von Kruger and his turncoat acolyte. Issuing this warning is a goal beyond the personal, a mission to transcend notions of glory. I vow to cross any barrier to achieve it. I've studied the chart and memorised my intended route.

When I return to the house Dufour is waiting and looking serious. I fear the worst. But no, I'm wrong. He says: 'We owe you. After the ambush you could have run – but no, you didn't, you came back to warn us. You raised the alarm. You saved us.' He beams at me and puts a grateful arm around my shoulder. 'It's only fair, we'll help you all we can.'

I nod my thanks, still wondering how to get started. Somehow I need to reach Marguerite's place at Freys, a bolthole from pursuit and, hopefully, a place where I can obtain help to cross the frontier, but this is still many miles away.

'How will you find your way?' he asks.

'I have my chart. It's a map.'

'But you might be out in the open, away from the road or the train...' At this, he disappears back into the house and returns with a small circular object. 'Best you have this,' he says, and I recognise a miniature compass. 'My grandpa's. Kept it all these years and never used it. Now's the moment to put it to good use. To get you away.'

I'm speechless, overcome by the gesture.

'I tell you what I'll do,' he says, 'we'll use the van tomorrow to get you into town. You need to get clean away from here.'

And then he tells me the rest of his plan.

'Male impersonation?'

I'm rocked back by this idea. I was expecting better shoes and maybe a change of coat, something less than a sex change.

'They know what you look like,' he says. 'They'll be on the lookout. You won't last five minutes as you are.'

'Yes, but most women get waved through the checkpoints.'

'Not you. You need a complete change.'

Can I carry this off? Swagger, bombast, ownership of *le pave*? In front of a mirror I try forcing my front teeth forward and pulling the lower lip back. Abandoning a feminine role is to forfeit a big advantage. The Germans are known to pay more attention to men, but the danger is that Bernard's treachery will shortly give them priceless insight into who I am and my appearance.

Inside the house I have my hair cut short – masculine short – by Madame Dufour. She's co-operating, I know, because she's anxious to get rid of me to protect her family and the little ones. I'm hot! The sooner I'm gone the better for them. And to send me on my way I get cast-off shoes, shirt, beret, suitably smudged overalls and a really dreadful pair of heavy spectacles, plus cigarettes. I don't smoke but a packet of Ecksteins will be useful to defuse awkward social moments. I dirty my hands in the mud by the door and scour my palms on a tree trunk while they pack a knapsack with sandwiches, screwdrivers and a selection of small tools to complete my pose as a workman. They even manage a small bottle of cough linctus to try and deepen the voice. Can I really carry this off? 'Good morning, nice day, might rain later, is this the way to the station?'

'You'll pass,' Dufour says, but I'm not so sure. All my life I've wanted to be equal to men. By this twist of fate I must now look and act like one.

At first light he takes the van as far as he dare, the outskirts of the next town. He has the right papers allowing him to collect flour for his bakery but has no way of knowing if von Kruger has raised a general alarm.

'What next for you?' I ask, and he says he'll ride out the storm in the forest, later emerging in a far-off village on an official transfer. I frown at this. 'Bogus papers,' he says. 'Contacts in the Mayor's office.'

Talk of papers and passes increases my sense of vulnerability as I walk into town, praying not to be stopped before reaching a certain bookshop. You can't exist in occupied territory without the up-to-date documents but I have it on Dufour's authority that the Mayor is willing to help people in trouble.

I scan the streets. A few scurrying figures are about, mostly working people showing little interest in strangers. How to conduct myself? I have to think this through. No use stepping gently down the road, I must walk like a member of the opposite sex. Be this man! This workman is used to climbing ladders and working with tools. He's confident, easy with himself, so I try stepping out in a rolling sort of gait but Dufour's oversize shoes are making me feel awkward. And no friendly smiles! No whistling a happy tune. This is Mr Grump on his way to fix someone's troublesome pipes.

Finally, after a couple of wrong turns, I find the Rue du Moulin and the Bookshop Girole. A bell jangles somewhere within as I open the door. Inside it's like a maze. Narrow passages lead off in different directions. The place is lined floor to ceiling with shelves and hundreds of titles. There are strange corners and unexpected dead ends and category labels I don't understand. It's only by chance that I find the tiny desk with a cash register and its seated occupant, a tiny, desiccated woman with scrawny hair, sunken cheeks and a gin-and-whisky complexion. This is Madame Girole. I recognise her from Dufour's description.

She looks up at me but says nothing. I cough, swallow and try for the gruff intonation. 'I've come about the account of Madame Legrand,' I manage.

She twists her mouth into a strange shape and I wonder if I've got the phrasing right. This form of words is meant to be the open sesame to people like me – people in trouble and in need of help.

'And you are?'

'Fabienne.'

Slightly ridiculous, since I'm dressed in male clothing, but it does the trick because she rises unsteadily and draws back a curtain, beckoning me into a private cubicle.

'Thought you'd turn up,' she says, 'there are rumours all over town about a runaway pilot.'

I nod.

'I suppose you need papers.'

Another nod.

'They all do.'

We proceed to the necessary fictional details – birthdate, place of birth, nationality, where headed – and some of Madame's air of perpetual gloom is explained. Husband missing, son in a labour camp, father shot as the Germans entered the country. 'It's all I've got left,' she says, 'getting back at those bastards in any way I can.'

I'm parked in the cubicle for hours while she minds the shop, not that there are many customers, and at midday she puts up the Closed notice and produces an old plate camera, clicking off two headshots before disappearing into a darkened room. Half an hour later she leaves for the Hotel de Ville.

The Mayor, it seems, leads a double life, secretly issuing passes for ID and travel, courtesy of the adjacent *Bureau de*

Population office, the German clerk who takes long lunches, a co-operative Belgian assistant and the duplicate key which opens the security cupboard containing all the blanks. He validates his illicit work with Madame Girole's photographs and an authorisation stamp he has no authority to use.

It's only when Madame returns from the *mairie* with her bundle of bogus documentation that I realise what a tightrope I'll be walking; there's a carte d'identité, the French equivalent of the basic ID for German civilians. But that's not all; you need a cluster of papers to travel legitimately in these parts. I look at my new employment certificate with my fictional company name of Gybels filled in, noting that I'm domiciled in St. Quentin, two facts swamped by the enormous blue official Gummistempel stamp. I pick up another: a movement document in the form of a company request for unhindered travel to Frankfurt on company business, but strictly only in combination with the ID card. Frankfurt? Nice touch that, hopefully makes me sound all cosily German to any inspecting bureaucrat. Add in another form allowing me to travel between France and Belgium.

'How do I pay?'

Another twist to the mouth and then a little ding as Madame Girole opens the till. 'We've had a run on people like you,' she says, handing over a sheaf of banknotes with a deep sigh. They're Belgian francs, much depreciated by the occupation. 'We're running short, you'll have to travel third class, I can only let you have fifty. That still gives you some extra.' She smiles a little wan smile. 'Just a *little* extra.'

I hesitate, feeling unworthy, looking down at this amount of money in the hand. 'We have generous benefactors,' she says, but adds that 'necessity money' is better. This is locally issued currency designed to beat the inflation, but they won't take it at the station. I look at her and blink, amazed at the level of assistance, generosity and bravery I'm getting from these embattled people.

Then I turn to my own problems. It's one thing to put on the clothes to look like someone else – that's just pantomime stuff. Acting the part for real, that's something else. How do I do male without giving myself away? And on a train in the close proximity to others and right up close to a suspicious enemy. Surely, they'll see through me.

I try to repress an outbreak of nerves and tell myself to get inside the head of Monsieur Fournier. Be this little man! You are this workman. On the way to the station I adopt his psyche. He's grumpy. He got up early, had a row with his wife, he's short of the normal things of life and he's hungry – we're together on that! He's going to work on someone's faulty pipework. He hates his boss and he's fed up having to travel to do this job just to make ends meet and he can't stand being up close to the Germans. He's a sourpuss, he doesn't pass the time of day, he doesn't smile and doesn't make eye contact. He just glares out of the train window.

I look down at my feet. Don't walk delicately! You're rough, swing those shoulders, walk with a rolling gait. I breathe deeply. I had no idea back at Vert that I'd be getting into this.

The station presents a scene that has me gasping. I almost funk it, wanting to turn back and flee. But then resolve kicks in. I have to get back to deliver my message – my vital message for the people at home – and the train is the best way to cover the distance to get near the Dutch border.

I look again and my throat constricts. Military police, soldiers, loiterers, vast queues. I'm an illegal with false papers, a hunted fugitive, a wanted woman, a female masquerading as a man. What chance do I stand?

The ticket hall is full of grumblers but I'm desperate to stay silent. They all want to moan. A large woman with a turned-down mouth speaks in an angry whisper. 'Hour after hour, day after day, standing about in line, waiting, waiting. Tickets, sausages, bread, ration cards. One queue after another. This is how I spend my life.'

'When will it end?' says a man in a beret. 'A life of torture.'

They're looking in my direction, seeking agreement, but I keep my expression blank, adopting a mask of docility and uncomplaining compliance.

'I wouldn't mind if there was something good at the end of it,' says the woman. 'But just scraps. Scrag-ends after they've had their pick.'

I don't want to be drawn into this conversation. Watchful, suspicious eyes under big caps are scanning the crowds, roving over the long line that snakes around this antiseptic, tiled and echoing interior. The queue moves with agonising slowness. The longer I spend here the greater the risk.

A uniformed figure sidles around the head of the line and takes position at the ticket hatch, sparking a renewed murmur of muted protest.

'Damned queue-jumper,' says the man in the beret, looking agitatedly in my direction.

I try to take a grip on myself, keeping hands hidden to hide the shakes. I crave anonymity. To reveal fear is to signpost guilt.

At last I'm at the ticket hatch. It's a tiny window with a shroud of dirty glass. Behind it an anonymous face stares back at me. I've been able to sharpen up my classroom French in the village but will this be enough to mask my English accent? I swallow and do my best to play the part: teeth forward, gaze steady, gruffing out my request. I silently plead for the ticket clerk to be on my side, rather than theirs, but who can tell?

'Frankfurt? Which Frankfurt?'

For a moment I'm thrown into panic, then remember there's

a city of that name on the River Oder and another on the Main. 'Main,' I croak.

I can see his eyes swerve away to search some distant part of his booth. Not many passengers to either Frankfurt, I'm guessing. Perhaps he doesn't have a ticket to such a distant destination. Perhaps he'll refuse me, begin an awkward inquisition or suggest I travel elsewhere.

Another curt demand: 'First, second or third?' This is followed by instructions on where to change and finally the key moment, the worst, the crisis point I've been dreading: has Madame Girole got the fare right? Will I have enough?

'Forty-eight fifty.'

I pass over my entire wad. A brief pause, then my ticket and a few puny coins appear.

Pity, I've no intention of going all the way to Frankfurt – either of them – but I nod my thanks anyway.

You'd think navigating the queue without a slip-up and getting a ticket without difficult questions would constitute a victory. A moment of huge relief. I permit myself a modest glow of success.

Mistake! As I step out of the ticket hall I turn a corner and run straight into a checkpoint. A line of trestle tables bars the way to the tracks. Behind sit an ensemble of sour faces, cold eyes and military field grey.

'Papers!'

The inevitable peremptory demand, spat out with routine disdain. How they love to intimidate and frighten. It feeds their twisted sense of superiority. I'd like to tell them this, that their power rests solely on the rule of the gun, but I don't.

Instead I fumble for Madame's freshly minted forgery, worrying that she may have given me a botched job. Is the ink even dry? The nearest inquisitor snatches my proffered paperwork and I hold my breath. Is he any good, or just nasty? He hands it back without comment and points to my tool bag.

'Open.'

He looks in at my hammer, pliers and pinchers, then stares at me as if he's just caught me carrying a bomb. 'What are these for?'

'House repairs.'

'Why are you travelling?'

'To my place of work.'

'Can't they repair their own house?'

'It's a very big house.'

'Show me your hands.'

I blink. This is a new one, but I've anticipated him. He wants to see if I'm a real workman. Smooth and delicate fingers will betray me, so that's why I rubbed them in soil and scoured the palms against Dufour's tree.

'Filthy!' he cries. 'Get in that washroom and come out clean.'

Another blow! This man does hysterical at full volume.

'How dare you arrive in a public place and use public facilities with hands like these.'

I'm genuinely shocked and stumble in the indicated direction, rinsing away the offending grime. I'd anticipated suspicion – but not meeting a hygiene freak. Outside once again I manage to avoid further interrogation. On the platform a scattering of people collect in small groups, smoking and murmuring quietly while waiting for the train. After my inspection scare, I'm on a taut wire of tension and decide that being solitary will look stand-offish and attract unwelcome attention, so I pick a young kid, give him a small smile and stand close. He's got pimples and unruly hair and radiates an aura of innocence.

He grins at me and says in a squeaky unbroken voice: 'Where you goin' today?'

My spirits drop. Bad choice. I've picked a wrong 'un here. 'Work. Shouldn't you be at school?'

'I know,' he says suddenly, like he's just figured out a crossword clue, 'you're a teacher.'

'No.'

'You're just like my old teacher, exactly the same, used to teach geography, are you sure you're not a teacher?'

'I'm not a teacher.'

He nods. 'Yeah. I realise now. He has a much deeper voice than yours.'

'Shouldn't you be at school?' I persist.

'No, not anymore, I work in a shop. Sell souvenirs to soldiers.'

'I see.'

'It's good. They're in and out all day long. I love the smart uniforms. We've got a full-length photo on the wall of the Kaiser. Must be great to have such a strong leader like that, don't you think?'

I look at him intently. Is this a trap? Perhaps this kid is a plant to catch the unwary. Or just a fool. Fortunately I'm rescued by a loud toot and the approach of the train. It wheezes to a halt and sits panting like an exhausted dog, the air pump working in overdrive. The carriages have clearly been retrieved from some railway graveyard and pressed into wartime service. They have open-ended verandas and shabby matt-green paintwork.

I detach myself from the kid and check the indicator board. A group of field grey push their way through the crowd. Doors bang open, figures disgorge and the military enter first. There's a little curtain of space around them like they've got the plague.

When I eventually climb aboard I see them sprawled across

an open area of wooden slats in postures of careless disarray. There are vacant seats close by but we locals stand apart in the gangway.

Don't make eye contact, I tell myself. Don't attract their attention. Instead I take a leaf from the book of Mooseface and look my morose best staring out of the window and into the far distance, pretending to be completely unaware of their existence but keeping a close watch using peripheral vision. Here I am, under direct gaze of the enemy, a fugitive in plain sight, but thankfully most of them don't speak the language. I'll be an object of little interest. Their hopes will be pinned on the possibility of teasing a beguiling mademoiselle or finding something tasty to eat at the next stop. If anyone approaches I trust all to a Gallic shrug of incomprehension. I must not speak. I cannot risk my voice again.

My biggest threat will be the train conductor.

The train rattles on and I reflect on this strange world of deception I've been forced to enter. So many layers of fraud are demanded here. I'm pretending to be innocent, which I am not; I'm pretending to be male, which I am not; and I'm pretending to be Monsieur Fournier who I am not. Just how many deceits can one person carry off at any one time?

'Papers!'

They never tire. However, this time the uniformed official requires no verbal response, simply a resigned handing over of documents. I do my best to strike a pose of bored indifference as the Ausweis and the permit are laboriously scrutinised. Could the Germans be sharper than the Mayor thinks? Perhaps they have new information. Perhaps they're already on the alert for an escaper, or have some extra unknown bureaucratic check that will bring about my undoing.

'Merci.'

The journey continues, achingly tedious and uncomfortable in this crowded, spartan carriage amid this swaying mass of bodies. The waiting time at each station seems endless, vast military transports carrying guns and troops pass in the opposite direction, and after about two hours the locomotive is detached to a water tower for refuelling. However, I'm beginning to be pleased with myself. The miles are racking up, I'm covering vast distances and pass the border into Belgium without problem, my array of documents satisfying all demands. I can't risk a glance at my map but instead create a mental image of the train crawling up the network of lines somewhere east of Brussels, higher and higher, getting nearer and nearer my objective.

'Tickets!'

This conductor is a rat of a man. He demands to know where I'm going, even though the ticket specifies my destination. And he doesn't like the answer. I can see he's suspicious. My fake voice hasn't worked. 'I'm not satisfied,' he says. 'I'm going to check on you at the next station.'

'Fine,' I say, 'there's really no problem to worry about.'

The train, which I reckon is still about 100 kilometres short of my chosen exit point, is now slowing. He beckons me to the end of the corridor and we stand by the door, ready to alight. I nod and grin and pose complete and relaxed co-operation. But inside I'm gripped by a sense of desperation, conscious that this threatens to be a key moment in my escape. And I simply cannot allow myself to fail.

I wait until the train stops and he's got the door open, then launch a hefty boot into his midriff and shove him off the step on to the gravel outside where he sprawls in the dirt. Then I yank the door shut and walk smartly to the other side of the carriage, open the trackside door and drop to the ground.

These continental railway stations are nothing like the neat and tidy layouts familiar to us back home. A vast array of trackwork is displayed here and a quick glance tells me there are no other trains approaching. Then I run as fast as Dufour's horrible shoes will take me, across the tracks and along the opposite platform until I come to the exit. I fly through and stop dead. A rake of horse-drawn hansoms is lined up for hire and the lead cabbie is away, presumably drinking or playing cards in some quiet back office. I leap up into the driver's seat, grab the reins and jerk the horse into life. Slowly, he gets the message and we start to move. I give it some more urgent tugs and the pace livens up as we dart out on to a road on the country side of town. I can hear shouts behind me but don't look back. I've always fancied myself in a pony race, but this is no time to indulge in youthful fantasies and it's not long before my antagonists decide to cheat. No horse this time. Instead, I catch the sound of the high-pitched whine of a petrol engine being worked at speed.

I jerk the horse into renewed effort and decide the situation calls for yet another layer of deceit. Round a sharp bend I whip my steed into greater effort, release the reins and climb to the top of the cab, ready to launch. I look down, the cobbles whizzing past, looking deadly. This is madness. Can I really do this? I'm not a trick performer – but the racket behind overcomes all doubt. A grassy mound is coming up on the left. I tense, hands over head, then roll off the side of the careering carriage, turning myself into a human football to minimise contact. The jolt is dizzying. Fortunately, no cobbles, more grass than grit. I keep rolling, dirt swirling around my head, espy a ditch and flatten myself into it.

A wail of moving mayhem – engine, tyres, furious voices –

banshees past the spot where I lay still. They're using an old Daimler even more ancient than my mother's, I note, heaving myself out of the ditch and wiping the mud from my eyes.

That's when I realise I've lost the big specs. I shrug. This is no time to hang around. Opposite is a driveway and a path leading up a small hill toward a copse. This will be my escape route.

The path is hard going and my footfall painful. I wonder how much head start I have before they overtake the carriage and realise they've been fooled. I'm not a long-distance runner and there's a limit to how long I can keep going. Finally, I have to stop and lean panting against a tree.

When my breathing subsides indistinct noises can be heard in the distance. I take a moment to think this through. I can't hope to outrun a group of determined pursuers. Instead I need to outsmart them. Images of Charles the Second hiding inside an oak tree come to mind, then stories of hare coursing, prevalent back in my part of England. How does the hare outwit a chasing dog? I recall an old hand telling me. It isn't just about speed.

The noises are getting nearer and I jog forwards, not in unseeing haste as before, but on the lookout. I pass a small pond and drop in a handkerchief. It floats nicely on the surface.

The path runs parallel to a hedge and then begins to open out into wilder country. I rip off my jacket and jumper, pull a sleeve of the jumper inside out, and toss the garment to the side of the path. A little further I drop my cap, some pencils, chalk and a wallet – minus the Ausweiss, I don't want to be identified. A few steps on and I stop to orientate myself from the map provided by the bookseller. I identify the station and see the direction I should be heading, then find a town off to one side and scribble the name of Abbaye on the inside flap of my packet of Eckstein cigarettes which I drop to the path.

Voices signal the approach of imminent danger. Time to play the hare. I get behind the hedge and begin to retrace my steps in the direction from which we've all come. It's bumpy, hard going, without any sign of a beaten path. Slow progress takes me a short distance back towards the road before I sense the presence of my pursuers and crouch low and still. Fortunately, they don't have a dog's nose and can't smell my new high aura of perspiration as they pass all unknowing on the reverse side of the hedge.

Their voices are telling. One sounds high-pitched, angry and up for the chase. Another placating, perhaps a shade less eager. The sounds fade and I find a shallow dip amid abundant vegetation. This is my hide, lying full length covered in grasses, twigs and a couple of fallen branches, but I have no idea if this will work. I'm a townie untutored in the wily ways of the countryside and unfamiliar with the close-up smell of the soil.

Time passes slowly, my tension rising along with an increasing sense of discomfort and I agonise over my tactics. Should I seek a more distant refuge? Will they find my false trail? The discarded cigarettes will surely be an irresistible trophy for them – but will they follow the clue I've given them?

Then, voices again. This time complaining – that's the voluble one. Mumbled responses from the other.

I should keep my head down but can't resist peering out. Through the bare lower stems of the hedge I catch a glimpse as they pass by. They're returning to the road. Two of them. One is tall, elegant even in the railway uniform of long blue overcoat with rows of gold buttons and yellow epaulettes. This is the placator, the senior man, still wearing his blue peaked cap. The other is dressed roughly, doubtless the cabbie furious at the sudden loss of his horse and hansom.

I'm triumphant. They appear to have bought into my fiction that this is the trail of a person fleeing in haste, lightening his load on the run, a quarry much too fast for them.

Silence. The relief of success. Gradually, I emerge from my hide. I'm straightening up, trying to pull away the detritus of leaves and mould from my clothing, when I'm startled by the snapping of a twig.

I look up, shocked, realising my mistake. There hadn't been two of them. There were three. And the third, staring at me, is just yards away.

I recognise him immediately. The suspicious travelling conductor who had tumbled my fake pass. Rat-faced and dishevelled, minus his pouch, coat and hat, but leering with pleasure at his discovery.

Who'll react first?

If he shouts loud enough he'll bring back the others. I can't allow that. Survival instinct kicks in. Without further thought I grasp a fallen branch, a stout piece of timber that becomes a makeshift club. I close the distance between us in three fast strides that takes him by surprise and bring my improvised weapon down on his head.

It's as if events have taken control, that my actions are directed by another mind. I stand over him. He's down, silent and unmoving.

'That's what happens to traitors,' I tell the recumbent figure.

I view this deed with a degree of detachment that surprises me. It's like I'm standing outside myself, looking in. On the one hand, the blow has been delivered with a cold-eyed ruthlessness born of necessity. My other self wonders what has become of the peaceable, humane Charlotte Dovedale, whose normality is to condemn violence of any kind.

I begin to move away. For certain it is, this action will spawn an even more severe reaction from the authorities. And will they link these two isolated incidents – a runaway pilot in one place and a violent rail passenger in another – and make the connection?

It slowly dawns on me that my options have narrowed to just one at a certain level of desperation; that travel by public transport with the aid of bogus documents is now an impossibility.

Urgency demands that I make as much distance from this point as possible. A cross-country trek is the only option. I must get off open fields and make for the cover of the trees, then travel only by night.

CHAPTER TWENTY-SEVEN

I'm lying up among the bushes at the edge of the treeline, closely watching the open fields on the slopes below for any sign of a continuing pursuit while also conducting a mental audit of my plight. In the chase from the station I've lost my cap and the knapsack and with it the sandwiches which could have sustained me in the hours ahead. No tools, no food, no proper clothing to face the vagaries of weather and night. Several pluses, however: first, moonlight fades but lasts for three nights and there may just be enough night light to guide me; also, I still have my pilot's chart tucked into a deep pocket. I spread it out, find a map covering all of Belgium and northern France and try again to fix my position. There's maybe a hundred or more kilometres still to go with no point of contact or help. I explore the forest and locate a pond. There are reeds growing at the water's edge and I rip up several long stems and try to pack them inside my oversize shoes to make a better fit, but they're rough and difficult to sculpt without a knife and my feet still hurt. At dusk, with no sign of any organised search party – perhaps they've written off the train conductor's injuries as a casualty of no consequence – I set off on my chosen course, but the going is hard: no beaten footpath, fields still not harvested, big clods of soil and uneven ground, which cause me to stumble and several times almost fall. In a couple of hours there's little progress to speak of, which leads me to a dangerous decision: that despite the curfew making illegal any travel after dark, I'll stick to the roads. These are deserted of traffic and I reason that any vehicle using headlights will afford me time to take cover. But do the Germans engage in unlit silent patrols? No idea! I watch my shadow moving along the road as moonlight silhouettes my progress, heightening an already acute sense of vulnerability. I worry about blundering into a concealed roadblock or the sound of my footsteps alerting a hidden sentry. Senses strained for danger, I get to think about the essence of what I'm doing and by now I'm sufficiently self-aware to realise the limits of personal ambition. It's not about me, it's about the urgency of getting vital information back to base. However, a sour taste in the mouth and an empty stomach do not make for the right sort of mood to cope with the ordeals ahead. The miles seem endless but the night is short. Dawn is not far off and the necessity of finding a safe hideout for the day becomes more pressing. On the approach to a village at first light dogs begin to bark, causing me to panic and raise the pace, but the rigours of the long trek are beginning to tell and when I spy a huge haystack in fields just ahead I make another instant decision.

Hay. It looks so mundane, so harmless. Should be good for a hideout, I reckon, and close up I can see this colossus is made up of man-sized bundles. I try forcing my way in by making a gap between them. Not so easy. I'm not too far in before I'm totally enclosed and the idea of spending the daylight hours in the midst of this heap of damp decay has all the appeal of sleeping in a public toilet. More pushing, more shoving and eventually the gaps close behind me. It's a tight squeeze but lying down may reveal gaps to a conscientious searcher or people working the fields. I hope a heightened sense of alertness will save me. Soon I discover sleep is a problem. I try leaning, kneeling, crouching. I try eyes open, eyes shut, counting imaginary Gauleiters, humming the long road to Tipperary and remembered delights of the Abbey Hotel cuisine. This is a true test of resilience. Despite my fatigue, blessed unconsciousness refuses to come. The stinky clinginess is a nightmare. I count off all my friends and relatives, think about my life back home, wonder about my many relationships and eventually speculate on whether all my troubles are down to the figure who's missing from my life. My mind is wandering back to childish yearnings, of letters written to this mysterious person. I recall imaginary conversations with the ghostly entity of my absent father.

It's not until I'm woken by discomfort – or is it the mysterious scratching noises or just the nauseating stink? – that I realise I've succeeded in dozing off. There's still daylight visible through the slits in the bales, making it far too dangerous to look elsewhere and I relapse, a sense of fatalism combined with fatigue so insistent that eventually body and mind cave in.

Later, when fully conscious once more and feeling wretched with sores and pains and broken sleep, I pray for the welcoming cloak of darkness. Venturing out too soon is to court disaster. Dark thoughts return about the prospects of returning home if, by some incredible stroke of luck, I survive this nightmare. I think about what's happened – the fiasco of the stranded plane, the spy's treachery, my act of violence against the ticket man and my diminished sense of mission – and compare it to the life I lived before; of campaigning at suffragette meetings, flying for flying's sake, the world of dares and challenges, the desire for speed and sensation. Can I be that former version of myself once again, or will I be a different person?

Night falls and it's time to move. The next stage is a test of my night vision, the moon having waned to a desultory glimmer, and hunger is setting in with a vengeance. At the edge of a field I forage for anything edible and find a turnip. I hate turnips, but hunger is the stronger imperative. I descend to the level of a trash scavenger. Such is my desperation that the high spot of the second night is to find a bin outside a cottage containing a crust of bread. A second turnip causes sores at the side of the mouth and a rumbling stomach. I also scavenge old newspaper to stuff in my shoes. I'm not sure which is worse: hunger or the cold? This August night contradicts any notion of summer and an evil wind has a bite that gives the ears a numbing sensation akin to toothache. I feel disgusting. So long without washing or changing! It starts to rain and I realise how ill-prepared I am for a long trek in the open. Oh for a hat, scarf or any form of warmer clothing. I battle on when the force of the downpour increases. With no shelter or trees, what else is there to do? The overalls begin to leak. The legs are flapping and splashing against my skin while the shoes are turning to mush. Hair streams sodden into my eyes and now I can feel water running down my back. By contrast my throat is so parched that I stand still, head back, mouth wide open, trying to drink in the raindrops.

It doesn't work.

In this condition I have to do better than a haystack to see out the day. Long before dawn I cut the trudge short when I spot a shed at the end of a twisting path from an isolated cottage and use a stout stick to burst the lock.

Inside it's dry if a little musty and I rip off my sodden clothing, find some sacking and towel myself down, hanging up the wet clothing on hooks and nails. But thirst is driving me crazy. I lean outside with an old bucket, catch enough rain to swill it out, then an idea forms. The roof is sloping; the rainwater will run off. Outside is a piece of broken gutter which

I place below the roof, propping it into the bucket, catching enough to moisten the mouth. Perhaps there will be more by nightfall. I bed down wrapped in the rough and scratchy sacking material and achieve a kind of repose and eventual unconsciousness stretched out on the wooden floor.

Luck holds and no one comes to interfere with my sojourn and when the light begins to fall I discover I have water to drink.

Problem! The sodden clothing has failed to dry. Another new experience, perhaps my most uncomfortable to date: pulling on wet clothing sends my spirits to the floor. It drags and clutches at aching, protesting limbs, seems to seep moisture down to the marrow. Only body heat from strong exertion will dry these things out.

However, there are some useful objects to be had in this shed: scissors, screwdrivers, a knife and loops of string. I use the latter to bind up my sagging shoes with the added advantage that this will cushion the noise of my footsteps.

Out on the road almost the first thing I discover pinned to a fence is a huge notice announcing *Wanted: foreign terrorist.* There's a perverse and eerie fascination in reading about yourself in the third person, learning, for instance, that I'm a dangerous female criminal dressed in male clothing, that anyone seeing me should report it immediately; that failure to do so will result in severe penalties and that I'm already responsible for the death of at least one person.

This last shocks. True or a lie? I cannot know the real fate of the little train conductor but cannot credit that my blow had been so damaging. Surely not fatal! My regrets extend beyond the conductor to the horse I'd whipped into a racing fury and to the next person I might have to cross in my quest to escape. This German poster forces me to acknowledge the steady escalation of ruthlessness around my actions and I wonder how Scott will view this.

Scott. My mind goes back to him. Did he get into trouble for faking illness? What's he doing now... will I ever see him again? I feel a certain guilt at my many past demands. Perhaps I pushed him too far and I vow to repay his friendship when – and if – we next meet. There's a rain-streaked grin as I recall a picture of his face and ready smile and that heady moment in the darkness of a London cinema when our hands briefly brushed. I relive the electric tingling of the fingertips, the thrill of the touch. Katie had demanded to know, during her visit to Vert Galant, about my romantic intentions. Am I still sticking to my vow always to put flying first? To be fated as an aviator and acknowledged by all?

I trudge on like an automaton, legs working as if they don't belong to me, and the road stretches ahead in an unending snaking line. I work to divert myself with pleasant images from our past – but the past refuses to emerge in glowing colours. My mood goes dark with the weather and I turn seriously inward. Perhaps I'm seeing my true self for the first time: ambitious to the point of becoming obsessional. And now I feel humbled by all those fine people who've helped me along the way; ordinary folk in occupied territory who have given freely at great risk to themselves. I see in the baker, the bookseller and the Mayor the true colour of humanity. All this does nothing to take away the blistering feet and aching limbs and I decide diversion tactics work for only so long and my mind is soon back with the debilitating cold that creeps under an inadequate and smelly gentleman's shirt.

I enter a small town, instantly alert. From my experience in Bouillon I know the Germans post sentries at each end of villages, but this one appears to be free of such perils. But it's eerie walking deserted streets during curfew and I'm alert for the first sign of trouble. This isn't long in coming. I hear the crunch of booted feet on cobbles and dodge into a darkened alleyway as a patrol clumps past. Shall I go on? While I'm debating the point, there's the noise of a vehicle. Clearly, the enemy are here in force, so I retrace my steps and use the map to work out an avoiding route. This, however, is going to add several miles to my journey.

Perhaps I'm not quite myself. I'm feeling weaker than yesterday, a bit woozy and a little faint and I have a headache, and when I see another example of that Wanted poster my anger erupts. Without stopping to think, I whip out my new knife and cut several big slashes through the words, find a pencil stub in a pocket and ring the unfamiliar signature with the word 'murderer'. Another damned vulture! I can't leave it. I have to send a message, so I scribble the words 'Soon you will face justice'. Only later do I think about the consequences of this act.

My whole metabolism begins to creak. I've never before experienced hunger like this, nor fatigue. My knees feel as if they're overlapping the bottom half of my legs. Eating another turnip is a form of torture, bordering on revulsion. There's a dull ache around my middle. It feels like there's a big hole there that the wind can blow right through. Once again it comes home to me that I'm not prepared for the extremes of this ordeal. Every fibre of my being feels shattered, my eyes want to close. And then the fear. I worry that the distance I have to cover may be insuperable. I'm a bundle of uncertainties, feeling all alone and thrown to the wolves. Damn that spy Bernard.

I entertain evil thoughts about this man and wonder if he still represents a threat. Perhaps he's in trouble with his new masters for his failure to entrap me and for the escape of the baker Dufour. Perhaps he's still on my trail.

I stumble on. I must be mad to do this. Easier just to give myself up, give in and claim prisoner-of-war status. Such relief. A warm bed, sleep, food... but then reality kicks in. No bed, I tell myself, just the firing squad.

A faint flutter of noise breaks into these thoughts and I'm instantly on my guard. I stop and listen. Hearing nothing, I nevertheless move to the side of the road, slide down into the drainage ditch and wait. Perhaps it was nothing – but then three silent figures cross my field of vision, treading silently, clearly wearing rubber boots. There's just enough light to see the tips of their rifles as they pass.

I grit my teeth. I remember who I am. I don't do failure, I always aim for first. Perhaps after all, there is a future. I see myself in some distant era of peace as a writer, an artist or an aviator. Better still, all three. That's a prospect to propel me forward, to fight for, to survive for. And Scott! Perhaps there is a bright future for us. I visualise us as itinerant soulmates, spending luxuriant hours in the company of old masters in the Rijksmuseum and gazing in awe at the Colosseum, the Parthenon and Versailles.

By the fourth day I'm so worn out I know I can't continue without proper rest or food. I've been drinking from pools of rainwater and paying the price with a grumbling gut. I'm still miles short of my target and shall have to risk throwing myself on the mercy of a stranger. For this, I select a neat and tidy cottage. It has white shutters and curtained windows and there are geraniums in a pot by the front door, which features a decorative glass panel. I decide such husbandry in wartime is the mark of a person of substance. There's no answer to a knock and no internal lights showing, so I go to the rear and try the back door. At a hard push, it opens into a neat kitchen with no plates or utensils on view, just a polished, gleaming surface and a vase of flowers on a window ledge. I pace through the house, looking but not seeing, just one thing on my mind: food. There's no one upstairs but what draws my attention is a large bed covered by a red-and-white patchwork quilt. I stand for many minutes looking at this soft and inviting vision of heaven, fantasising about dream-filled hours of warmth and comfort, then turn downstairs to raid the larder. I find small neat containers of cheese and ham and sit at the table with milk and fruit juice, indulging my immense need and ignoring another pang of guilt.

Then sheer unreason drives me back upstairs. This bed cannot be resisted. It's just too good to miss. I won't sleep, I won't close my eyes, simply rest my weary body while I await the arrival of the person who I trust will turn out to be my saviour.

Scott and I are making short work of enormous plates of grilled Suffolk venison with parsnip purée and juniper berry sauce and he's checking the champagne bucket to make sure the maître d' at the Abbey has got everything just right and we're laughing uproariously at an immensely funny joke although the precise details of the story are cloudy and elusive and I can't quite grasp them and there's a strange pricking sensation in my right shoulder. 'Stop it, Scott,' I hear myself murmur and then a shocking loud noise erupts in my right ear – a shout, no less – and I register a strange voice – female and not male – swearing in some odd patois version of French and I open my eyes and discover it's not Scott but a strange woman glaring at me with a pair of open scissors in her hand and looking as if she's going to jab me with the razor-sharp point.

'What do you think you're doing?' A screech this time, clear and as brutal as any wake-up call.

I swallow and try to shake off the effects of deep sleep. 'I'm sorry...' I stammer.

'Who the devil are you?'

'So sorry but I couldn't resist...'

'I come home from my mother's place and find a man in my bed.'

Honesty and a plea for sympathy are all I can manage. My best tactic, I instantly decide. 'I'm not, I mean, I can explain...' The soft voice has given it all away.

'But you're not, are you?'

'No.'

By now I'm more alert and take in the full picture. She's young but has lines across the forehead, short mousy hair and beginnings of bags below big eyes. She's wearing a shapeless black smock and has a young child on her back with its arms around her neck. It too is female and, like its mother, has immense green orbs for eyes.

I try sitting up as she exclaims with sudden alarm: 'Now I know who you are! I realise now, you're that terrorist in the Wanted posters.'

I shake my head. 'Not a terrorist, I assure you...'

'You go around killing people.'

'No, no, no! It's not true. That poster is all lies.'

'Says you.'

'You can't trust anything the Germans put out. It's all lies. I'm not dangerous, I just want to get away. Get out of this country, that's all.'

'It says you killed someone.'

Who knows the truth of it, but I do my best. 'He's not dead,' I say. 'I did hit him but only in self-defence. He would have dragged me off to jail.'

'The poster says anyone who gives shelter faces a long spell in jail.' She swallows, fear writ large in those eyes. 'I don't want that. What would happen to my child? I would lose her! You, just being here, you're a danger to us both. I didn't invite you in...'

I sigh. Another stage has arrived in my burdensome path

across other people's lives. 'I'm really sorry,' I say. 'I know you're right to be angry but...' And here I embark on the obvious line of persuasion: I'll only be in the house for a few hours, I seek sanctuary only until darkness, I'll steal away and no one will see, no one will know...

'But someone might see you and report me,' she wails. 'I must give you up. To save myself. And her.' Pointing at the child.

'Please,' I say, 'just a few hours.'

'And you've eaten half my rations for the week!'

I'm on tenterhooks for hours, hoping desperately she's not going to betray me. And what are the chances of this frightened mother raising the alarm the minute I'm gone? All I can do is calm her down, engage her sympathy and empty my pockets of the coins from the station. In the course of a difficult conversation I gather the Germans are out looking for me, quizzing the customers in a café in the next village and even searching houses – the consequence, I realise, of my thoughtless act in slashing the Wanted poster. Perhaps I've succeeded in winning this woman over, because I leave at dusk with better shoes wrapped around with wool, some clean underclothes and an old bike for which she has no further use. So now I'm back on the road, still dressed in my dried-out workman's overalls, and within biking distance of the big house at Freys and my hoped-for bolthole.

CHAPTER TWENTY-EIGHT

I'm not sure. Maybe, possibly. The black iron railings look familiar but when I was a young visitor here I never knew them on the outside looking in, rather the opposite. Closer still and then, yes, this is it, the old lodge and beside them, the big wrought-iron gates topped by an ornamental crest. Glancing behind to check I'm alone, I place a grateful palm on the handle and heave.

Nothing. And the pain goes right up to the shoulder.

The handle won't move. I rattle it some more without result, and then see the chains. Not just locked but anchored. The weeds growing round the stanchions confirm it.

I stand rock still for a moment as the fear takes hold. It's obvious: there's no one at home because the family have fled. It makes sense. Why would they have stayed in the face of the German invasion? In my mind's eye I can see them hurrying across the border into neutral Holland just hours or perhaps even minutes before the grey hoards descend on their home territory. I hold my breath to control a sudden flood of panic. It means the chance of a bolthole is gone, signalled as never before that I'm utterly alone with no prospect of help.

Checking behind once more, I force aching limbs to move on to the lodge, expecting to see it similarly shuttered, but a small hope returns when it appears outwardly much as before. And there! The glimmer of a weak electric light bulb.

I burst up the path, brushing without noticing the straggly hedge, and hammer at the door, breathing heavily, willing a release from my sense of pursuit and torture, quite forgetting my appearance, heedless of the male handyman pose. Then, heart pounding, I wait. And wait. The silence is ominous. Hope begins to fade but finally, after a scuffle and a creak, comes the sound of a voice. An old voice. Faint and reedy.

'Who is it?'

'Charlotte,' I boom, breathless with relief, a smile beginning to form.

'Who?'

'Charlotte. You know, Charlotte Dovedale. From England.' The last added in a pathetic pleading tone.

'Go away,' answers the reedy voice.

At this, desperation sets in. I hammer on the knocker again. 'Look,' I say to the blistered wood of the door, 'it's Charlotte, please, I'm desperate, let me in!'

A crack appears where before the door jamb was closed. One beady eye. 'Who are you?'

'Just told you, Charlotte!'

'Take me for a fool?'

And then realisation dawns. The tatty overalls and dishevelled appearance have thrown him, so I put my head on one side and grin insanely at the old man. 'Sorry, Gilbert, recognise me now? Had my hair cut short. I assure you it's me, me, Charlotte Dovedale, you remember...' By now I realise I'm almost gibbering with anxiety to convince the old retainer, fearful he might close the door those few precious inches. 'You remember, when I was here as a girl with Marguerite and Jules and Dr Leger in that summer, oh goodness, how many years ago is that now?'

The reedy voice cuts in, displaying a dismaying indifference to my pleadings. 'I'm not to let anyone in.'

'But it's me!'

'No one comes through here. Strict orders from the boss. No one.'

'I'm desperate, Gilbert, don't turn me away, please, or they'll catch me sure as eggs is eggs and turn me into old rags. Please, tell Marguerite I'm here.'

'You do sound a bit like Charlotte.'

'I am Charlotte!'

The door opens just a little wider but it's not an invitation to enter. He's peering over my shoulder and I realise he's checking for watchers.

'Come to the side gate.'

The ancient wood and hinges creak with rust, that's after countless bolts and chains have been unleashed, and I am ushered inside and out of public view. The old man peers at me questioningly, as if he's still not sure he has made the right decision, and I can't blame him because I'm beginning to realise I don't look anything like the Charlotte Dovedale he knew as a bright young thing cavorting around the estate with the master's children. He repeats his orders for a blanket refusal of admission but consents to ring 'the house'.

Sitting on a stool in his tiny kitchen, the shivers set in. Looking as I do, I feel a fool, relief giving way to shock and fatigue while I await some reaction from the family to my unexpected arrival. Eventually, a door opens and there is Marguerite, looking older, her hair up in the usual pompadour style and dressed in what I can only describe as a dowdy brown dress made of tussah silk, a quizzical expression in place. This quickly dissolves into a smile of recognition.

'I can't believe it's you,' she says, hand gestures describing circles of incredulity, 'but what are you doing here?'

We embrace but my explanations soon bring a frown. 'This is dangerous,' she says. The grounds are locked and barred to keep out marauding German soldiery and to deflect interest from the local Gauleiter. 'And the fact that they're looking for you makes it even worse. We're trying our best to be completely invisible to them here at L'Abri. I'll have to tell Father. He won't be pleased.'

We walk the long gravel driveway to the house, still as I remember it – a hugely turreted medieval manor with extensive grounds, but I'm also thinking of the man I've fondly regarded all these years as the person closest to being a father figure. Wise, considerate, caring. But that is not the image I receive today. Instead, a frown, a cold exterior.

'I'm sorry, Charlotte,' he says, 'you can't stay. You're too hot! We're all in danger, every day. I doubt you realise what you've done, coming here...'

He shakes his head and I'm stricken at this rejection. From such a man! 'You must realise,' he says, 'these days we're not masters of our own fate, so I trust you haven't brought your pursuers to our door.'

I drop my head and swallow. 'I'm so tired, so hungry, I've been trudging for days.'

That I should have to beg!

'I'm sorry,' he says, face still implacable, and with these words all my hopes of sanctuary are destroyed. All my illusions, the dreams and treasured memories of those idyllic early years, are smashed with this one brutal utterance. Golden memories fall like leaves in winter.

'You see, the occupier is relentless,' he says, looking away, gazing from the window, perhaps fearing the imminent appearance of field grey. 'A dragnet in this district?' A deep sigh.

'Your presence invites a search, and if they were to find you...
Any hint of resistance is met with draconian reprisals. People
are shot and jailed and deported every day.'

'Just until I'm fit to go on?' I'm desperate for respite: rest,
food, clothing, assistance for the onward journey. I take his
rejection hard, as a betrayal, even though I know he's protecting
his family. Back then, in those halcyon pre-war days, I'd
foolishly imagined that I was almost part of his family.

He sighs and turns to Marguerite. 'You'd best find
somewhere to put her,' he says, 'perhaps the attic, but she'll have
to go straight after dark.'

Marguerite looks at my gaunt appearance and doesn't
need to be told of my most urgent need. I'm still hungry.
Ready to steal, grab or bribe for food. The Legers themselves,
like everyone in occupied territory, are short of supplies but
she manages to find some cheese, a hunk of black bread and a
tiny slice of sausage. I can barely contain myself to observe
the normal civilities between friends before ripping into these.
While I assuage my empty stomach she tells me how they're
only staving off starvation themselves thanks to relief supplies
from neutral nations. And then she explains the family
situation: that both she and her father work in the medical
laboratories of the city hospital; that their status as key
workers is on a knife-edge; that shootings, imprisonment and
deportations are daily events. It's a shock when she insists that
on no account must her father be addressed as 'Professor'.
The Germans have no use for professors of history or
literature and have closed almost all the universities in a
rampage of arson and destruction. Now both she and Dr
Leger, with the willing complicity of friends at the hospital,
have turned themselves into lab technicians assisting the
search for methods to prevent the spread of infection. So far
antiseptics haven't worked, she says, with chemists currently

chasing solutions for the battle against pneumonia, gangrene and trench fever.

'Where's Jules?' I ask, but Marguerite is vague and warns me to stay well clear, that I must not make myself known to him. Her anguish is obvious as it transpires that Jules has turned full-on enthusiast for the Germans – thinks they're the future – and might well give me away.

So much for my image of the hero Jules, of the brave resister, defying the might of the enemy. I won't be getting any help from him. Another destroyed illusion. It's one thing to adopt a policy of minimal collaboration sufficient to ensure survival, but quite another to become an enthusiast for this alien cause. A stage beyond forgiveness, I decide.

Later there is a relaxation of tension and I find myself once again admitted to the big sitting room. My gaze runs over the familiar ornate stone fireplace and screen, the cluttered mantelpiece, the giant mirror and side tables laden with photos. Dr Leger, still dressed formally with a large white collar and tie, is seated on his favourite ornamental oval-back chair, glass in hand. He's evidently now in a mellow mood, more the figure of the mentor I once knew, and there are greetings cards on display, symbols of his wide circle of friends and acquaintances, a wide circle I've never had. At that, bitter thoughts turn to the role of fatherhood; to love, protection, concern, wisdom, advice, guidance. I've had little of these.

I try to explain the urgency of my situation. He still has the full head of white hair I remember. 'It isn't just about me and my survival,' I say, 'I have urgent information which must be got back to the authorities. Secret stuff, vital to the war effort, you understand.'

'That makes you all the more dangerous to us,' he says.

I can't argue the point. I'm scared enough myself, been living on my nerves these last few days. Even so, I can't repress a sense of deep disappointment at his attitude. I had anticipated a more resistant response to the invader. I venture: 'You can't like this situation, surely?'

'Hardly! Their murderous intent, invading my country, incinerating the greatest university library in the land at Leuven, bleeding us white of our every possession, kidnapping our sons...' This is more the Dr Leger I had anticipated. 'But danger forces you to reassess all your easy peacetime assumptions,' he says. 'Collaboration might be a dirty word to you, but when the devil appears to like you, should you spit in his face? To us, it's the only way to survive.'

He sighs, more reflective than hostile and apologises for his earlier abruptness. 'But you see, you are one and we are three.'

'Perhaps,' I reply quietly, 'in terms of peril and threat, that's really only two.'

He doesn't need to be told to whom I am referring. 'Each individual has to make their own accommodation with the new circumstances,' he says, 'and to the young there is a certain spurious attraction around strength, vitality and modernism. To some extent this may be keeping the wolves from our door.'

I know better than to expect a father to criticise a son, especially since the future now looks even more bleak. Suddenly, his manner is confiding. 'My country is being ravaged by a monstrous machine and I fear we may soon become a battlefield.'

'They'll evacuate you, surely?'

'I wouldn't count on them for anything.'

We have apparently arrived at a key moment in our conversation. He leans forward to tell me of the latest rumour doing the rounds at the hospital: that the Kaiser is planning for the ultimate German victory; that he intends to clear out the indigenous peoples of Belgium and northern France and repopulate this part of Europe with German settlers.

'Well then!' I challenge. 'How can you collaborate?'

He defends his lab researches. 'I like to think we can do some good. Searching for remedies to the maladies of the age. That's why I'm here. To save lives.'

I repress a tart rejoiner – that he's primarily out to save his own skin – and I'm glad I didn't say it. Disappointed though I am at my treatment at L'Abri, who am I to challenge him?

And just now I'm not feeling so very brave myself.

CHAPTER TWENTY-NINE

Marguerite knows someone in the village who knows someone else who, it is said, helps people in trouble. 'But don't tell Father!' she says, and cycles off into the night on her mission of inquiry.

I should be happy that I may receive help with the next, and most difficult, part of my journey, but somehow I'm not. I swallow and nod my thanks and take to a bed in the attic. Such relief! Food, drink, warmth, rest, sanctuary; what I've craved over the last few days, and the prospect of going out once again into hostile territory begins to shoot spasms of panic right down to my core. I want to sleep, my body craves it, but the perils outside the walls of this house are too real for anything more satisfying than a few snatches of brief unconsciousness. Instead of the anticipated relief of sanctuary, I feel more like a cornered fox with the hounds at my throat.

Marguerite returns a couple of hours later in an almost conspiratorial mood. Her eyes sparkle with achievement but there's something bothering her. This second 'someone', she has discovered, runs an escape line that includes sending alerts to people on the other side of the frontier. Some sort of secret reception can be arranged.

'But you have to understand, it's a huge risk,' she says, her tone heavy with warning and concern. 'Very risky, you could get killed on the wire.'

'What wire?'

'The border, it's shut off, the Germans, they've locked us in. They've put an electrified fence across the frontier. Hundreds of people have been electrocuted on the wire trying to get away.'

Just what I needed to hear. The near impossibility of escaping from occupied Belgium into neutral Holland. In my present state I'm not sure I'm up to it. And if that isn't enough, the promised help is available only to people considered to be of great importance.

Am I a person of importance?

I swallow and nod.

Someone will be in the lodge in the evening to test me out. 'To make sure you're worth it,' she says, 'and that you're not a German plant.'

I snuggle down again and finally drift into sleep, but it doesn't last. Some time in the early hours serious fright takes hold. Images of my journey to the border and patrols along the electrified fence. Images of my scorched and broken body. Images of torture and a police cell. Images of the firing squad. I'm shivering, sick of the chase, fed up with being pursued, scared stiff at what will happen next. And when dawn creeps into my attic bolthole I can't get out of bed. An inner voice tells me this is foolish, having come so far, having got so near to the crossing, that to lose my nerve now would be tragic. But I just curl up into a foetal ball. I lay still. Can't move. Screw tight my eyes to keep out a terrifying reality. There's a loud and not-to-be-repressed thought blasting through my head; that I simply cannot take any more.

Marguerite reappears at my bedside. 'Okay?' she asks, all concerned. 'Sleep well?'

My nod is an absolute fib and she probably knows it. My eyes almost certainly tell a different story. She's brought me a cup of their precious coffee. When my hand clasps the saucer it begins to rattle and I'm ashamed to let a friend see my funk.

Marguerite says: 'I'm so sorry we can't do any better, really I am, I wish we could do more...'

'I know, I know,' I say.

A sudden thought: what if I persuade her father, against all the odds, to let me stay? What if I simply refuse to go? Then I take a grip on myself. This is a shock reaction to the constant state of nerves I've been subjected to over the last few days. I tell myself I have no option but to go. I can't put my friends in danger. Could I really risk seeing them in serious peril of their lives? Another ghastly image chokes me up: Marguerite or her father whipped, stripped, degraded and perhaps shot, simply because of my failure. I cannot repay them in this fashion.

I give her my best effort at a reassuring smile, take a deep breath and climb out of bed.

The 'someone' in the lodge turns out to be a tall and forbidding figure let in by the same side gate I had entered. He's aggressive with no trace of sympathy for my plight and does not announce himself. Instead, he glares at me in an intimidating manner, trying to rattle me, but I'm too fascinated by his lived-in features to be impressed: a shiny bald pate, black bushy eyebrows and a squashed boxer's nose that seems to flatten out all over the lower half of his face. If only I'd kept that stub of a pencil!

The big man demands to know the details of my squadron, the planes I fly, the name of the hotel at Hyde Park Corner and which club won the First Division this season. This last, of course, is the oldest of trick questions. Answer: league cancelled in 1915. I have the distinct impression that a single wrong answer will have serious physical consequences but tell him I have vital information to take back and can he pass that message on?

'I'm not a damned telegram service.'

'How are you going to...?'

'Don't ask questions, just be ready at nine tonight.'

Later, speculating on how he would get his message across, I'd put money on a pigeon, and just hope no alert crack-shot German sentry is on hand when 'my' bird flutters over the wire.

Suddenly the Legers are all concerned and anxious to be as helpful and sympathetic as possible. If I were in cynical mode, I'd say their dangerous guest was on her way. Certainly, I'm grateful to be wrapped up in a voluminous cape, hat and gloves and with fresh female attire. I'm still nervous but with the help I'm promised I'm determined to make a go of the final leg of the journey. At nine I'm clenching fists and stamping nervous feet by an estate side gate, fearful I could still be the victim of a fraud. By now I've seen enough deceit to acknowledge the possibility of a trap, of being sold out to the enemy, but what choice do I have?

This time I'm met by an anonymous figure almost completely masked by hat and scarf and huge overcoat. He says he's Matteo. Probably an assumed name. I'm in the midst of a group of people known only by their forenames: Matteo, Oscar and Luca. Who next, I wonder. This Matteo thrusts a cycle at me. 'You can ride?'

We zoom off down a lane and I worry some more. At the rate we're going we could ride straight into a patrol or a roadblock with no chance of getting away, but Matteo raises my hopes when he stops and listens intently to the noises of the night. This man knows what he's doing. He tells me I'm fortunate to be part of the escape line; that the Germans have had patrols out for days searching for me and they're especially piqued by what they describe as 'terrorist messages' left in the district. I rue my headstrong poster protest.

Finally, we're by a river, wide and fast flowing with a faint hint of moonlight glinting off the lapping swell. 'This is where you get off,' he says.

I give him the bike and he turns without a word and expertly cycles back towards the village guiding his two machines, leaving me standing on a wharfside staring down at a big black shape at the side of the river.

CHAPTER THIRTY

Slowly, when my night vision improves, the big black shape transforms into a long narrow barge. Then I'm conscious of a small figure by my side and I'm taken by the arm and led across a small plank and descend several creaking steps into a tiny cabin. As soon as I duck past the door the figure grabs me by the arm and swings me around, his grizzled face close up to mine. I can smell his breath, tell what he had for dinner. 'If you're a provocateur...'

I try to shake him off but his grip is like a metal claw. 'I'm not and you're hurting...'

'We have a way with traitors!'

'I'm not!'

It's clear I'm in danger of being dumped over the side in a weighted sack. I insist: 'I've already been cleared by your people.'

'You may have fooled them but you don't fool me.'

In the flickering low light of the cabin I can see him now, a small man in a black boatman's hat, the wrinkled leathery skin of the face revealing someone who's spent his life on the water.

'I'm vouched for,' I insist angrily, finally pulling free of his grip. 'And I didn't come all this way to be bullied by a...'

'By a what? A mere boatman?'

'By anyone.'

We stand glaring at one another. A sullen silence. Then he says: 'If I'm going to risk my wife, my life and my boat to you, I need to be sure you're not one of them.'

I breathe in. I can do without all the hostility and a bruised arm but prepare myself for another test, though I'm a little short on civility.

'What?'

It takes a hard telling: where I'm from, who I've been with, my knowledge of Belgium, my personal history and why a mere girl is supposedly flying an aeroplane. Did I expect him to believe that? At this, I give him the aero talk although how much he understands is another matter. During this terse exchange I'm vaguely aware of an unobtrusive presence in this gloomy space, a comely middle-aged woman. Quiet words are spoken.

'She thinks I'm too hard on you.'

'She's right.'

At last he drops all the aggression. 'I'm Lars,' he says, 'and I've been given the job of getting you up close to the wire.'

I nod in relief.

'A lot of arrangements have been made for you, so I hope you're worth it.'

I nod. 'It is important.'

Somewhat grudgingly, he lays out the details. 'You can't get near the wire on foot, a forbidden zone blocks all approaches, roadblocks and patrols are out night and day.' He gives me another glare as if he's still unsure about me. 'You'd never make it on your own, the river is the only way.'

The Meuse, I soon learn, is a busy highway of trade. The Dutch are shipping in desperately needed grain, vegetables and foodstuffs from a humanitarian supply line set up by a group of neutral nations, plus coal, steel and timber of their own. Trade must go on. They need the business, they say, to put bread into the mouths of their children. I'm despatched to a hiding place beneath the floorboards, lying on sacking and covered by a tarpaulin, to evade inspection from German river patrols and any sharp eyes along the shore. By now I should be inured to discomfort, but the past few blissful hours of warmth and repose have weakened my resolve, so I find my new berth hard to take. It's damp and there's enough swell on the river to rock the vessel even at its moorings, causing bilgewater to swill about close by. Pieces of rotting potato from a previous voyage lie scattered in corners, there's a nauseating stink of diesel and oil and I can hear scratching noises not far away. At daybreak the barge casts off and the rhythmic deep chugging noise of the marine engine adds to the ordeal of the next twelve hours. Some time into this I'm allowed up for a brief respite and a sandwich during which I'm on the receiving end of another Lars harangue.

'If we're stopped and searched you stay very quiet.'

I swallow. How many more perils on the way to the wire?

'And if they find you, you're a stowaway,' he says. 'We don't know you and you don't know us. Mind you, we'd be in a heap of trouble, and you...'

He makes a face and doesn't finish the sentence.

Then I'm returned to my dank dungeon and the monotonous thudding continues. When at long last it dies away I anticipate relief, only to hear the high revs of another vessel, then jarring bumps and gruff voices overhead. This is followed by the sound of clattering big boots on the staircase over my head. I curl silently in my corner as an inspection hatch is prized open and from the corners of the tarpaulin I can see a light sweeping around the interior. I dare not move, try not to breathe, fearing at any second some imperious command of discovery. Worse still is the screeching sound of protesting nails as a floorboard is prized up, followed by grunts, heavy breathing and protesting voices. This is it, this is where they get me...

I hold my breath, close my eyes, and earnestly pledge to myself never to utter a caustic word to another soul.

More indistinct sounds, the resounding hammering of restored woodwork, the click of a switch, then darkness restored.

Sometime later I'm allowed up in the cabin again, now that it's night once more. I feel like some prehistoric species emerging from the deep. What a relief it is to feel the fresh night air and see this wide-open waterway and the dark shapes of the trees lining the shore.

We tie up once more and set about cutting reeds which grow in great profusion at the side of the river. These we lace around our shoes and tie with string as a means of deadening the sound of footsteps. From now on, the irascible Lars is my stealthy guide into the forbidden zone. We start off along the towpath but soon branch off. This is the most dangerous part of the journey, moving cautiously across open country. Movement can be detected here even in the dark of a moonless night, even with heavy cloud cover. We walk slowly, stopping every so often to check for movement ahead. The German patrols don't always move. For the same reason they too stand still. Our aim is to keep to the protection of the treeline and the hedges but this is not always possible. We take a tortuous path to avoid known static roadblocks and pace slowly through a small copse. I find it frightening and spooky and the crunch of our shoes over fallen cones seems magnified in the stillness of the night, the reeds having been worn and stripped from our shoes. However, this is the perfect cover, according to my guide. Across a field I almost stumble when a foot snags in a rabbit hole. In the grass we can hear the rustle of small animals – stoats, weasels, voles, hares.

There used to be deer out here, Lars whispers, but 'those bastards' have shot them all. Meat is in short supply.

The wind is getting up and rips through the trees of a second copse, thicker this time, setting off a shrill symphony of whipping leaves while wildly thrashing briars snatch at my face, tearing the fabric of my cape.

Disguise at this point in the journey is pointless. Anyone found in the forbidden zone can expect to be arrested or shot, and possession of a pair of wire cutters is the biggest provocation and telltale of all.

We cross a wide stream and the mud at the bottom clutches at my shoes, trying to suck me in. The wind, which has numbed my ears, suddenly drops and Lars whispers that this is a mixed blessing. The storm stood a good chance of forcing the patrols to take shelter. In the silence we're more cautious and progress is slow. I'm beginning to tire but eventually he points to a hollow in the ground. 'This is it,' he says, 'this is as far as I can take you. The wire is over there, just about a kilometre away.'

These are my instructions: lie up in this hollow until 4am precisely, an hour before the guards change shifts – the time supposedly when they're least alert – then make for the wire in a straight line, using a gulley for cover.

As Lars slips silently away, leaving me alone, I look at my hollow. It has an overhanging cliff of branches and bracken. I settle down as best I can in the dirt. Five hours to wait.

Just then it begins to rain.

The hours pass in tortuous procession. Nothing to read, nothing to do, no movement permitted. And the rain never lets up. Pretty soon the limitations of my little hollow become obvious and water streams down my face. I can feel it dripping off the end of my nose.

At first I'm protected inside my new set of clothing but gradually I feel the clinging coldness of deep saturation, followed by the icy hand of an early morning frost. I'd put great faith in the quality of Marguerite's cast-off grey woollen cape, seen better days but with a full set of buttons and a generous collar turned up against the weather, yet this too eventually succumbs into a sodden deadweight. I pull the foliage of a bush across my trunk, hoping no patrol ventures this way, hoping that they feel as miserable as I – wet, tired and demoralised – but in their case, with the imminent prospect of a warm bunk. With luck, that should keep them preoccupied.

I'm conscious of the smell of wet soil and the sound of dripping vegetation. With time on my hands and the last and most difficult obstacle just ahead, my thoughts take a bizarre turn back to Freys and my treatment there. I think again about the disappointing father figure of Dr Leger and once again find myself blundering about in a fog of conjecture over the continuing mystery of my absent parent. And now my imaginative curiosity takes me to some very strange places. Am I legitimate, or perhaps adopted? I shrug. I'd take illegitimacy in exchange for certainty. In my dripping misery a door opens on more painful speculations. Once I'd been close to the Leger family. Could this man have been more than a friend, in fact my biological parent? The idea, once half formed and vague, is now dismissed. A man diminished, his authority spent, his integrity in question.

Perhaps foolishly, my mind wanders ever more widely, even to Jonathan Cowper, that other benign figure of my early years in whose home I'd been welcome, the man who purchased so many of my paintings, the man whose generosity allowed me to pay both fines incurred at Bury's suffragette rally. I try the idea of pairing my mother up with either of these two men but shake my head. These ruminations, at once absurd but persistent, have a paralysing effect on my state of mind.

In a few hours I'll face my greatest test. Now I worry about the Dutch crew I've been promised. They're set to meet me at the fence. It's crucial they appear at the right place and the right time and I get to wonder about their escape device – an object I'm told will get me across the border, an elaborate piece of woodwork I pray will save my life.

I'm quivering all over. Is this damp or nerves? Will courage fail me at the vital moment of the crossing? I have a great fear of electricity, at the prospect of such an horrific death. I worry too about capture and maltreatment. Then I wonder if you feel the bullet in your back.

I tell myself I'm too young to die.

Three hours to go.

There's no let-up to the misery of the rain as the hours drag by. I'm in a pitiful condition and begin to doubt my ability to make the final run to freedom. I look at my watch for the twentieth time but time stands still. The wind gets up but the rain doesn't ease. Minutes ago I could hear the squeaks and grumbles of the local wildlife, considerably more kitted out for these conditions than I, but now an angry gust is howling through the trees overhead whipping the branches into a dangerous dance. I can hear creaks and groans as ancient boughs threaten to break and crash down on my inadequate hiding place. With a rising sense of alarm I hear something else above the racket of wild nature. Maybe a metallic clink. Maybe the snap of a treading boot? I'm shivering from cold and from the fear of discovery by an enemy search party. Is it instant oblivion – or do you feel the bullet tearing into flesh, slicing through limbs, dismembering you? In my mind's eye I see a group of desperate men, water dripping from their capes, cocking their long rifles, no compassion in their hearts. I'm an active person. This stationary, inert and cramped retreat is utter anathema. Spirits could not be lower. I know that when I emerge from this muddy pit the danger will go sky high.

I clasp sodden hands together and think back over the long trek that has brought me to this place. Vert now seems so very far away, a lost part of my consciousness, almost a lost world. In this dripping hell all ambition, all pretence, all arrogance is seeping away. Lofty notions of a future filled with aviation glory don't seem to matter anymore. I'm left with a single strand of hope. If there is to be a future it is for friendship, recognising that I've been reckless with my most loyal supporter, the selfless rock who's backed me all the way. Scott deserves better than how I've treated him and now I'm ready to reciprocate. He deserves recognition, loyalty, commitment. This trek has demonstrated more than any other how threadbare life is when conducted alone.

I think again with a shiver of apprehension of that electrified horror and decide that if, in a few hours' time, fate allows me to cross safely with just one wish – just one – which is it to be?

No contest! After all, he and I have so many things in common.

It's time. A final check on the watch, then I creep forward in the gulley, bent low, praying my blackened outline will be lost to any watching eye. The closer to the wire I get the more likely is the prospect of interception. The border guards patrol the fence with orders to shoot to kill without question. I keep by the trees and stop every few minutes to listen, but can detect no follower or direct threat. Still, I have the feeling they're shadowing me, that they know I'm here, that my arrival at the fence is entirely expected. An ambush... will they pounce or shoot? The chaotic sense of panic, the terror of the hunted prey, is in full flood.

Nearer now, a faint outline up ahead, the silence of the night broken only by the patter of raindrops on my clothing. I skirt a strange rectangular shape that might be an old shelter and then, as I round the corner, something creaks.

I freeze, a pain shooting through my chest. A door has opened and a figure is standing stock-still, barring my way. I must look the frightened rabbit caught in the glare of a spotlight. I certainly feel the frightened rabbit. And then, despite the gloom, I recognise the figure. I'd know that lopsided leer anywhere.

I'm utterly aghast. It's him, the spy. My betrayer, my most detested individual. It's Hugo Bernard.

CHAPTER THIRTY-ONE

For the moment my brain is as frozen as my movement, then some mental cog clicks into gear. Don't wait for the detested turncoat to speak, I tell myself, don't give him the chance to dictate the pace of what happens next. Seize the moment! I have my plan. I'm grinning madly but behind my back nails are digging into the flesh of a painful palm. I'm back in control, I'm past his power of intimidation and I step forward, suddenly flinging up outstretched arms.

'Hugo!' I say. It comes out like a damp croak in the eerie silence of this hour. 'Thank goodness, it's you!'

'Hello, Charlotte,' he says and it's impossible to read the tone. Not menacing, not friendly, just neutral.

My mouth is a pit of bile. This pretence is acid to the heart. There's every reason to treat him with disgust. To demand why he's betrayed me and the network, to denounce him for turning traitor to his own people, to accuse him of cowardice.

I come up close. Rain streaks my face, everything drenched, feeling wretched, but I force the biggest smile of my life and fake relief and joy. 'So you made it out! Brilliant! What a coup!'

His face is still a mask bereft of reaction. I stare into it. I examine the eyes of the betrayer and try to read what lies behind. Is he still the egotist of old – still full of himself, playing to the self image of the big personality always in command? Or do I detect a glimmer of guilt or uncertainty?

He has his arms firmly around me and I pretend to be relieved and pleased to see him. 'I thought they'd got you,' I say. 'Only just escaped myself.' While murmuring this I wonder how it is that he's managed to position himself right at the key point of my crossing. Then I remember. Of course! He's done it before, this is the best crossing point on the frontier, he's anticipated me, he's been lying in wait, another ambush, just like the churchyard back at Bouillon.

'This is wonderful,' I murmur. 'That we've met up again.' And trying for my plan: 'We can go across together.'

I see a twitch in his left eye. Is this a prelude to violence? I have no illusions that I can prevail in a physical struggle and I realise with an increasing sense of despair that this plan to play him is naive. He's playing me and I realise with a sudden dread that now I'll never get across that wire. How bitter that my nemesis should be this man with blood on his hands – already responsible for God knows how many deaths and others still to come. How desperate to be defeated by such a person, that it has come to this.

In the distance I can hear the barking of a dog, so perhaps he has already alerted the guards. How foolish of me to think I could get across. Common sense should have told me this was always one challenge too far.

Somewhere a searchlight is switched on. Will there be shots to follow? I close my eyes in surrender. So this is the end of it all. A feeling of total desolation overcomes me. That it has all been for nothing, all the sacrifice, the pain, the ordeal. They warned me, back at Vert, but I didn't listen. I slump in utter desolation. It's my collapse at the end of a long and tortuous road. I cannot fight it any longer. Wet, fatigued, scared, hungry. I admit it to myself. I've come to the end of the road. This man is blocking me and very soon half the German Army will arrive to complete my humiliation. What can I do?

And Bernard confirms it, whispering quietly into my ear: 'Sorry, Charlotte, I can't let you go over.'

CHAPTER THIRTY-TWO

Bernard is making soothing noises, has me clutched in his arms, and I have my eyes closed, as if to shut out the humiliation of surrender.

'So glad to have found you,' he says, 'and don't worry, I'll look after you, you don't need to go over that wire.'

Even in my state of near collapse something jars about these words. Didn't he once promise to get me out of the country; to get me over that wire into the safety of neutral Holland?

'We can't go over,' he says, 'we have more work to do here.' He grips my hands. 'Hold still, we must think this through. Going over is foolish. You could get shot. Better this side, this side of the wire is safest.'

Suddenly, the sheer duplicity of these words brings me up short, brings me to my senses. Why give in to such a liar? Isn't he just about to hand me over to the enemy?

He says: 'We'll do much better work this side of the wire.'

I open my eyes and stare into the face of treachery. This devious little trickster whose self-confessed pleasures are fraud and betrayal is now grinning in triumph at his latest victim. Me.

This is the moment the spark returns. No, I decide, I won't cave in.

For some seconds I remain submissive, reviewing the situation. I don't have much time. His new friends are closing in, I need to act now and I need to act fast. And just when I need it most inspiration comes to my rescue.

I wrench free from his grasp and sprint for the wire. 'Got to get over,' I cry over my shoulder. 'Got a big secret to tell.'

He's recovering from his surprise, pounding after me, demanding I return and Marguerite's old cape is slowing me down. He reaches out and yanks me to a standstill. Face to face in the shadow of the wire. I can see the line of the fence now in my peripheral vision and I know I need to outfox the fox, to deceive the arch-deceiver.

'We must get back,' I say, emphasising the first person plural, as if I'm still convinced we're on the same side. 'Such a lot to tell. Got word from the networks. A whole lot more to come.'

His arm is clutching mine but I can read uncertainty. 'More?' His brow furrows.

I'm convinced now I've got it right; my insight into the devious workings of this duplicitous mind. I can see the cunning little weasel running to catch up. 'Word is,' I say breathlessly, 'another big Allied push is on the way and more agents will be coming down the pipeline.'

'How d'you know this?'

'Explain later, but come on! We need to get across.'

He's weighing up his options: either turn me in to play whatever game he's set up with the enemy – or go for the bigger stakes, a return with me to the Allied side to score a major espionage coup and gain even greater glory. The ace double agent. The man with the biggest pot of gold.

Time to clinch it! I tilt my head to one side, look imploringly into those Judas eyes, try not to spit and in its place project an adoring and admiring gaze. 'You're a hero back in Blighty, Hugo, a real hero. They'll be delighted you've made it out. That you've come good on the King's award. Living up to your gong and that mighty reputation of yours.'

Does he have a hand on a whistle in his pocket? Will he summon the grey uniforms, the precursors to the firing squad? Which way is this going to go?

'Who's telling you all this stuff?'

'Network Matteo.'

'Never heard of 'em!'

'You surely will.' I smile knowingly. 'They're big round here. And fired up with all the messages they've received.'

'What is this information exactly? You must tell me.'

'Not now. No time. When we get to the other side.'

'I must know, I'm head of network, I decide if it's right to cross.'

'Course it's right to cross.' I register his uncertainty, clock the mental battle going on behind the eyes. Keep going, an inner voice yells, ladle it on, convince him I'm totally trusting, that I still believe in him. I must banish all his suspicions and doubts, so I touch his face gently in a fake gesture of emotion and relief. What an actor I've become!

'Big reception for you,' I say. 'More gongs at the Palace, shouldn't wonder.'

He looks at me closely, clearly surprised that I don't know of his duplicity, awash with the possibilities. At first, I can see he's ready to go with it, to return with me and play the double agent in London, but he's still conflicted. What will his German masters make of his absence? Will they think he's still on their side, or will they conclude that he's fled? What's he got to lose? I'm conscious of the battle going on inside his head. He's torn. He draws in a deep breath and looks uncertainly in the direction of his approaching 'friends' while releasing his grip. Even if he blows his whistle – or whatever alarm he's arranged – I'm banking on making it over before any guards arrive.

'Can't stand here talking,' I say and resume my run for the fence. Once again, he's grumbling, lagging. Round a corner the path divides. I take a right fork, veering off from my original trajectory, past some bushes before the ground opens out. And there it is, just ahead, in all its ugliness. Three lines of wire. In the middle is the barbed one, the deadly one loaded with 2,000 volts. Thousands have already died there.

A hand is waving a white piece of cloth. My rescuers.

Two huddled figures lying low on the far side, stationed just as they said they would, ready to get me through.

I veer to a stop, happy to register that Bernard is not behind. Must have taken the wrong fork in the path. I have my clippers out to start snipping at the first line of wire, the one without the power, but hesitate. Something has just come under the fence, some sort of package done up in string, then I spot the long pole that has delivered it.

'Put them on,' says a voice from across the wire. 'Rubber boots, coat and gloves.'

I check behind. No Bernard. I rip off the string and pull on the boots.

'Get rid of that old cape,' says the voice. 'It's wet. It's lethal.'

I'm into the new coat and gloves just as a panting Bernard arrives, desperate at having taken the long way round.

'Stop! I can't let you go. Must stay with me!' He's grabbing at my left arm but I still have the clippers in my right. They have a sharp edge. I'll use it if I have to.

I shrug him off and start on the wire. Snip, snip, snip. 'I thought you were in on this,' I say, 'but if you're not, if you've given up on the network...'

'I haven't. But hold still, we must think this through. Going over is silly, you could get shot. Better this side, this side is safest.'

I ignore this. 'You coming?'

Hugo is still torn by uncertainty. He's not sure which way to turn as I get ready for the next move, the deadliest part of the crossing.

'Hurry, hurry!' voices issue from the other side and I crouch down to get my first glimpse of the magical escape machine. I've been assured that an insulated expanding mechanism will force the electrified wires of the fence apart sufficient to create a space to climb through. Six pieces of wonderful wood are arranged with slots and rubber grooves to fit the electrified wire; side pieces are set to expand to push out the wires and create the escape channel.

This is my live-or-die moment. I can hear the expander stretching the wires, forcing them apart. I clench a fist in tension as I register the creaking, straining and groaning strands while the hole gets bigger and bigger. I can hardly breathe as the gap expands. Will it really be large enough?

'Why are there two of you?' questions the voice on the other side.

I ignore it, hoist myself across the first obstacle and concentrate on the size of the clearance in the centre section, praying for it to grow. 'Take care,' warns the Dutch voice. 'Keep well clear of the wires.'

As I turn to head through to Holland and freedom, Bernard is also clambering across the first fence and tries to pull me back. I flick the snips at him, catching his hand. He cries out, releasing his grip and I go gingerly and oh-so-very carefully through the centre gap, holding my breath, fearing a killer flash.

Halfway through I can feel a hand clutching my leg, pulling me back.

'Get off!' I scream.

This bloody man, this crazy Judas! This is desperate.

'D'you want to kill us both?'

He must have let go in alarm because the pressure is off and now I'm through.

On the other side I see the third line, the Dutch wire, is already cut, ready for me to pass.

So now I'm safe and raise a fist. Then I turn to face Bernard. He's still reaching through, trying to grab my arm, trying to pull me back. 'No, Charlotte,' he says, 'come back, we should collect more intelligence, cross later, send a pigeon.'

I explode with anger. 'The Pigeon Man's gone, been arrested, there are no more pigeons.' I keep my eyes on him, holding his gaze. 'Well? Are you coming through?'

This is the moment of truth. If he crosses into Holland I'll denounce him as a traitor, but if he stays he's a threat to what's left of the network – the postmistress and other survivors of Cicero still unknown to me. I can't let him go. The men at Vert were right. This is war, you can't play soft. I hold my nerve. I'm ready. I know what has to be done. I'm fully committed to the cause.

Still holding his gaze, my hands creep up the sides of the big wooden device and wrap around the hinges.

His arm is still reaching out for me.

'Careful,' warns the Dutch voice once more.

It's finally time to be plain with my nemesis, to give him a chance for honesty, his last and final moment to confess. 'What's the matter, Hugo, what's bothering you, time to tell me, time to be honest, what's this all about?'

He's swallowing, chewing, still conflicted.

'Why, Hugo, why, tell me that. Is it about your old mum?'

There's a strange look in the eyes I haven't seen before.

'No,' he says, still reaching for me, 'but you must come back with me.' His words tumble out in a spate of desperate urgency.

'I'm also on to something big, back here, this side of the wire, before you go we should investigate, another great prize for us...'

The final closing of the circle, the final deceit, the last lie. Even if he's protecting the old lady I can't allow him to do so at the cost of lives and a massive betrayal. This is the moment both Scott and the adjutant Gambier warned me about. No court of appeal, no quarter given.

'Hurry,' a voice repeats behind me.

'You've brought this on yourself,' I tell Bernard, silently stating that what I am now about to do is harsh but necessary. No need to debate. No need to hesitate.

I release my grip on the hinges of the escape device and flick the side struts free, instantly collapsing the frame.

There's a blinding flash, a huge arcing light bright enough to be a lightning strike, accompanied by a searing animal wail, as the electrified wire twangs down from the frame and strikes his arm. It seems to burn him apart, blasting and contorting him.

I look away, no wish to see the burns, the scorched flesh and the tortured limbs as the body falls back into the no man's land between the lines of the frontier wire.

CHAPTER THIRTY-THREE

W e're in a room somewhere, I assume it's the British Legation, or perhaps it's just some hangout for spies. I've gleaned the fact that Holland is a hotbed of espionage, mostly of the British variety, so that figures. There's a portrait of the King looking glum and doleful above a mantelpiece and several armchairs filled with a group of silent people. They seem to be staring at me, as if waiting for some kind of pronouncement. I'm aware of a trance-like quality to this occasion, as if I'm frozen, like I'm outside of myself, that this is not really me, just a person looking on as a spectator. That wasn't the real Charlotte Dovedale out there on the wire who just despatched the duplicitous Bernard. That was some escaped person. It had to be done, of course, no question, I absolve her of blame.

I've glided rather than walked into this room and now I take note of the faces: there's my big supporter from Whitehall, Waterman. Doesn't strike me as strange that he's here; quite logical, in fact, since he had a hand in sending me to Vert and Scott made some mysterious reference to his involvement. But talking of Scott – there he is! Now that is a surprise. How could he know when and where I was coming out? Then, to my left, another shock. My brother. I had expected some kind of welcoming committee but this is quite a turnout.

I look long and hard at Marcus and note that Brother Dear appears bothered and uncertain, as he usually is whenever we meet these days.

I shake my head, trying to clear the fustiness. Something else begins to bother me. Scott's expression.

No welcoming smile, no happy greeting. No glad to see you're okay, more one of horrified shock, an expression that says that while this person he's staring at may look like the Charlotte he once knew it really isn't her. That he might shrink away at any moment without a single word of greeting. That he and I are to be in a state of estrangement. His mouth is open, his finger pointing. 'You...'

I nod. 'Yes.'

'Deliberately! You did it deliberately. You executed that man. You meant it.'

'Yes.'

He shrugs disbelieving shoulders.

'Because he deserved it, that's why.'

Scott turns away as if he doesn't want to continue this conversation and his lack of recognition of my predicament is raising the temperature. Back there at the frontier wire I was as cold and wet as an Arctic whale, but right now my inner temperature is soaring. Getting very close to boiling point. But before I can react there's a cough from the older man and I turn my attention to Waterman.

He says, 'Quite apart from what's just transpired at the crossing, there's something I want to say.'

I wait for it. What now? More condemnation, more accusation?

259

'It's only fair to record that we owe you a massive apology,' he says.

I blink.

'We left you all alone to do what you had to do without any help or assistance from us, totally dependent on your own resources. To get to this point is an amazing achievement and we're sorry we couldn't do more. At one point we did consider putting a man in to help...'

I interrupt. 'No! Would have been a disaster,' I say, 'only made matters worse. Turned Kruger even more brutal, caused more trouble for the people in the village, my best hope was staying invisible.'

He agrees. 'That was our conclusion too. Another landing behind the lines might just have been possible but would have been far too dangerous, given that the enemy would have been alive, ready and waiting for it.'

At this I feel slightly mollified. Some sort of recognition at last – but how can they be so short on understanding?

Then, another voice, another turn of the screw.

'I have to say,' says the new voice, 'this is all very well but we still have a major problem with you.'

I swivel and identify the speaker. It's Huckerbee, my Mr Reluctant from Vert Galant, the man from the shadows and the little secrets hut. And he isn't looking any more thrilled to see me now than on the night he allowed me to take off in the Parasol with the spy on board.

He steps forward, eyes blazing, pointing an accusing finger. There's going to be no apologies from this source. A small bead of sweat has just appeared on his brow.

'Do you realise what you've just done?' he asks in a hectoring tone, and he doesn't wait for my reply.

'You've just terminated our very best agent. A man who was precious gold!'

CHAPTER THIRTY-FOUR

Momentarily, I'm taken aback and before any more accusations can fly Waterman steps in with a softer, more considered tone.

'You don't actually know that, Jon.'

I clench my fists. I'm not having any of this. What do they know? 'Precious gold?' I shake my head. 'An agent who's just been responsible for rolling up the whole network,' I say with some vigour. 'The Pigeon Man's been arrested and the rest of us only just got out in time. We were on his list for betrayal. The man's a killer. A traitor. A turncoat. Some best agent!'

From the corner of my eye I can see Scott's shocked expression at my continued vehemence and the way I'm addressing government VIPs. After what I've been through I have no fear and no deference left in my locker.

'You can't possibly know all the circumstances,' says Huckerbee. 'There could be other explanations for the arrests. You can't be sure that what you think has happened is an actual established fact. You're not in a position to know the complete picture.'

I hit back. 'And you are?' I snort at him. 'You were sitting under the hedge at the church when the nasties turned up, when Bernard was planning to ambush me and get me arrested by the enemy?'

'Maybe other explanations... And now we'll never know.'

'I'll tell you what you need to know. The explanation?' I don't disguise my disgust. 'The explanation was deceit.' I positively shout the last word, careless of who's listening. 'The Judas thing of selling out his own friends and greed at the fees he was being paid. You've misjudged your man. What he wanted was to set himself up in a nice way of business.'

'But he brought you all the way to the fence, got you out...'

'He didn't!'

Huckerbee is still shaking his head. 'We were notified, rather late in the day, I have to say, by our sources that you were safe with friends.'

I laugh. 'Safe?' Time to give it to them straight. 'My friends were in a funk over getting caught and couldn't wait to get rid of me. And back at Bouillon, you didn't get any messages because Bernard or his new pals killed all the birds. I saw the carcases myself.' I take a breath. 'I've had some help from people along the way and I'm grateful, but mostly I've got here by myself. Been on the trek almost from the moment we landed.'

There's a long silence at this. It's obvious. Huckerbee is the worker bee but Waterman, who's keeping silent, is the man in charge, quietly weighing up the situation, assessing both the damage and the value of his agent whose life I've just extinguished on the wire. But I'm past caring about their concerns. Now that I've achieved sufficient allegiance to the cause of total war to be able to commit the ultimate act of ending a life, a deed I once thought was beyond me, I'm certainly not going to be worried because this has upset the plans of some government department... I draw another long breath. Perhaps they're thinking of having me charged with murder. The idea seems both absurd and possible all at the same time and in this mood I'm not sure I give a damn. This whole experience seems weird. Perhaps my impetus to truculence is the natural aftermath of hostile action.

Waterman retreats to some chairs and says in an even quieter tone: 'Perhaps we should sit.'

Scott and I join him. It's a rather self-conscious moment. I don't know quite what to expect. I look at Waterman inquiringly. I study his features, still a pleasant open face that seems comfortable and untroubled by its place in the world, despite the fraught atmosphere of the last few minutes. I also look at the well-cut suit, a small red smudge just above his stiff white collar and a rather flamboyant blue bow tie. These are features which I might sketch later from memory.

'Yes,' he says, 'on reflection I think we can put this unfortunate business behind us. You may be right. You've been up close with this man and we should take your assessment of his true character as being the more realistic.'

I give him a non-committal nod. The full import of what I have just done will sink in later, as will realisation of my escape from its consequences.

Later I find myself sitting alone with Scott. Perhaps they've arranged it. I make direct eye contact and hold his stare. It's my challenge to him: say what you have to say!

He looks as if he's seeing a stranger, an enigma he can't quite fathom. He sighs and murmurs in a quiet tone: 'I never thought...'

'That I had it in me?' I interrupt.

'That you could.'

'It's your strategy!' I say hotly. 'What you were all asking me way back. Was I truly aggressive and prepared for war? And then at Vert you told me I had what it took. And to expect ruthlessness on the ground, remember?'

'Yes, but their ruthlessness, not yours.'

'I couldn't let him go. No choice! He wasn't coming over to us and I couldn't allow him to go back and cause more mayhem.' I hold Scott's stare. 'You should be pleased. I'm cured of my inhibitions. I can fight the war now like anyone else. And anyway...' I shrug. It may have looked like a petulant gesture. 'The spy would have been a dead man if he had come over to us, denounced as a traitor, so I've simply saved the hangman a job.'

At this Scott looks even more shocked. Visibly shrinking in distaste. Even as I say it, I feel like a spectator to the conversation, fascinated by the spectacular demonstration of hard-faced cruelty that this version of Charlotte Dovedale is giving. And I watch, equally fascinated but also with increasing regret, as my hopes of a blossoming relationship melt away with every blunt and brutal word issued from this mouth.

Later I'm in a room with a healthy fire in the grate and a huge sofa, left to my own devices while Waterman is apparently busy on the telegraph to London warning them to break off all contact with Network Cicero and not to send them any more pigeons. I think about those poor birds, the ones we dumped by the side of the stranded Parasol and feel guilty that we left them to starve and die. Just one more example, I know, of my tendency to irrelevant thought at times of crisis. Then I think about Waterman. Who is he exactly, why is he here, what does a civilian ministry man have to do with spies? Scott, somewhat reluctantly, has supplied some of the answers, mostly in a confidential whisper in defiance of yet more regulations. The Department of Information, it seems, is a somewhat shadowy and insubstantial institution. Perhaps a sideline, one might say politely – a sideline of a much more significant, if equally shadowy, organisation.

'Waterman is C.'

I shake my head in puzzlement.

'He's Control.'

'Of what?'

A hesitation, a second's silence, then a reluctance overcome. 'Thought you would have guessed. His Majesty's Secret Service Bureau.'

'Aha! I see. And now you're also part of this... bureau?'

But Scott looks away, as if enough has been said.

This warming fire, so comforting now that I've dried out after all the hours spent in the rain, seems like a gross indulgence. Such inaction contrasts with the chase, the stress and the peril of my journey, and now that I've managed the great escape I ask myself, what do I feel? I'm still stricken by an immense sadness that was precious to me, the relationship with Scott and its hopeful signals of a bright future now seems in severe jeopardy. He sees only the hard crust I present to this new world, but I know that taking a life will leave a mark on me. I'm never going to forget. I'll live out my days with the recurring image of that body falling back into the wire. Perhaps I'll make two separate compartments in my head; one labelled Justified, the other marked Remorse.

Later there's a stuttering conversation with my brother. When Marcus tells me my mother has been concerned about my absence and is relieved I'm free, I can't repress the retort: 'My goodness, has the world turned on its axis?'

Marcus also seems shell-shocked about something else, telling me that Waterman has something personal – 'something very personal' – to tell me and makes his excuses. He won't enlarge.

Someone else walking out on the hard-shell Charlotte. Perhaps Waterman too is shocked by the new me.

I shall see.

CHAPTER THIRTY-FIVE

Waterman has returned from his urgent tasks in the communications room and is now all attentive and concerned for my welfare. He hopes I'm comfortable and that I'm getting over my sense of shock, though he says it may take some time to recover from the ordeal. What's more, he's going to fix me up with somewhere quiet for a few days. 'Lots of relaxation and stress-free comfort,' he says with a grin.

I'm overcome by all this solicitude and my suspicions are up and crackling. As he sits back into the depths of the sofa I stare at that mark on his neck and there's something about it that disturbs me. Some little hint from the past that's niggling at me.

'They say you've got some sort of news for me,' I begin. 'My brother seems a bit put out by something. Maybe it's just me.' I shrug and look at him expectantly.

He smiles back and nods. 'I hope that what I'm about to tell you isn't too much of a shock. You've had enough of that already.'

'I'm not a delicate wallflower,' I snap. 'Haven't I proved that?'

'Indeed you have. And I want to tell you that I'm very proud and impressed by what you've achieved.'

I can feel a frown forming. This stuff doesn't sound like the sort of chat you expect from a Whitehall mandarin or a boss man of any kind. Sounds far too... I strain for the right word, then it comes: mumsy.

'We've been keeping a careful eye on you,' he says. 'And on reflection, I think you're right about Bernard. I have to confess we were worried about him, had our doubts about him, and when you two went missing there was a problem.

'You see, you're very special to us. We've tried supporting you in any way we can. I've talked to your brother about this as well.'

My brow furrows. I can feel the heat rising. I'm beginning to steam, wondering if this is the helping hand I've always suspected was at work; how my rejection at the War Office turned suddenly into the newspaper opportunity afforded by this man. 'Please!' I demand, 'where is this going?'

He's smiling at me and changes tack: 'Have you ever wondered about your father?'

'Frequently. In fact, all the time.'

He's regarding me with the sort of gentle, benign and appreciative smile that has little to do with a high official of the Department of Information or of this strange new nomenclature of C. Now he's nodding at me, a picture of indulgence, and murmurs: 'Surely, by now, you've guessed it.'

And finally the penny drops with an almighty clang.

Now I remember old George's description of a tall, distinguished, well-spoken man.

And that damned birthmark on his neck.

For a long while I stare blank-faced at him, at that birthmark, feeling just as shocked now as when it first dawned on me seven searing days ago that I was stranded behind enemy lines. He's regarding me gently, saying nothing, and I begin to feel foolish. Very foolish, given all the clues that are now falling into place: tall, distinguished, well-spoken, slightly bald, the birthmark. How could I not have put it together?

Then the anger flares. How could he do this to me? All these years... all these frustrating years when I questioned my own identity. Who was I, really? Where did I come from; where was I going in life, what's my destiny? Not knowing was a mystery I did not enjoy. My brother had even less idea, being that much younger than I, and this I regarded – still regard – as a form of torture, as nothing short of gross parental neglect.

'You've told my brother?' This is my first spoken reaction.

He nods and I wonder why Marcus has said nothing to me. Perhaps he, too, is awash with confusion and uncertainty.

'You got my letters?' I blurt, before thinking this question through.

'Letters?' He's frowning now.

Of course he didn't get my letters. Those childhood missives to a mysteriously absent father figure, yearning for the day when he would get in touch. *'If you're reading this...'* And then the imaginary conversations with the missing parent and the fantasy answers that came back: heroic, adulatory, enviable images of knights and statesmen and national leaders. Of course he didn't get my letters, because to whom could I send them?

He sees my confusion and begins a softly-spoken explanation. 'I anticipated you'd be shocked and probably angry and I've been trying to figure out a way of breaking it to you gently.'

'Why now?' I interject.

He sighs. 'This has gone on long enough.'

'You're right there.'

'I can't keep up this pretence, of sitting back and watching the progress of you and your brother from afar.'

'But why? Why the absence, why the mystery?'

Another deep sigh. 'Your mother and I... we were not suited... in truth, we should never have been together. It was constant war between us. I don't know how we thought it would work. Completely different backgrounds, the relationship was a disaster from first to last. The only thing we could agree on was not to make the children a battleground.' He looks at me, defensive now, almost seeking sympathy. 'This was the one thing we agreed. That it was best not to bring you up in a severely divisive household. A clean break with no emotional fallout. Not allowing the children to be made pawns in some horrible domestic warfare.'

Is this really true? 'But you liked dancing,' I insist, 'I know you did, I heard about it.'

He gives a rueful smile. 'Conflict temporarily suspended in favour of the foxtrot.'

I'm growing impatient with this. Years of frustration and anger erupt. 'So you think disappearing from our lives was the right decision, cutting yourself off from us, denying your very existence?' I'm aware my voice is rising. 'Why? Isn't it normal to want to care for your children? Nurture and oversee their formative years? Have you no paternal instinct? What was wrong with us... were we defective in some way? I suppose we must just have been some unfortunate unintended accident. Makes us feel like rejects.'

'Your mother insisted. It had to be a complete break. That was the agreement.'

'You could have got in touch later. When we were old enough to be adult about it.' I'm conscious of breathing heavily but carry on: 'I can tell you, when you don't know who you really are, you feel there's a great chasm, a great hole in your life, as if you might be anybody, you might be the daughter of some really dreadful evil person, a mass murderer...'

'Hopefully not,' he says.

I persist: 'I had all these horrific ideas when Mother wouldn't open up. My imagination... it just took off.'

'I'm so sorry about that.'

'But why wait so long? Until now? I'm twenty, you could have told me four, six, maybe ten years ago. This is an abrogation of responsibility. Don't you realise the damage you've done? Watching us from afar, it's unnatural, like some voyeur...'

He seems to be shrugging off my display of hostility. Perhaps he expects it. He says how pleased he is with my progress into adulthood, how it confirms his sense of a family strength of purpose.

I can no longer relate to this man. Before I perceived him as benign. Now he is revealed as the monster who's ruined my childhood and I challenge him on legitimacy. Was there a marriage?

'Oh yes,' he says with a sigh, 'and there was also a divorce, all conducted in secret to save her from any shame.'

'Your shame as well,' I say hotly. 'But why is there nothing in the public record? Or the census. I know, I searched. Nothing except a blank on my birth certificate where your name should be.'

For a moment he looks a touch embarrassed. 'I have to admit I did make use of my position as head of this bureau. As a special arm of the state, we do have rather extensive powers and a capacity to – shall we say? – to adjust the public record and to make inconvenient facts go away.'

I'm taken aback by the sheer effrontery of this admission.

'But why get together with Mother in the first place?' There's a taste of acid on my tongue. 'A very strange union.'

A shrug, even a slight grin. 'I really don't know. We never really hit it off. From different worlds. She was petty bourgeoisie... not me at all. I suppose we were just young and stupid.'

I think back to my childhood, still seething over the deceit of it all. How we children had to say that our father was dead so that she could maintain her pose to business associates as the plucky little widow still carrying on in trade. Both Marcus and I understood this to be a lie of respectability to engage friends and neighbours.

I sniff. 'When you've got a mother like mine,' I say, 'you want to know about your roots. You worry about your roots! Could be that's why I find engaging with some people difficult. Not knowing all these years, it's like an open sore, I don't think I'll ever forgive you for that.'

I'm being spoilt. Recovery leave for a week in a luxurious bungalow looking out on what's probably the only upward slope in Holland, topped by a line of cedar trees, and a woman who comes in twice a day to cook my meals. I lounge in a chair in glorious static indolence with the added luxury of the soothing ministrations of a chiropodist for my wrecked feet. I don't feel ill and the sense of being outside myself has disappeared, though I can't get out of mind the image of Bernard's body flailing away from that electrified wire. Maybe I'll never get over it. Maybe, after this, I'll never be sure of the person I am.

Waterman, who has revealed his true name to be Willoughby Munroe-Carter, is still on hand and I have a clutch of visitors.

First, a long talk with Brother Dear who fills me in on his exploits and the nation's pioneering attempt at an aircraft carrier. Taking off from the static tower on a ship at sea – now that's a dare, for sure, and so too is landing in the sea and trusting to the ship's crane to hook you back on board. I take my hat off to my brother and we're all pals again. I can see he's as shell-shocked as me by the revelation of Waterman's paternity. It's too soon, too raw, too indigestible to know how we feel. I'm still angry with the man for the damage he's done not only to my childhood but to Marcus. My brother is two years younger and has always been needy, a mother's boy. He's the centre of her attention and she is his. Confusion and resentment are now writ large on his face. Who is this strange man who's butted in on our lives?

'Odd feeling,' Marcus says, 'to discover that he's got a whole different family out there. Three daughters... strange!'

'Three stepsisters,' I say.

'Can't say I really warm to him.'

It's clear to me. Marcus perceives Waterman at a subconscious level as a threat, perhaps fearing that Mother may go off with him, perhaps a rival for her undivided affection. We don't speak of it much. Instead, he insists I should visit her as soon as I hit Bury.

I consider the prospect of reconciliation with Mother. Maybe the ship trick would be easier.

Next day Katie Snow springs a big surprise. She arrives dressed in a spanking new matron's uniform. Wow! Working-class girl made good, and she's rightly proud of her achievement in a forward military hospital. It's validating the efforts of women in this war, she says. 'And they won't be able to refuse us the vote after this little lot!' And who can disagree?

There's going to be big changes after this war, whenever that glad day arrives. When she's gone I think about Bury and images of Guildhall Street and Tenement Row come to mind. How small and confined they seem! I'm not sure I can return after this.

Waterman is back. My anger towards him has cooled and he gives me an update on the wreckage of Network Cicero. The baker Henri Dufour has resurfaced in another village and made contact, but the postmistress has been pulled in by the Germans. However, word is that she's completely confounded them by refusing to speak in anything but an incomprehensible local dialect and they've let her go. It seems von Kruger is cracking down even harder on the villagers at Bouillon and I vow to myself that one day, if I ever get the chance after the war, I'll wreak vengeance on this particular tyrant.

Waterman is still apologetic about my time spent on the run. 'I feel really bad about our inactivity on this,' he says.

I shrug. 'It was just not knowing. That was the devil.'

He nods, contrite. 'Must say I regret this whole business, sending you off to Vert, should have known you'd fall prey to temptation. A mad keen airwoman was never likely to stay a spectator for ever.'

I smile at this, surprised at his lack of reproach, but he's clearly feeling something approaching guilt about the whole business of sending in people to spy behind the lines, given the appalling conditions of the occupation. 'Must say, I shudder every time I think about those poor people who have to live there. I hate to imagine what it must feel like to have soldiers billeted in your house, invading every room, stealing your prize possessions, violating the most treasured places, carrying off food and wine.' He sighs. 'I tried to imagine it happening to my own village, my daughters in constant peril, my wife's jewellery snatched, the hearth and home invaded. A nightmare vision of booted oafs slouching in my rosewood armchairs, vandalising my treasured collection of timepieces...'

That's when I hear about the treasures of the Waterman household: an Empire clock with figures representing Justice sitting between Slavery and Liberty, and the bronze-and-gilt piece with the Father Time figure.

'Best thing,' I say, 'win the war and kick out the enemy.'

However, when Scott comes to say farewell I'm a lot less sure of myself. He's returning to some other duty, whatever that might be, and I feel intensely frustrated that events have soured our friendship; that my reaction to his advice at Vert is the very thing that's driven a wedge between us. He's no longer accusative. Says, 'I want to stress how very sorry I am for my reaction yesterday.'

I realise I'm blinking a lot and having trouble swallowing. He's been my mentor, supporter, loyal acolyte, my right arm. His turning against me sends a prickle of pain shooting under my eyelids.

He shrugs another apology. 'It was a surprise – but I can see it now. What you did was an operational necessity. It had to be done.' He looks at me earnestly and adds: 'Being put in that situation must have been truly awful. The hardest test anyone could face. Amply proves your mettle.'

I want to tell him that my hard shell is just a defence mechanism, a protection against personal collapse triggered by guilt. At least, that's how Waterman explains it. And I want to say that he – Scott – is still a prisoner of his own primitive preconceptions of how a woman should act in the 20th century; that if he's a fighter then so am I.

But I'm too choked to say any of this.

'I've got to get back,' he says, glancing toward the door. Is this the end? Are all those sunlit dreams of a bright relationship to evaporate on the rocks of this new reality? A golden future done to dust? I'm wishing fervently that he'd cool off, think better of me, and return. My eyes implore him: don't throw away this bond, don't desert me now.

There's a silence between us.

What's it to be? He doesn't say.

Instead, he wishes me all the best but I can see he's shrinking away. I hold tight on to my chair, clutching the back to maintain control.

Maybe one day, his expression says, and slips quietly from my life.

Some time later Waterman reappears to talk about my future. I almost spit at this but manage to stay civil. He doesn't know that my most precious hopes have just walked out of the door. Life has delivered another bouquet of thorns. How will Waterman's ideas of the future shape up against this experience? Surely, an enormous anticlimax! Perhaps I'll spend the rest of my days looking back in regret.

Waterman – I can't yet think of him in more familial terms – is being brightly conversational and talks about his home and everyday things. I wonder about his daughters. Might I get to meet them? I breathe in uncertainly, not quite sure how to cope with the idea of having three stepsisters. I know this doesn't appeal to Brother Dear, but I'm beginning to soften toward this man and his engaging descriptions of life at the big house deep in the Sussex countryside. I can't yet bring myself to say, or even think the word *father* and I'm still annoyed about his long silence through all the barren years of my life, but he is doing his best to wrap me in a welcoming, sympathetic and caring embrace. As I said once before, a modern man.

Beyond the unfortunate history of his relationship with my mother, and here I instinctively place myself in his corner, I can't really see another fault to find. Perhaps, in time, I will get to forgive him his long absence.

He's also being encouraging about what happens next. 'You've so many talents in your locker,' he says, and tells me how pleased *The Planet* is with my supply of human-interest stories on the ordinary men and women caught up in the war. 'Just their cup of tea, they love it,' he says. 'And you'll have a big hit with this story, that's for sure. A bright future there, if you want it!'

I shrug. I've come down off my high, struggling with the awful memory of my action at the electrified fence, feeling anything but bright or optimistic. Waterman is also talking about flying and how no blame attaches to me for losing the Parasol in Belgium. 'Could happen to anyone. Always an unknown quantity, landing behind the lines.' He clasps his hands in a gesture of encouragement. 'A flyer of great ability and a specialist with the Morane Parasol. Think pilot instructor,' he suggests. 'Or test pilot. Or, as you say, women may one day fly in the military. Maybe you'll get that chance.'

I think on that. A flyer now ready to fight, ready to kill again?

We're both silent, then he says: 'The war's a long way off finished. Plenty more still to do. There's lots of scope for a clever young woman.' He gives me a mischievous grin. 'You could even, if you were interested, join me in the secrets business.'

I make a face. Haven't I had enough of cloak and dagger? Nevertheless I get a small, enticing glimpse inside his world of secrets, though I prefer his cover name, or C, to the double-barrelled reality.

My post-action bombast has left me now but I'm not the person I was when hostilities began. Do I like the new me? A shrug. But would I want to go back to being the person who would have caved in and lost it at the wire?

Once again I consider where I am. In relationship terms, it's as simple as it is stark. I think of it in the style of the pithy journalism I've perfected at *The Planet*. Penning my own headline, I might just have summed it up like this: A lover lost but a father found.

THE END

ACKNOWLEDGEMENTS

I would like to acknowledge the following for assistance in researching this novel:

Mike Webster of the Cambridge Flying Group, Johan Vanbeselaere from the Air Museum at Leper in Belgium, Debbie Land and colleagues at the Shuttleworth Veteran Aeroplane Society, Liz Tregenza of the Colchester and Ipswich Museums, Carolyn Felgate of Anglia Research Service, Alison Lee, Dept of English, University of Western Ontario, Fiona Bourne of the Royal College of Nursing and Tim Mobbs for flights in his Jodel light aircraft.

A NOTE FROM THE PUBLISHER

Thank you for reading this book. If you enjoyed it please do consider leaving a review on Amazon to help others find it too.

We hate typos. All of our books have been rigorously edited and proofread, but sometimes mistakes do slip through. If you have spotted a typo, please do let us know and we can get it amended within hours.

info@bloodhoundbooks.com

Lightning Source UK Ltd.
Milton Keynes UK
UKHW031544010622
403836UK00004B/897